I0604944

REALM OF ILLUSION

THEA ATKINSON

Copyright © 2023 by Thea Atkinson

All rights reserved.

ISBN: 978-0-9921489-8-0

No part of this publication may be reproduced, distributed, or transmitted in any form or by any means, including photocopying, recording, or other electronic or mechanical methods, without the prior written permission of the publisher, except as permitted by U.S. copyright law. For permission requests, contact [include publisher/author contact info].

The story, all names, characters, and incidents portrayed in this production are fictitious. No identification with actual persons (living or deceased), places, buildings, and products is intended or should be inferred.

Book Cover by Christian Bentulan

Get updates and news at theaatkinson.com

 Chapter 1

Somehow, I'd become Prometheus, and pain was a raven digging into my bowels with a hot beak of molten iron. The stench of my own liver searing with each twisting stab made me roll and twist, trying to get out of range of both pain and stink.

There was no escape, and I rolled and writhed, and groaned, to no avail.

It was the moans that woke me. I came alert so swiftly, so abruptly, I was grabbing for the carrion bird perched on my ribcage before my eyes even flew open. Grappling bare air gave me the first hint that I wasn't Prometheus at all. That the gods weren't punishing me for trying to save humanity.

I was just a drug-sick junkie coming down from too many days' glut of a drug no mortal should have business ingesting. And I wasn't even in a human realm anymore. The hunter I once was, no more than a tool of assassination for the Shadow Court of the Fae.

The drug—Bloodmist—was one I'd kicked in the mortal realm with the help of my mentor, Gideon. So it was distressing to think I'd had to go through the ritual of cleansing once more. In Fae. With a far worse addiction to kick, and far stronger withdrawal.

But what choice did I have? Abducted into the Catacombs of the Dread wearing nothing but the cotton shift supplied to a tavern owner by the gang of Base Fae who'd taken me. Put on auction block after auction block in that God-forsaken, hope-deprived place. That inhaler filled with Bloodmist was the only thing I had to level the playing field.

I used it. Lots. Until it was empty of even a last misting of breath. Until the addiction I'd fought and won against so long ago bloomed in my belly like a water lily on a serene lake, comparing the pain of withdrawal to a raven's sharp beak and myself to a hero of old. I would have snorted at the thought, except it hurt too damn much to breathe.

I was left on the banks, somewhere in Fae, coming awake beneath a tree with rose-colored leaves and moss green eyes staring down into mine in alarm.

It didn't take long to realize the moaning had been coming from me, or that I'd slept through my last moments of pain-free existence. How long I'd been sleeping, I had no idea. I suspected it hadn't been long. The drug was a demanding bitch if it was anything. And now, with the withdrawal advancing, consciousness would not be pretty.

Plus, those eyes anchored me to my agony in a way that had me begging their owner to kill me.

The only answer I received was to be scooped up into the powerful arms of the Shadow Court's dark enforcer. And when I didn't have the strength to fight him off, I let him carry me to the horse that brought us onto the Shadow Trail, and I did my best to stay upright without falling off.

The way back to the tavern they had taken me from was a haze of pain and nausea. I blearily recalled his warning about wendigos earlier, when I was still slightly high on the last dregs of buzz. I even prayed we'd find some of the creatures, that they'd put me out of my misery.

To my disappointment, the ride was uneventful except for the stew of misery that broiled around behind my eyeballs and inside my gullet. Each roll and lurch of Nutkin's trot was agony. The only thing that kept me from passing out was my battle to fight Blade off as he wrestled me against his stomach time and again to keep me pinned against him. I would have given up every tooth in my head and trophy chest to fall off Nutkin's back where I could lay on the hard ground as immobile as I needed to.

I wanted to be lying curled on my side into as tight a ball as I could manage. Preferably on a cold tile floor around a porcelain toilet somewhere. Back home. Where civilization might offer me something more in the way of pain relief than a bit of breeze beneath my hairline. Not here in Fae, where the whistling of birds pierced my ears each time a shrill note of a cardinal or robin filled the air. Even the breeze made my eyeballs hurt. I bit back groan after groan until, in an unexpectedly hushed voice, Blade whispered to me, "Hang on. Almost there."

He held me still with a gentle hand as if he understood the pain of movement so intimately he was part of my own skin. Without comment, he slowed Nutkin to a free walk, giving the horse his rein as the dark enforcer pinned me with his thighs, cushioning the jostle of movement in the horse's stride.

I wasn't sure which was worse: the horse's plodding step or Blade's unyielding and uncharacteristic gentleness as he urged the horse ever forward. I decided it was neither of those. The touch of his body on mine was far, far worse than any of those things. Parts of me wanted to twist around in the seat and hold onto him so tightly he could share my shivering.

He deserved that for making me move at all.

Even the free walk Blade gave Nutkin made a roll of nausea slosh back and forth in my stomach. Pins and needles rose and fell at the dark enforcer's touch. My scalp hurt. The only blessing was that we rode in silence.

Twice, I had just enough time to lean to the side and let a stream of stringy vomit cascade over my thighs. The horse skittered to the side as he felt the liquid dribble onto his belly and ribs. I didn't have enough energy in my body to feel shame or embarrassment. I couldn't even mumble out an apology to the poor beast.

That was when I remembered I was still dressed in that shift and it was filthy and bloody, and now vomit-drenched. Nice. I wished I had it in me to do more than shudder.

By the time we made it to the tavern, I was trembling so badly my teeth were clacking together. I'd long ceased to be able to feel any individual part of Blade's body on mine; instead, his entire back, arms, and thighs were shards of glass embedding themselves into my bare skin where the tunic rode up, and burrowed in to chafe me raw where the fabric covered me.

Nutkin halted in a slow, smooth motion beside the hitching post, either because the beast was indeed sentient and didn't want to get splashed again, or because he felt pity for me. I supposed it was the latter. My head hung to my chest, and I had good view of his mane as he lowered his head to the trough for a drink. It was matted with sick, and I cringed at the sight.

"I'm afraid what awaits you inside might make you lose your stomach once more, Ponytail," Blade said as he slid off Nutkin's back, leaving me to sway on the saddle alone. "But do try to miss my feet, won't you. I don't fancy it squelching through my toes."

Right. He was naked. Even if he'd glamored himself a set of clothes before we set off, they were mere illusion. The only person who was dressed the entire ride was me, and the linen shift I wore would need to be burned.

Not that I cared about that right then, either.

"I'm not afraid of a little blood," I said in a whisper that hurt my ears.

He made a humming sound and rolled his eyes. That red snake in his eyes tried to swallow its tail around the silver lining his irises. "I can't honestly say it's just a bit of blood," he mumbled.

When he extracted me from Nutkin's back, it shocked me to discover he wore no glamor at all. Each raised bit of flesh from the rune-ish symbols he'd branded on his skin stood out plainly on his body. Perspiration ran in rivulets down his chest between the hollows of muscle and, seeing it, I felt some slight horror. It was my sweat that coated him.

In some deep recess of my mind, I wondered if he was still burnt out of magic and couldn't raise a glamor. Then I decided it didn't matter. Not right then. I couldn't imagine much mattering to me in that moment except my own damn misery.

"You might want to close your eyes," he said as he scooped me once more into his arms.

I was already doing so, but not because I was afraid. His touch was agony for so many reasons, and I needed to shut out some of the stimulus just to bear the pain.

The stench hit me first.

We weren't even inside the tavern yet and I knew by the unmistakable stink of rot that at least one creature had died in the yard. My stomach spasmed, and I gagged so hard my gallbladder clenched and threatened to slide up into my esophagus.

"Hold on, Ponytail," he said. "Don't use up all your energy before you get inside."

I sucked back on the bile, tightening my eyelids against the wont to puke, inhaling slowly through my nostrils to filter out the rotting smell. Held it. Repeated it.

The creak of his feet on aging boards indicated we'd reached the door of the tavern. I might have felt victorious at holding down my nausea, but I was past feeling much but a desperate desire to just. Stop. Moving.

I felt him shift me in his arms so he could grasp the door handle, and all I could think was: finally. He'd drop me on some hard chair inside or onto the wooden floor and all the horrific movement would be over. I had already decided to curl up right where he put me.

Then he yanked open the tavern door with a creak of its bones against the ligaments of its hinges.

That was when the full force of the smell really hit me. As if he knew how bad it was, he angled me forward, probably expecting me to upchuck the last of whatever fluid was left in my belly.

But there was nothing left. I hung there in his grip, dry heaving and gasping until I felt as though I'd wrung myself inside out. Beneath me, on the wooden floor, blood had clotted and turned black. Small pools of it led in rivulets out of my line of sight. Flies flitted around, landing and lifting.

I groaned at the buzz of them in my ear.

"All finished?" he asked quietly.

I shook my head. "No, but your delicate princess feet should be fine because I'm empty."

He made a thoughtful humming sound in his throat as he lifted me back up against his chest. A perfect view of the tavern swept over my vision like a panoramic movie cut as he did so, and what confronted my eyes shocked me so much I went limp in his arms. Well. Limper.

What met my gaze was more violent gore than I'd ever witnessed and that was saying something, considering I'd seen what he'd done in the catacombs. Body parts littered the floor and tables. A large, hairy creature, indistinguishable as a man of any sort, sat still slumped in a booth. His head sat between his hands on the table in front of him. His mouth was open, as if he'd been killed mid-protest.

"The women," I croaked out, a frantic sort of panic seizing my insides as I remembered that fae taverns all kept mortal females as chattel. "Were there human women here?"

He made a thoughtful sound that vibrated against my chest. "No mortals were harmed in the making of this murder," he said in a flat tone. "I gave them time to run."

So much death. So much violence.

"Put me down," I said in a small voice.

"In due time," he said, and I felt him stride through the room. Blurs of color—mostly red—swept past my gaze as we progressed to the staircase.

"Not here," I said. "I can't stay here." I rammed my fist over my mouth and nose to block out the stink, a smell that didn't seem to bother him one bit. One that couldn't be stoppered up no matter how far I shoved my fist into my mouth.

"You need to get clean," he said in a tight voice.

Clean. Not washed. Meaning he knew exactly what was causing my suffering. I made some small protest about preferring to sleep in a mound of hay in a stable or the dirty furrows of a garden. Anywhere but this.

"There isn't a safe space for miles until we get to the Iron City," he went on. "Would you prefer to ride the rest of the way without stopping?"

My stomach, my ribs, my entire body shouted the answer. "No," was all I said through my fingers.

He grunted an 'I thought so' in a grouchy tone and climbed the stairs. His footsteps fell heavily on each step. "The room is untouched," he said, as if that somehow mattered.

As he kicked the door to the room open, the fresh air from an open window wafted over me. I sagged in his arms, grateful for the respite.

By the time he laid me atop the clean bedspread, I was already curling into a ball. He stood back and regarded me, a carefully blank mask of neutrality on his face.

"You didn't tell me you were an addict," he said.

I peered at him through one eye. "No one's business," I muttered.

He crossed his arms. "Bloodmist," he said, and didn't wait for me to nod my confession. "I know why you used it. Why you had to."

I said nothing.

His gaze captured mine, and the intensity of the look actually stilled the shivering. "It's my fault you had to take it."

The tightness of his voice made my chest hurt. Sympathy? Remorse? From the dark enforcer of the Shadow Court? I had to be delusional. Without the experience of knowing what to say under such circumstances, I just nodded. I needed to sleep. I wanted nothing more than to fall into a coma. All he was doing by hovering over me in that creepy way delayed that. I was willing to agree to anything at that point just so he'd leave.

I knew this was just the beginnings of the suffering. In time, without another hit of Bloodmist, I'd soon be begging him to kill me.

"I don't need you to opine on whose fault it is," I said in a voice I hardly recognized as my own. There was no confidence in it. No strength. "What I need is a hit. Just a small one. Enough to push back the withdrawal. Then smaller and smaller doses. Wean me off."

He knelt by the bed instead of sitting on the mattress beside me. "I can't do that," he said. His eyes were level with mine. I could see straight into the depths of the pupils, and there was flame there, in the deepest shadows. So unlike Stone's gaze, filled with a cool promise of ocean water.

"If you can't do that, then get out," I grumbled. "It's not going to be pretty."

He chuckled with a dark humor. "What makes you think I care about pretty, Ponytail?"

He pushed himself to his feet and looked down at me with hands on his hips. "I know something about addiction," he said. "A woman I knew. A mortal." He hesitated, and I thought he wanted to say more, but then he huffed out a long sigh and changed the direction of his thoughts, obviously knowing I wasn't worth confiding in.

"This too shall pass. I promise you. And I'll stay with you. Ease your suffering when I am able. Once my...once my magic returns."

I didn't expect the confession of vulnerability and I might have found it interesting, might have marked it as a point of interest in my plan for vengeance, but it skimmed off me like a bead of oil on a hot griddle.

That was the last thing I heard before the cramps came and I lost time. In some vague awareness of my mind, I knew time had elapsed. The fire had been lit. The light had grown dim. But I was lost in my own world, alone, terrified, with demons of my past slithering over me in waves of sticky pain.

Sweat coated my skin, mingling with fluids I didn't even want to consider. Tears, surely. Maybe urine. Every fiber of my being screamed for relief.

And yet when I called out, he was there. A thorn needling its way beneath my nails. An itch that wouldn't go away. I begged for more Bloodmist, promising him anything if he'd get me more. I just wanted the torture to stop.

"Hold on, Ponytail. Almost there." A whisper of touch along the skin of my cheek that felt both agonizing and rapturous.

Peering at him through half-open eyes, I caught sight of worry in his face, and it made my throat ache all the more. I wished I deserved all the concern that painted his expression.

It might have made the weight of withdrawal easier to bear. As it was, the look just made me feel more miserable.

"I can't do this," I said as another wave of impotent, unrelenting sick took me. "I can't live through it again."

"You can. You will."

A command. Not a request. Not a modicum of sympathy in the voice this time, as though he'd had enough of my whining. Maybe he realized pity just made me angrier. It hardened me, that cold tone. Callousness I could take. I understood it. I swore at him.

He swore back, shooting me a pitying look that just made me hiss at him for his trouble.

"You're wasting your time on me," I ground out. "Just get me a hit and let's get back to business. It's all I'm good for anyway."

I tried to roll away, unable to bear the nursemaid facade, any more. It hurt as much as the twisting of my bowels. He held me by the shoulders, forcing me to meet his gaze.

"We'll speak of my time and your worthiness later," he said. "For now you will clear your system of that trash. And you will do it like the warrior you are, and if I have to, I will climb into that bed with you and hold you until you are too tired to fight anymore."

"Don't you dare," I said.

"Don't make me."

I pulled my eyes from him, and he released me to my agonies.

At some point, he dressed, either by glamor or by physical means. He looked too fresh to be the man who had brought me to the tavern, who had mauled an entirety of a dark cavern and beyond. Not an inch of blood marred his skin.

Fabric clung to him like a lover's embrace. He might have stepped into the tavern for a pint and pleasant conversation and nothing more.

I noted a pitcher of water on the nightstand at some point. Suddenly, the thirst overrode the cramping of my intestines. He must have noticed because he lifted it and poured some water into a kiln-dried tankard.

"Here," he said, urging the cup to my lips. "You need to hydrate. You're burning up inside."

I let him lay the tankard against my trembling lips. The coolness of the pottery was a welcome respite. His touch, gentle.

Something stopped me from opening my mouth, however. Even though my throat was crying out for a drink. All I could think was that one belt of too-cold water might send me cascading into another tsunami of vomiting. I felt weak. Vulnerable. If he wanted to, he could have executed me with a breath of hateful words.

"You've nothing left," he urged, easing the cup closer again. "If you puke again, you need something to bring up. Your body can't take much more."

I eyed him warily. "You want to kill me," I said.

His eyebrows climbed to his hairline. "An hour ago you were screaming at me to slit your throat and now that I haven't, you worry I will?" He rolled his eyes in a way that had to be just for show because he wasn't one to do that. "Mortal women. So strange."

I eyed him through slits this time, my eyelids no longer able to stay open. "I won't do it."

His groan was less indulgent this time. "If I wanted to kill you, I'd have done so by now." He tipped the mug and water spilled down my chin. "Drink," he said, but his tone was gentle even if the feel of the cup was more demanding.

I opened up because the water was coming like it or not. I let a dribble enter. It tasted salty and cold and disgusting.

I sprayed it over his chest. "You laced it with salt."

He offered a long-suffering shrug. "You need the electrolytes. And it's not that strong, you big baby. Just drink it."

"If I puke on you again, don't say I didn't warn you."

"I've been covered by your fluids several times over the last twenty-four hours," he drawled. "I'll manage."

At that moment, I realized he wasn't actually wearing physical clothes, but using a glamour. There weren't enough changes of clothes in the tavern to look that fresh. I narrowed my eyes at him, trying to decide if the water would feel as bad coming up as it felt good going down.

"I hope I do puke," I muttered.

He grinned, showing tiny points on his incisors. "Me too. It's been pretty dead in here the last couple of hours."

Dead. Was that his idea of a joke after the dozens of bodies he'd left scattered about? I sniffed, realizing that of all the smells lingering in the chamber: vomit, sweat, and piss, that rotten flesh was no longer one of them.

"The bodies have been burned and the tavern, cleaned," he said, sensing my thoughts with a shrug. "After the first two times you tossed your cookies on me, I figured the ripeness of all those carcasses was doing me no favors."

At that, he reached out, his touch gentle against my heated cheek. "You can do this," he said, his voice steady even at the low rumbling note it possessed. "You're almost there. If you can survive the catacombs, you can get through this."

I decided I must be hallucinating it all because I was sure I heard begrudging admiration in his voice.

With a force of will, I maneuvered onto my elbows so I could drink without the cold water dribbling between my boobs.

He held my gaze, warmth brimming in his eyes, and leaned in closer. "Good," he said as I swallowed mouthful after mouthful, taking my time between drafts to breathe. He pulled back when I gasped for air, and he tilted the cup forward again when I caught my breath. My core was trembling. My elbows worked to keep me inclined. He was patient, letting me take the time I needed.

Eventually, I managed enough to know I would not bring it back up, and I felt markedly refreshed.

He smiled with his lips pressed together, a brush of movement across the muscles in his jaw. He was pleased. Satisfied. Good. I was exhausted.

"Now sleep. You're safe. I'm here. Fighting right alongside you." He gave me a long look that I thought might be awe, but decided was more relief. "Till the end, Alathir."

I had the feeling the end was near.

Chapter 2

Blade was sleeping in the wing-back chair when I woke. Evening had crawled its way into the tavern, casting shadows into the corners of the room. The fireplace had died down to a few red embers and a damp chill shivered through the chamber. The oil lamps cast fairies of light all over the walls and a deep, mellow glow over the ceiling.

What it did to Blade's body was enough to make my heart squeeze. This brutal, horrible fae had rescued me, stayed by me, forced me to face the darkest cloak of withdrawal. I felt the stirrings of gratitude and regret, and something else, something that made me want to hide in a dark closet and sleep for a dozen years rather than inspect what it might mean.

He looked less ferocious with his eyes closed, I thought. A quiet sort of peace played over me too as I studied him, taking in his chiseled jaw, the bunch of muscle around his shoulders that on Stone looked almost too big, but gave Blade the look of a wolf or a massive dog—something powerfully predatory.

His arm hung down, showing that one pink nail with its chipped edge. I glanced down at the worn out pedicure I wore, and noted it was nearly the same shade. A match. I felt a tingle in my belly at the thought.

And then there were the brands that peppered his skin. Asleep, he'd not glamored himself any clothes but was sitting beneath a wool lap blanket, so his chest was bare. From my angle, I could make out several raised and silver bits of skin.

If I traced the tiny lines from wrist to shoulder, I could make out five clearly. A straight line hunkered into the hollow next to the bone of his wrist. It was companioned by two dots on either side. That lead to something that looked like an arrow pointing up and the next looked very much like an H except the two horizontal lines were diagonal. The next one—

"Should I get you an easel and some charcoal?" came his husky, sleep-swelled voice.

Even if the room was chilly, my face heated just the same, as if the fire were right next to me. Embarrassment shoved aside all notions of gratitude.

"If you're inferring you're a work of art," I countered. "Then you're delusional." I propped myself onto my elbow, surprised the world didn't spin. "I'm merely assessing my enemy."

He swung his head toward me and those eyes, those chunks of emerald with their silver and crimson serpent turned on me. "Are we still enemies then, Ponytail?"

"Are you still going to keep my sister hostage to the Shadow Court's demands?" I didn't mention Jasmine. I wasn't ready to let that ghost float out from the safe place I'd put her.

"I'm not keeping her hostage; Flint is. But yes."

"Then we are still enemies."

I swung my legs over the edge of the mattress and stretched. I didn't exactly feel normal, but I wasn't about to throw up my stomach lining, so that was something. In a few hours, I might actually stand without shaking. My hands and wrists were sticky, but I felt much better.

It was the act of moving that informed me of my own nudity, not the way his eye trailed over my skin like a hot wash of molten wax. When his gaze fell below my throat, it took everything I had in me not to drape a shamed arm over my breasts.

"You stripped me." Not quite an accusation, even if the sharpness in my tone would have made Gideon cringe.

Surprise, that's what put the edge to my voice. I should have tempered it, I supposed, knowing all the things he'd done for me, but I was always such a dolt when it came to things like gratitude.

His hand jerked beside the chair, but that was the most re-action he showed. "You would have preferred rolling around in that stinking bit of linen?"

"At least I wouldn't be naked."

"I burned the tunic," he said, nodding toward the fireplace. "It stank of vomit and sweat."

I was willing to bet it stank of far more, but that wasn't the point.

"I'd think it a common courtesy to dress me instead of letting me lie here all splayed out like a trollop."

A single tick of his jaw and that was all to suggest he was doing his best not to react. "That comment predisposes a sense of chivalry that a monster like me doesn't possess, Ponytail." A flash of his eyes that had the muscles of my core weakening. "It also suggests trollops take issue with splaying their wares whether they're snoring like a dog as they sleep one off or not."

"I don't snore."

He snorted. "Believe what you like, Ponytail, but I saw several rats leaping to their deaths from the window, for fear a wolf had come for a picnic."

I huffed a sigh at him with a curled lip, and he lifted a single eyebrow. "Would you like me to fetch you a jerkin from one of the bodies in the compost heap?"

He no doubt saw the shudder that went through me as I clutched at the pillow, aiming it for my chest to cover myself up. I knew my cheeks were flaming and no matter how I tried to tell myself that my discomfort was just the result of considering sliding into a dead man's shirt, I knew that the tiny flare of emotion that seemed to clog up my throat was the real culprit. And I wasn't ready to mull that over either.

It was bad enough knowing the energy between us had changed, that my dreams had been filled with the scent of spices and a dark, shadowed figure loping after me through a lush forest until I longed to surrender myself to its teeth. I wasn't entirely certain I hadn't cried out in my sleep.

And that ticked me off. Any sort of emotion other than vengeance would just get in the way.

"In case you haven't noticed," he said dryly, cutting into my thoughts. "I am not wearing anything either."

I had noticed. I wished I could pretend otherwise.

"And why is that, exactly?"

He shrugged. "I'm all about equal rights."

"And so you thought if you stripped me naked, you might as well be too?" I said with a toss of my hair over my shoulder. "Seems sketchy to me."

At that, he rose from the seat of the wingback slowly, taking his time, letting each inch of his own skin show itself to me as the blanket slid from his lap. The fabric fell to the floor in a puddle around his feet, and I had a damnable time forcing my eye to follow along with it, because it wanted so badly to linger on those hips, that muscled stomach.

He prowled toward me with such predatory intent that my fists clenched automatically. "I didn't think you'd want any reminders of that place," he said in a low voice that dragged my gaze, thankfully, back to his face. "Nothing remains of it. Not from the wounds you took there or the clothes you wore."

His gaze was hard as ice for some reason, when it was usually like flames about to raze a village. "So I got rid of all the evidence. Whatever happened in that place resides only in your memories."

His throat bobbed as the muscles tightened and let go around a deep swallow. "I can't do anything about those."

My chin trembled. No. No one could do anything about those. What mattered was that I was out of there. I was alive. Whatever psychological evidence remained of that place could be stuffed into a dark closet the same as the rest of the things I didn't want to remember. And I could be thankful for that. Thankful. Not this damnably irritating desire that curled inside my belly like marshmallow dropped onto a fire.

Because those thoughts felt strangely traitorous considering the things he'd done. The violence. The death. The suffering.

Those things should not light up desire in my body; not unless I was just as much a monster as he was.

And yet it did. And since it was difficult to hold his gaze, those thoughts swirled about like ashes trying to find a place to land. I had to force myself to seek out the hearth with my eyes and away from his powerful thighs as they crossed the room toward me with an agonizingly slow gait. My chest felt tight at the anticipation of his approach. My jaw clenched. I didn't want him to come any closer. I wasn't sure what I would do if he touched me. I didn't even know how I'd react if I caught his eye.

So I stared at the ashes in the hearth and the way they held together in a clump that still clung to the form it might have been when tossed inside. The tunic. Oh god, those ashes were in the shape of a linen shirt those damned fae had dressed me in, and all it would take was a breath to crumble them into nothingness.

"I stripped you," he said in a hoarse voice that dragged my eyes from the white ash and to the bruises I knew should pepper my skin. "And washed you off dozens of times. Yes. I did that. I had to. You were covered in blood and cuts and bruises."

My mouth went dry at the comment, at the preternatural movement of his approach. I knew each and every abrasion I'd taken as I'd fought back in that cursed place each time they displayed me as an item for inspection. I'd broken my nose at one point, I was sure. Breathing had been difficult and restricted.

My sinuses were clear now. I couldn't remember when I'd started breathing clearly again.

All of the wounds, bruises, and broken things were gone or healed.

He came within a foot of the bed and held me frozen in place with a fierce look. "I didn't inflict the wounds, so I had no idea where they might be. I had to see them to take them from you."

My mind reeled back to the City of the Dead and how Terran had ordered him to hurt me as punishment. While his father had wanted to show me Blade could heal as well as harm, I recalled I hadn't felt one iota of pain during the attack.

"Your magics allow you to heal as well as absorb pain?"

He nodded, a red glint in his eye. "It's one of my natal magics, yes, but even that can be depleted if pressed hard enough."

Hard like shifting multiple times, like killing an entire tavern, like tracking me down into an underground of hateful creatures doing hateful things. Like erasing wounds that were numerous enough that even I'd lost track.

Part of me wanted to say I didn't need his help. That I would have been fine. But I knew that was bravado, and I knew it was a lie. I wouldn't have made it out alive, let alone been able to heal on my own. Even if all I was to him was a duty, something he had to protect until I did what his father wanted, I was grateful.

What he'd done for me there...it was so much more than I could have ever imagined—no matter what his reasons—that I didn't have the heart to pull up the mask of stoic callousness that kept me protected from most horrific things.

All I had left was the genuine sense of gratitude. He'd gone to bat for me. Except for Gideon and Kit, no one had ever done that for me before. And both of them had turned their backs on me eventually just so they could survive me.

The trouble was, I had little experience with gratitude. I didn't know how to act, what to say. Pulling from my childhood, I knew the words. I'd been taught to say them. I'd heard others, innocent folk Gideon or I had saved from some horrible creature or other, say them in a rush of emotion that seemed to slide easily from their tongues.

"Thanks," I said, trying to smile through that residual pain and show him how I felt. "It couldn't have been easy having me taken from you by a few Base Fae."

"Those few Base Fae were trows," he said. "Or at least half-breed trows. Whatever else they were is lost now." His voice was still somber and sullen, and he was making me more nervous.

"Yes, well, whatever they were, I imagine it wasn't pleasant to find me in the mess I was in, knowing I'd be useless by the time you got me back to your father. Using up all your magic to get me out of there...to put me back together...it was nice of you."

"Nice," he said in a flat voice.

I nodded, hurrying to clarify. "Yes. For whatever reason you did what you did for me. I appreciate it."

A light flared in the depths of his eyes and disappeared. "For whatever reason," he said.

"Do you still have blood clots in your ears?" I said, feeling a bit annoyed he was repeating everything instead of taking the damn thanks like a normal person would. Couldn't he see I was struggling? He could have tried to make it easier instead of showing me that expressionless face, that dull gaze.

I rolled my eyes. "I imagine your father would have been ticked to see his assassin in such a mess under your watch."

His jaw slid to the side ever so slightly as he shrugged, an offhand movement that made my chest ache, more so when he spoke, a comment of dismissal so cold, I shivered.

"My magics don't just absorb pain, Ponytail," he said in a low voice. "That's far too passive a description for what it does. I felt each blow you took, every cut. Here in this room, I lived your agony, and I knew your suffering." His voice broke and something cracked in my chest. I didn't want to think about those things. I didn't want to bring them to mind. If I let them see the light, I was terrified I'd know how bad the damage was.

To think he'd suffered them as well as he took them from me...I couldn't breathe for the guilt and sorrow that rooted in my chest, cracking open a dark and hardened place that hadn't been tilled in a long time. No one, not even the dark enforcer, should have had to endure that.

I shrank away from him and if he noticed, he either didn't care or refused to acknowledge it. Fast as a lighting strike, his fingers coiled around my wrists, tugging me to my feet in a rough movement. The pillow dropped to the floor with a soft thump.

"You think I resented using my magic to take their lives?" He rasped out, his voice a grinding of stones. "You think I did what I did because of some oath I swore to my father?" He laughed, a dark sound that sounded like it belonged to the pits of a grave. "I enjoyed every moment of their deaths, Ponytail. I relished it."

With one firm tug, he had me against his chest. I felt the muscles of his chest twitch against my forearms as he pinned my hands between us. Within the space that cushioned our bodies, energy pulsed and snapped. The serpent in his gaze came to life again, sliding along a spark of silver that rimmed his irises, and I was close enough to realize it was a true inner light that flared the metal to life.

Light. Thick and disturbingly bright. I almost squeezed my eyes closed against the glare.

He dragged in a ragged breath that shuddered his body along every inch of skin that met mine. "So yes, I did strip you. I took off that filthy garment, and I saw your body, a warrior's body broken and bruised, and I knew the moment that I saw those injuries that I would do anything to relive the violence of the caves again because what I'd done to them was not enough."

His body molded to mine. Fingers once on my wrists, moved to my waist, peeling away like Velcro trying to hold the flesh together. Our breath came as one inhalation, and when he laid his mouth against my ear, I thought my whole body would go to a viscous puddle of quicksilver.

Blade's kiss tasted like warm cinnamon and cloves just the way I expected. It was agonizingly leisurely, almost exploratory at first, but as it deepened, it quickly became apparent the laziness was for my benefit and not his. Within seconds, he demanded I open to him, and I did so without compunction, letting the warmth of his breath invade me, the sweet slipperiness of his lips claim mine.

I wasn't ready for the complete claim he made on me in the languid moments his lips pulled submission from me. Surrender wasn't something I expected, but his mouth demanded it and I gave it so automatically, I was afraid when he let go, I would stagger on knees too weak to hold me upright.

I was terrified he'd see by the hollowing of my neck just how much it ached, that I was having a hard time taking in air. That I was afraid of facing my own reaction.

He eased his mouth from mine and it horrified me to discover my eyes had closed. I snapped them open to see him staring at me. A rush of heat moved up my throat as he nestled his lips into the corner of mine, his breath washing me with that cinnamon scent.

His eyebrow quirked, a lazy sort of smile taking possession of his features before he lowered his face again. A single pause, letting me know he fully comprehended my surrender.

I wasn't ready for the ferocity of the way he claimed my mouth then. I didn't have a chance to protest or even try to fight him off. He just took me, took my lips, took my breath, took all the space between us with a searing violence that spoke of the passion he'd inject in that careful punishment. His kiss and the brutality of it held all the violence I imagined he'd deliver to those fae who'd taken me.

And in that moment I stood helpless beneath that kiss, I wasn't sure which of us deserved the punishment more.

CHAPTER 3

Blade's kiss was like nothing I'd ever known. Gideon had been a masterful lover, and the inexperience in me responded to the expertise of age. When we joined, it was a melting pot of survival lust or the soft, gentle coupling that spoke of love and trust until that eventually wore off. My one night stands were swift, stress-relieving quickies, sometimes in the backs of cars along a dark street.

Blade made my marrow cry out as if my bones were hollow shells only he could fill. My shins, my femur, even my spine threatened to crumble to the dust they were made of. If he hadn't been holding me aloft, I wasn't sure I'd be able to stand. And that made me panic.

A flash of violence played behind my eyelids. The chaos of screams played in my hearing. And all the while, as my stomach clenched with lust and my brain screamed at me that danger was in every flick of his tongue against mine, every suffocating draw of breath, my skin tingled. The very soles of my feet ached to run. A whisper of threat brought to me the voices of the dead from that cavern, carried it to me on wings that seemed very much like the chalky paintings on the stone walls.

This kiss, this intimacy, it was too much. It was dangerous on a visceral level that terrified me. And I knew if I waited one second more, I would offer everything I had, everything I was, to him. One more breath and I'd let him use me in ways I wasn't sure I was ready for.

And I hated myself for it.

It took a magnificent amount of will to reach down into a well born of decades of cultured coldness, and extract the resolve I needed to pull away. I jerked away sharply, tearing myself from his embrace, and gods above, if he didn't let me go.

"Back off," I said, inflecting acid into my tone but failing miserably. All that came out was a choke of syllables so garbled I found myself reaching behind me for the bed so he wouldn't notice how shaken I was. "Back off or I will cut you."

I sank onto the mattress, grasping for the sheets because my entire body was flushed with so much heat I needed to feel the coolness of cotton just to bring the redness down. I clutched the fabric against my chest and it pooled along my ribs in a path to my legs.

"Thank you for cleaning me up," I said, angling myself so he didn't have a clear look at my face or the shaking of my hands as they gripped the sheet. Only when I felt like I'd gathered enough composure to look at him without begging him to fall on me, did I toss a dismissive look over my shoulder, lifting my chin.

What I saw of his face was almost as terrifying as the sight of him tearing into the fae in the catacombs. The column of his long and muscled throat grew hard as his jaw blanched to white. The serpent buried itself beneath the silver and his pupils clenched into pinpricks.

"Think nothing of it," he said with a long look at my throat and the rope scar that I knew was flaming red. "It's not like you could go to the King's fancy dress ball looking like a junkie brawler from the Kennel."

A dull ache bloomed in my chest like a mushroom. It was a hateful comment, a dig at the nasty addiction I'd barely survived. But I'd asked for that hate. I deserved it.

Hate was something I could work with. Even if my stomach was bottoming out along with every ounce of my self-control. At least I wouldn't have to worry anymore about losing myself to him. He'd never touch me again.

"Indeed," I said, my voice shaking as much as my core. To distract him and maybe myself, I tugged at the sheets, pulling them over my chest as I stood onto quaking legs, doing my best to look unaffected by the hurtful slur about my addiction.

"So," I said, pulling the haughtiness of a cold and calculated hunter about me like a comfortable sweater. "What now? Am I expected to ride back into the city like Lady Godiva while you just glamor yourself a nice riding suit so the unwashed masses don't get a good peep at your nasty bits."

He scooped the blanket he'd dropped from the floor and tossed it in the chair. His back was all I saw for long moments and his shoulders knotted and let go several times before he turned back around. The Blade I recognized stood before me, his mask, like mine, carefully placed.

"First," he said. "The unwashed masses should be pleased to get a peep at my nasty bits, and second: you won't exactly look like Godiva," he said. "She was a lot chunkier than you think. Most fae wouldn't look twice at a mortal woman, but physically, I think she warranted a solid nine out of ten." He waggled his hand in front of his chest as he looked at me as if he was ranking me, and my jaw ticked at the study.

So he liked them chunky, did he? Well bully for him being all woke and all. I had never been on the thick side. I had too much muscle and I tended to excesses that stripped weight off me rather than put it on. Even so, I knew I had a decent body except for the scars. Gideon always told me I was attractive. I didn't have any trouble finding lovers.

It was the scars that made me leave the lights off when I took a lover, not shyness of my body. I let them roam those things in the dark where I couldn't see the revulsion in their eyes, or have to try to explain away the multitude of thready silver lines that couldn't be the result of martial arts practice.

"Are you running me through your slide ruler right now?" I asked.

A muscle fluttered in his cheek. "Maybe." He shrugged. "And maybe someday I'll tell you where you rank, Ponytail," he drawled, just as cool as he'd ever been. "But right now I don't think you could handle it."

I snorted, a show of how much I cared what he thought, all the while knowing I'd probably suffered a bout of Patty Hearst syndrome. He'd been kind to me. In the midst of violence and fear, he'd given me hope. He'd even somehow tricked me into believing there was some goodness beneath that ruthless facade.

I knew better than to believe that the way I knew monsters and their tactics. No matter how my body called to his, I had to remind myself that he and his cadre had taken my sister. I couldn't forget that. Neither could I conveniently forget what he'd done to his mortal lover, a fate that would be mine at some point regardless of whether I let my guard down or not. It was time to get down to business.

I slid onto one of the two chairs that companioned the table and gestured at the pouch that had at some point without me noticing been laid atop it. It looked how I remember it, with gold lacings that felt like satin as I let my fingers trail through them.

"Maybe it's time you dumped those things out and told me what they're for."

He eyed me cautiously. "This is what you want to do right now?"

"I will once you get some clothes on. Or are you waiting for me to measure you on a scale?" This time, I didn't shy away from sending him a pointed look directly at his hips. A zing went down my spine and settled at the base, making me ache all over. I ignored it even as both of his eyebrows cocked up.

"I don't think you're prepared to see how I measure up," he purred, and I got the feeling that now he'd taken my measure, he was going to torment me with it as punishment for rejecting him.

Not to be manipulated by my own lusts, I leaned back and crossed my arms over my chest, purposefully ignoring the innuendo despite the flaming of my skin all the way from my chest to my scalp. A flaming he had to see and one I was determined to brush off because I did not need that complication right now. I wasn't so innocent to realize most men would screw a bullet hole if it had hair around it.

I doubted fae males were much different.

"I don't know how it is in your world," I drawled. "But in mine, some are growers and some are show-ers. Don't forget. I sat on that gigantic horse with you for hours. I have a good idea which one you are."

His single raised eyebrow suggested he wanted to press the question, but I was done. He could try to use sex to torture me if he couldn't use violence, but that didn't have to mean I had to pine about every time he decided to try.

With a wave at the chair opposite me, I said, "Just sit down." I leaned back in my own, crossing one leg over the other. "And give me my karambit back. I want it."

I rubbed at my wrist absently with one hand, feeling the tackiness of my skin. Despite my outward calm, at my own mention of Nutkin, the streak of several images, all of them bloody and violent and darkly reminiscent of the catacombs started playing behind my eyelids. My neck prickled along the base of my skull.

I had to blow out a long breath just to speak without my voice breaking because what I had to say, I wanted him to understand there was no refusing. I felt much better. Much more like myself.

"I'm done being in this realm without a weapon," I said. "You can trust me or you can release me." I let my gaze run lazily up his torso to his face. "But it's time this thing got done already."

There was a moment when I thought he might be watching the play of those scenes over my face as if it were a movie screen. His jaw clenched. Then let go. Finally, he dipped his chin in what looked impossibly like agreement.

"Whatever you say, Ponytail," he said with a nod then prowled closer, garments of black-colored fabric collecting around him with each step. By the time he reached the table and had pulled out his chair, he was fully clothed. And damn if he didn't still look like raw sex. Fuck me and my ridiculous, traitorous body.

"Better?" he asked, though he hadn't sat down at all.

I swallowed down that unwanted throttling of lust and splayed my fingers over the table top, grounding myself. "Better would be me at home on my sofa binge-watching Outlander."

"So you're a romantic," he said in a soft voice. "How peculiar for a such a cold-hearted monster hunter."

My gaze flicked back up to his face, where a muscle feathered the corner of his lips.

"I like the violence," I countered. "But I find it interesting that you know what it is."

His grin came fast as he reached out and snagged the leather pouch from the table. "I make it my business to know what mortal women like," he said as he bounced the leather in his palm. "But for now, I think any further discussion on that front requires both of us to be dressed." He pointed at the knot in the sheet I was still clutching.

I clutched at the knot in the sheet, yanking it up high enough to indicate I still wasn't wearing real clothes. "Please do find a way for me to accommodate you. I assure you, I won't mind."

This time when he smiled, it was filled with mischief and the pouch dropped to the table, his hand slack as he eyeballed me. "There's always the dress if you need something to wear. It does bring the woman out in your killer eyes."

Without waiting for my response, he laughed, reached under the table and pulled out the blade from beneath with a noisy tear. He laid the karambit on the table between us, a frayed bit of duct tape sticking to the handle.

My left eyebrow crawled toward my hairline. It had been there in the room with me the whole time. Not a great look for a monster hunter, I supposed, but I told myself I did have the extra distractions of withdrawal and exhaustion keeping me from bringing my A game.

"Duct tape?" I asked.

He shrugged. "I don't abandon useful mundane tools when I come to Fae. Duct tape can be very handy when it's necessary to hide a knife from a woman begging to die." He grinned boyishly.

So that was why my wrists were so sticky. A huff of comprehension slid free of my lungs as I eyeballed him and that stupid grin that was so disarmingly charming on him, that I smiled back before I could stop myself.

My knife. He was giving it back to me. I scooped it from the table before he could change his mind, and tucked it beneath my leg while he watched me silently. I almost closed my eyes in relief of how it felt with its cold steel warming beneath my thigh.

I blinked back at him, daring him to comment. His response was to drop his gaze to my bare chest where the cleavage was no doubt peeking above the knot. His swallow was audible. The way he grit his teeth was reminiscent of a woman on a diet eyeballing a huge chunk of chocolate cake.

Long before his eyes left my chest, he was standing. With his gaze still on my chest, he grabbed the leather pouch by its laces from the table. His own chest was expanding and contracting very slowly, as though he was drawing in bracing breaths. Then he dragged his gaze from my cleavage to my eyes and I had to grip the edge of the chair until he spun on his heel and headed for the door.

"You're right," he growled. "You should get dressed. A few of the mortal women returned a few hours ago," he said in a tone of dismissal that made my hackles raise. "I told them if they cleaned the mess they could run the tavern for the Shadow Court. One of them will be here shortly to fill the tub for you so you can have a proper bath." He nodded to where the copper tub still hunkered into the corner of the room. "She's about your size and might have some clothing stashed somewhere."

I wasn't sure what to think of the information, except to wonder just how far the Shadow Court's influence reached if he could gift an entire tavern to a few mortal women. "You can do that?" I asked.

"Well, I asked her very nicely to draw the water," he said. "Not a single cut throat among them."

"No, not that," I said, waving away the misunderstanding. "I mean, it's possible to just take what you want?"

He took hold of the latch on the door and looked back at me over his shoulder. "It's been my experience that once I murder an entire building filled with low Fae, base Fae, and high Fae, that land claims on the property go uncontested."

He blinked at me owlishly.

I narrowed my gaze at him, curious. "Is that your idea of a joke?"

A tug at the corner of his mouth. Just that and no more.

"I suppose you'll have to see," he said and swept out the door.

It took several more moments of me clutching the corner of the sheet and staring at the door before I heard someone in the hall on the other side. Expecting the rap on the wood, I strode to the door when the sound came, and opened it.

She was tiny, the woman who waited on the other side. So petite, the buckets of steaming water sitting on the other side of her on the floor looked too big for her to have carried them all the way up the stairs by herself.

I looked both ways up and down the short corridor and as far past the railing into the tavern below as I could. Blade was gone. That unearthly speed seeming to have returned along with his ability to glamor himself. But the scan showed that while the downstairs bustled with two more women cleaning and clearing debris and bodies, the hallway outside my door held just this one woman and her buckets of water. A disquieting thought that she'd been in the tavern long enough to hear me begging to die ran through my mind. Maybe they all could.

I swallowed through the tightness in my throat and bent for the buckets, payment for what had to be pretty terrifying.

"I'll get them," I said.

She tapped my fingers away. "It's fine," she said in a husky voice that befitted sultry prostitutes everywhere. "Just go over by the tub." She jerked her chin toward the interior of the room and bent to retrieve the water.

I watched her cross the room, carrying the water with little effort. Muscled in places I couldn't see beneath the shapeless cotton shift, then. Probably lean from her time here and having to do things the hard way instead of merely turning on a tap or pressing a remote.

Steam billowed over her head as she upended the first bucket, the sound of water sluicing over cold copper putting an itch in my spine. Despite the obviously cursory wash-ups from Blade, my skin was coated in old, dried sweat, and it fairly crackled when I moved.

I inched closer, drawn by the steam even as my mind ran to the women I'd caught sight of downstairs. "How many of you are here?"

She looked at me over her shoulder as she set the first bucket down by her feet. Bare, I noticed, and covered in grime and bits of broken leaves, dried blood, and what looked like sand. Her eyes held a haunted look that she couldn't disguise with the desensitized stoic expression masking her face.

"There were six of us in the cellars," she said and picked up the second bucket.

"Cellars?"

She paused, setting the bottom of the bucket on the lip of the tub. Water sloshed over the side into the bowl.

"It's where our rooms are," she explained. "We had just started our shifts for the night when..." She swallowed and for an instant, a tic took over her lower lip. Then she straightened her spine and inhaled, bracing.

"He came into the tavern just as the sun set. I'll never forget the spray of crimson over the horizon that showed through the doorway before he closed and barred it. It was so beautiful, it caught my eye. At first no one but me paid attention to him. People come and go in the tavern all the time. But then...then Ely noticed him standing there. I saw Ely's face when he did. I knew something was wrong. And then everyone seemed to notice him at the same moment. Like a movie scene or something." She cocked her head at me. "They still make movies at home, don't they?"

I nodded, my throat aching at the thought that she'd wonder such a thing.

She adjusted her stance next to the tub, leaning her hip against it as she balanced the bucket. She closed her eyes, her expression going blank with memory.

"It was if he was waiting for everyone to notice him, standing there in the doorway. And when they did, you just knew there was no way out of that tavern. He said, 'I am not here to ask questions. I am here to make a statement.' And I swear the hair went up along the back of my neck."

I was mesmerized, seeing it with her, imagining the room below and the way Blade would fill the doorway and soak up all the energy of the building without so much as moving. I waited for her to continue, knowing there was more.

She opened her eyes and held my gaze with an unflinching bravery despite the emotions I saw moving across her face. "He told us chattel to go to the cellars and not to come out. 'Go below,' he said. 'And no matter what you hear, no matter who calls for you or how badly you want to run to find escape, do not come back up until it is deadly silent for at least an hour.'"

"He said that," I asked. "He used the term: deadly silent?"

She blinked, freeing herself from the throes of memory. "Those were his exact words. I'll never forget them."

She turned away from me and poured the water, leaving me standing there with the words hanging in the air.

I edged closer still, near enough to feel the steam on my face. Close enough to touch her, but I didn't. I didn't want to spook her. I wanted more. The part of me that still ached from the time in the catacombs wanted to hear it all. Part of me wanted to bask in the story. The other part wanted to run from the memory.

"And then?" I asked. "What happened afterwards?" I didn't need her to describe what happened after she'd gone below with the other women. I'd seen the evidence with my own eyes. It had been a massacre and nothing less. What I wanted to know was why, after all that, she came back.

"Blade said you came back. I would think you'd run away and never stop."

She snorted. "Run? Who would have dared with all that screaming. We were frozen from fear. Clinging to each other. Screaming ourselves blue down there, all six of us."

"Six," I said, eyes narrowing. "I only counted two more downstairs."

She let the empty bucket hang in her grip as she sat on the edge of the tub and faced me once more.

"When he came back, he offered us a ferryman coin for our troubles. Told us we could use it to find a portal home again but that we'd all have to go together." She eyeballed me as though she were studying my reaction to the information. "They're rare, you see. A ferryman coin will create a portal to the mortal realm anywhere you want, and it will create a shade of the traveler as well, leaving a doppelganger behind. A changeling." This last was whispered, a hoarse sound that reminded me of sand paper rasping over soft wood.

I was speechless. A coin. A coin that could take a mortal home. Leave a doppelganger behind. Blade had possession of such magic. A hiccup stuttered my heart. I blinked, the only part of my body that dared to move.

"And what did you do with the coin he offered?" I asked in a careful, nonthreatening voice. She was obviously still in Fae. Maybe the coin was too. I couldn't risk spooking her. I wanted—needed that kind of magic.

"Three took it. Three of us stayed." She spread her arms out to her sides, the bucket dangling in the air over the tub. "Where would we go at home? What would we do? The life we had there is long gone and for some of us, there was nothing worth returning to. We chose to stay. Take over the tavern." She dipped her chin toward the floor. "We can make a go of it here. He told us we'd have his protection."

I sagged against the side of the tub, my mind churning from the knowledge that there could be a way out of Fae, maybe even a way that could create a double of Kit, a means to protect her. And now it was gone.

 Chapter 4

I bathed and dressed in the simple jerkin and breeks Sylvia left me. Once we'd broken the ice, she was a cheery sort, and friendly. She'd left with a promise to send something up for me to eat before retiring for the night, but I'd yet to see evidence of it by the time full dark had smothered the tavern.

With nothing to do, and antsy as a game-show contestant running down a clock, I took to pacing the room, my mind running over and over again to the vape pen I'd lost in the catacombs. I couldn't remember if there might be just one small hit of Bloodmist left in it. I hated the thought that there might be even the slightest drizzle of drug left unused. I hated the thought that some fae might pick it up and use that last bit.

As I paced, Erachne's gown caught my eye several times. Some part of me wanted to touch something lovely, and it was lovely. It was smooth and tactile in a way that velvet could be, the way a lover's touch could feel on the softest parts of your skin. I wanted to touch it. I wanted to fill my restless mind with something other than the horrors of the catacombs and the tavern below.

And if I didn't fill my hands, my head, with something, I was going to wear a trough in the wooden floorboards deep enough for pigs to eat from. Half of me wished I could have gone to sleep and woke up not wanting, dying for, the Bloodmist. But I knew even if it was possible, no amount of sleep could curb the mental dependence on the drug.

So the gown became a sort of surrogate. The fourth time I checked it, I had the gown in my hands before I realized I'd taken it out of its bag.

The fifth time, I decided no harm could come from trying on the dress once more. Just to see if it still did the things to my body that Erachne had made it do.

I stepped into the skirt and pulled the bodice up over my shoulders the way Erachne had, so the sleeves trailed down my arms. When I smoothed out the material and turned to the mirror to check the fit, I saw that I looked very much like I had in the woodsprite's mirror.

Not only that, but for the first time in hours, I didn't look like a leather sack pulled through a keyhole. And I felt a buoyed elation at the way I took my own breath away. As a replacement for the magic-infused drug, the gown did something the drug never could: it put a smile on my face.

The silvery sheen of the material clung to me in all the right places. The skirt was more evening gown style than princess, which was a relief. My body had never been completely athletic no matter how hard I trained or what I ate. I had muscle, sure, but I tended to curvaceous over lean, and the dress favored that quality.

The vine tattoo had returned, disguising the rope burn scar on my throat, and extending to each and every wound, scar, or scuff that had imprinted itself on the skin of my torso and stomach over the years—minus the ones I'd acquired in the catacombs, I reminded myself. All evidence of those was gone, just as Blade had promised.

My navel peeked out from the inked foliage above a broad V cut that spanned my hips. A long slit ran the length of the left side, ending just above the knee and giving me room to move, and hopefully to run.

It was wholly fae and vixen and bad ass all at once. I felt like I could do anything in that dress, and for the first time since the catacombs, my lungs expanded all the way open.

I flipped the skirt back so I could see if I could strap the karambit's sheath to my thigh as a test. I twisted in front of the mirror. Not one hint of bulk showed against the material no matter which way I turned. The lines were as smooth as if I was naked beneath.

Health and vigor appeared in the mirror, a woman who was hale and normal and maybe just this side of half-way OK. Maybe I'd be alright. With enough time, enough therapy in the form of rigorous training and hunting, I'd be able to put the entire ordeal into a stuffy dark closet where a monster of my own making devoured it, never to see the light of memory again.

I swallowed, watching the bob of my throat, the slender columns of muscle, and dared—challenged myself—to lift my gaze higher.

The eyes that looked back at me told the real tale.

The tightness at the corners gouged out hard lines that seamed their way to the expanse of emptiness that looked back at me like tributaries led into larger pools and then oceans of water. There was no affect in that gaze. Just a constant ripple of failures.

Inside, where the tightest coil of color pooled around my pupils, I recognized the kid who was too ashamed to go to her parents' funerals and hid out at a crack house getting high. A teen who made her sister's life a breathing, combustible hellfire. A woman who didn't deserve to feel safe and divine when her sister was in danger and completely ignorant of exactly how much danger it was.

In my eyes was the entirety of my awful life, right there on display.

My fist rammed into the glass before I realized I'd even moved. It was so fast, so unexpected, that I jumped at the sound of crackling, splitting shards. My fist was at my side, gripping the material of the gown as the webbing of cracks began to spread out from the center of that wound, just like the ripples of pain in my gaze.

I didn't hear the door open, just saw Blade filling out the door frame through the looking glass, a lacework of cracks breaking him into dozens of shards.

He held onto a tray laden with a slim bottle of green liquid and two long stemmed flutes. Correction. He wasn't holding the tray; it was floating in the air in front of him. His hands were balled into fists below the tray.

Like mine were. Both of us ready for battle.

Except my hands shook as I stared at him, and his did not. They flexed. Once. Twice. Then the alarm on his face softened and his hands opened all the way to hang at his sides. Maybe he'd realized there wasn't a threat. Maybe he saw the way I was trembling, a stupid girl shaking in her boots at some specter she couldn't fight.

Whatever it was, the way he stood there watching me made my throat ache.

"Can't bother to knock?" I asked in a shaking voice that I hated...hated to hear, but damned if I was going to just stand there letting him look at me with that...pity in his gaze.

His Adam's apple plunged down his throat as he reached for the tray and gripped it with white knuckles. He saw me too, the real me, the one in the mirror, not the one in the gown. I know he did. The revelation was all over his face as he scanned me hair to heel.

My heart dropped to my stomach.

"That's not how you looked when I left," he said in a gravelly voice.

I dragged my eyes from his and turned away from both him and the mirror, dropping it to the floor. Just having my gaze released enabled me to breathe again. I bent to retrieve the nightgown from the floor. I didn't know what to say, so I stayed silent.

His approach was soft and sure as he advanced into the room, the door closing behind him with a soft click.

"I told you before; I prefer the ponytail, but you do look beautiful in the gown, Ava."

No mention of the broken mirror, but my head jerked up at his use of my name, my fingers clutching the bodice of the gown. "You called me Ava."

"It's your name, isn't it?"

Straightening my back, I pulled the plunging neckline higher. The room got suddenly too hot. I couldn't move for the suffocating air.

His mouth twitched almost imperceptibly before he crossed to the little table beside the fireplace. The items on the tray vibrated with his steps. Once he set it down, I could see it held not just two flutes and a tankard, but a plate of meat and cheese and two hunks of rustic bread. Melted butter ran down the crust in rivulets.

The yeasty fragrance mingled with that of butter and strong cheese, reminding me I hadn't eaten in forever. My stomach growled. Loudly.

"Sylvia was going to bring this up to you," he said. "But I figured it was time we both ate and had a little talk."

I groaned as I sat on the chair. The skirts left enough slack that I could cross my legs, but doing so showed more than an average amount of skin. I uncrossed them quickly.

"That sounds like an 'it's not you, it's me' thing."

He cocked his head at me, confused, and I waved my hand at him, gesturing that it wasn't important.

"If it's about the mirror, you can forget it," I said. "It was broken like that when we got here."

He tapped the table with his fingers without so much as shifting his expression. "I'll let Sylvia know," he said without missing a beat.

I scanned the table for the best place to tuck into the meal. The bread looked the most inviting.

"So what do you want to talk about?"

"We have to be on the road early in the morning."

I stuck my finger in a pool of melted butter and poked it into my mouth. Still warm and flavored with some herb or other, it tasted better than divine. I reached for a small plate.

"If we have to be up early," I said. "Then it might be best if we just eat and go to bed." I eyeballed the bottle suspiciously as he slid the tankard from the tray onto the table and partnered it with the glasses. "I hope you're not planning to get me drunk and take advantage of me."

He glared at me. "I'm a monster, remember," he said in a blistering tone. "I don't take advantage. I just take." His gaze shuttered as it dipped from my face to my cleavage. "Are you inferring I should try."

"Do it," I said, my face heating. "And see what happens."

"Have a drink," he said flatly.

"I'd rather have a hit of Bloodmist if you don't mind."

It wasn't a test, not really. I hadn't asked him earlier how he knew about the drug. But I wanted to see how he reacted, because if by some miracle he had my inhaler, I wanted it. If there was just one hit left, I wanted it. One hit. I could handle that. I had to. It might be the only chance I had of surviving this God-awful realm.

And if he didn't, then maybe, just maybe, he'd be pissed enough that he wouldn't notice when I dug for information about those ferryman coins.

But when he chuffed out a short laugh that sounded as though he'd actually found my comment funny, I realized he'd heard a joke in my words and not the earnest hope I intended.

"So you're going to ply an addict with booze then," I said, eyeballing the bottle. "Haven't you ever heard of AA?"

He quirked a black eyebrow. "Of course I have. It's some sort of power source that runs on energy instead of magic. Powers flashlights and clock radios."

"Sweet Jesus," I snorted. "I thought you were familiar with the mortal realm."

A fleeting pull of one side of his mouth made me roll my eyes in slow comprehension. "You're joking."

He reached for the bottle while I sagged in the chair, watching him. His hands were as thick and calloused as Stone's were, but somehow graceful at the same time. I imagined they could be equally at ease holding a blade or a brush. I certainly knew he could offer a gentle touch as well as brutal. And the realization left me gawking at him like a love-struck teen.

To disguise the sudden discomfort at realizing I was thinking about his hands at all, I grabbed for the closest piece of bread.

His gaze flicked to my face as I broke off a piece and stuffed it into my mouth. Even without butter it tasted divine.

"I had a piece below," he said absently. "It's good, isn't it."

I dropped my head back, savoring the flavor as I moved the cushion of bread around in my mouth, not wanting to swallow it too soon. I didn't care how crass I looked, talking with my mouth full.

"Like baby unicorn tears," I said around a mouthful.

He pushed the loaf toward me with a single finger. "Maybe," he said. "If baby unicorn tears weren't poisonous."

I stared at him. A slow, languid smile crept over his face. His eyes flashed.

"Are you joking again?"

He shrugged, a movement that lifted one shoulder, bunching up the muscles in a knot that drew my eye. I had to force myself to stop staring, so I broke off another piece of bread—too large a piece, really—and stuffed that into my mouth.

It took a good deal of wrangling to get the bread broken down enough to swallow, and thankfully, he pulled his gaze from mine to the bottle as his fingers wrapped around the neck.

His lips pressed together as the cork popped and a sigh came from the bottle that matched the one that escaped his lungs.

So released, I had time to relax, to enjoy the fizzing effervescence that danced in the air above the mouth of the bottle. To watch his hands and the muscles of his arm as he worked.

"We need to talk about the king," he said absently, startling me as he rolled the bottle around as if it needed to be mixed. I thought of the Rot Gut Tavern and its drink with a spelled chunk of crystallized absinthe and wondered if he'd cast magic into the bottle.

The mere thought of it had me pushing the chair back. The squeal of the legs on the floor caught his attention and he leaned sideways to inspect the chair. I kept my shoulders rigid.

"It's about time someone decided to supply information on the mark," I said.

He swirled the bottle, eyes on me. "Stone and Terran plan to give you information when we return, but they won't be able to tell you all the things you really need to know."

"Pretty sloppy of them to hire an assassin and not educate her on the target," I said, mentally substituting the words hire and assassin for other, more apt terms that he didn't need to hear if I was going to get him to confide in me about those coins.

He poured from the bottle into my glass until it was full and pushed it toward me. The depths of the drink moved like something swam within it. "So much depends on what they can gather from their sources. But even then, there are things they don't know about Ferranus," he said.

"Again," I said. "Pretty sloppy work."

He sighed as he sat back in his chair, stretching his legs out and crossing one ankle over the other.

"To be honest, they do know a lot," he said, reaching for a piece of cheese with blunt, calloused fingers. "And they've told you the main things. Namely, that he beds mortal women like an addict and that failing a flat out attack, getting into his bed might get you closest to him for you to complete the job."

I tried not to squirm at the analogy, and held his eyes steadily, with a determination I feared would wane if tested too long.

Seemingly oblivious to my discomfort, he continued.

"What you don't know and what they won't tell you is that the Shadow Court has been supplying him with those women for over two centuries. The best candidates are selected over a few weeks of grooming, and those who don't quite fit end up in the taverns and bars or are sold into Indenture. Those who are a match to the king's taste, go to him."

"Like cases of expensive Chianti," I said with a note of bitterness. "How lovely. But how does that help me?"

He pursed his lips. "Chianti would accompany a good meal, it wouldn't be the meal."

My fingers froze with a chunk of bread an inch from my mouth. "He's going to eat me," I said and blinked long and hard at the shocking words coming from my mouth. "Eat me." I echoed it because this was too surreal and I needed to hear it a second time.

Blade's hand snaked over the table and grappled my wrist, pulling the morsel of bread and my fingers away, exposing my face to his scrutiny. "No one is eating you, Ponytail. At least not in that sense of the term."

I yanked my hand back, despite the way a jolt of energy moved up along my arm. There had been far too much insinuation in the way he consoled me, and I wasn't in the mood to deflect all that again.

"Damn straight," I said. "I'll slit his throat first." More bravado to hide the squelching feeling in my chest, the one that brought back memories of trudging through the dark in my bare feet. Again, I found myself aching for a hit of Bloodmist. Just to calm my nerves. To boost my confidence.

Blade relinquished his grip on my wrist but he did not drop his gaze. "I believe you," he said. "And I'm counting on that."

"So what's the trouble?" Besides me being completely terrified now of facing the king.

"Ferranus knows someone wants to kill him."

I sucked the back of my teeth in a dry retort. "I'm sure every king and every queen in all the realms in all the wheel of time expects someone to bump them off."

He made a thoughtful sound deep in his throat. "Ah, but not every king has the power Ferranus does." This said with a fierce gaze over the table. "And not every assassin will know what you will."

"And that is?"

"That you won't live an hour past the assassination."

I stared at him, willing my face into a mask that gave away nothing, least of all my lack of surprise. I'd long suspected Terran's cadre would want me dead once I killed the king. I'd be a loose end, and loose ends got cut. So long as Kit was safe, I didn't care.

What surprised me was that Blade was admitting it to me, especially after that passionate kiss. A picture came to mind, unbidden, of Jasmine's arms coiling around his neck while she hooked her ankles over his waist. No matter how much he might have cared for her, his blood vow to his father and the Shadow Court had been stronger.

I couldn't let my feelings for him cloud that fact.

Keeping my expression carefully neutral, I held Blade's eye. "I suppose you'll be the one to kill me, then," I said, casually running my finger along the rim of the glass. Bubbles rose to my touch and tickled my skin. It was such an odd feeling, that I had to pull it away and tuck my hands on my lap. Regular booze didn't feel quite so alive.

Blade watched me, his gaze dropping to the rim of my glass and then along my arms to where my hands lay beneath the table. His scrutiny was careful, intentional, a general mapping a conquest in his mind.

Oh, the balls on him. He could at least have the decency to admit it out loud. After the things we'd shared together, the fighting, the rescue. He at least owed me that. But he would deny me the bald truth, hiding it behind silence.

I felt the rage rise like a phoenix threatening to consume me. But I swallowed it down like a hard knot of unbaked dough.

"And Kit, then?" I asked, because my own demise was nothing to my sister's future. I couldn't forget that either. I'd been living on borrowed time all my life. If I died here in Fae, then I needed to know it wouldn't be a useless demise. "At least tell me she'll be free when it's over."

He leaned over the table toward me enough that I could make out the flecks of silver in his eyes, matching the lining of the irises. "I have a feeling you won't believe me even if I said yes." There was grit to his voice and I blinked, trying to see through the expression, so carefully put on, to the truth beneath. I found him impossible to read. He hadn't answered, and we both knew it.

Crossing my arms over my chest, I leaned onto the table as well, propping my elbows on the surface. "Swear you won't touch her after you're done with me."

"I just did." Not a single movement. No shifting of his body. Eyes steady enough that my heart started to hammer, squeezing something within my chest so hard I thought I would have to fan myself just to get enough oxygen to breathe.

I did my best not to watch him as he nonchalantly rolled his sleeves up to his elbows, exposing the first of the brands he'd seared into his skin. He reached for the bottle again and poured himself a glass, that smoldering gaze dropping to my cleavage over the rim.

My mind automatically conjured the canvas of brands on his arm as I'd seen it growing from his wrist to his neckline and below and I found myself tracing the raised lines I couldn't see. I was aware of a nasty lump settling into my stomach, because while there was no denying something had shifted between us, it was also clear that he would be burning a new symbol into his flesh.

And I couldn't help wondering what sort of symbol that would be when he killed me.

CHAPTER 5

I knew I was going to die, but that wasn't the thing that bothered me most as I sat at the table, watching Blade set the bottle back down. What troubled me more was knowing it was going to be him who did it. I'd seen his work in the dungeons with Jasmine. I'd heard her screams. Facing monsters was one thing; facing a hellhound quite another. I'd seen grown hunters quail in a battle against werewolves. Even a simple Pitt bull could make a man piss himself.

So when Blade came for me, I wasn't sure how I'd manage to stand against him. Maybe I wouldn't. Maybe those last moments would be a relief.

I'd fight him, of course. Tooth and fist, but I couldn't kid myself no matter how badly I wanted it to be true. I knew I didn't have a chance. Not against a monster like that, with speed and agility and magic I didn't—couldn't understand or access. And without an ounce of Bloodmist, I was even more vulnerable.

It was a hard, icy realization, but one I'd learned for real after the catacombs. I'd come to terms with that truth long before I'd been a limp rag soaked with the perspiration of withdrawal under his watchful eye.

It was hard not to pretend I'd been taken by a gaggle of base Fae who couldn't even use their own magic, and still I couldn't do a damn thing to protect myself. Blade could have ended me right then, and it was still such a strange thing that he'd treated me with such care. Begrudging, grumpy care, but care nonetheless.

It was as if he was trying to piece something back together that he'd accidentally broken. Like a child with a favorite toy, smashed to pieces in a fit of anger. An image of Jasmine in those cellars pressed up against my memory, begging to be noticed, and I stuffed it back down into the depths.

But it wasn't just the thought of the violence he was capable of. The thought that he would have to take my life felt like more of a betrayal than Gideon's or Stone's. As much as I hated to admit it, I felt something for the bastard. It was still a big mash of mixed up emotions, but I had the feeling if I could ever pull apart the strands of sticky rubber, I'd find something in there very much akin to Gideon on steroids.

With a stomach that suddenly felt like the savory bread had somehow baked into a brick, I reached for the glass, thinking I needed something to soften the clay in my stomach. But then I realized he'd not so much as touched the stem of his own. I reconsidered taking a drink and pushed the glass back toward him.

He lifted his chin and the silver lining of his irises flared to crimson. "You don't want to share a drink with me, Ponytail?"

My eyes narrowed to slits. "Sharing a drink with you implies you'd be drinking as well," I said, giving his glass a pointed look. It wasn't as if I thought he planned to poison me, but who knew what sort of magic might be in that bottle. It even felt alive on my skin.

His jaw moved side to side, ever so slightly, but I noticed it. "You don't trust me."

I pushed away from the table, my palms flat on the top. "I'd trust you more if you swallowed some of that booze."

He held my gaze but didn't pick up his glass. I waited.

A cloud of suppressed emotion moved across his face for an instant before he mastered it. "Even after everything, you won't trust me."

He sounded hurt, but hell, he'd also sounded like he cared for Jasmine before he'd torn her throat out.

"No offense," I said, standing up. "But I don't trust anyone. And especially someone who just told me they were going to kill me."

His head tilted to the side, very canine-like. Even his eyes held the same sort of lapdog softness. "I told you I was going to kill you?"

I snorted. "You do still have clots of blood in your ears. I heard what you said: I won't live an hour past the assassination. I understand how the mafia works."

"Do you, now?" he asked, and his voice was cold and tight. That was fine with me. My entire chest felt exactly the same way. "And you're comparing the Shadow Court to your earthly counterpart?" He sucked the back of his teeth in disdain. "I'd take the time to educate you on the differences, but I have the feeling it would make you trust me less."

I worried the inside of my cheek with my teeth. "I'm tired," I finally said because I was and because sifting through all the contrasting emotions was exhausting.

"You think you can just dismiss me, Ponytail?"

"What happened to Ava?"

"Ava is a rational, thoughtful woman," he said. "She in front of me now is a cold, calculating, damn hateful hunter."

My chest tightened into a knot even as I lifted my chin. At any other time, I might have taken pride in that description. Now? I wasn't sure. "I'm not cold."

He snorted as he rose from his chair and towered over me. My poor heart beat out a nervous tic the way Thumper would have warned Bambi.

"You're a damn stubborn female," he said in a low voice that sounded very much like a growl. "I should have left you in the catacombs to find your own way out."

I snorted. "Like you would have," I said. "That ego of yours would never be able to stand that a few base Fae stole me right out from under your canine nose."

His face blanched and his jaw clenched, turning whiter than a herring belly before he snarled in response. "You think I endured your cursing and puking and sweating and ... pissing on me...for fuck's sakes, because of my ego?"

I crossed my arms and said nothing. He pretty much had the gist of it, after all, and I wasn't going to give any credence to his hateful comment about my withdrawal by saying a single word. Those bodily functions, that aching and sweating and nearly dying of want was something I'd feel shame over for the rest of my days. They weren't within my control, and I hated myself for it.

But I didn't balk and I didn't back down. We stared at each other for several long moments, waiting to see who would give in first before he finally huffed loudly and rose from his chair with a preternatural slowness, as though he wanted me to see each inch of movement, each flex and twitch of his muscles as he rose like a beast from the depths of a pit.

His lips pursed together so tightly that his jaw turned white around his earlobes. Then, as if he'd taken enough time and had suddenly decided he wanted to be gone, there was a flash of movement and the bottle, glasses, and bread were gathered up into his arms.

He shot a shuttered, heated gaze at me, then pivoted and headed for the door.

Without a single denial, he strolled his way across the entire room in a lazy retreat that all but equaled his agonizingly slow rise from his chair. Bastard was going, alright, but he was taking his sweet time. By the time he pulled the door open and disappeared into the shadows of the hallway beyond, I was seething.

I stood there beside the table for a long moment, swaying on my feet before I dared breathe. Only when I knew he wasn't coming back did I sink back onto the chair's seat and drop my head onto my forearms.

Now that he was gone, whatever steel I'd found in my spine had rusted and crumbled. Exhaustion dogged me like a beagle on a rabbit. I told myself it was the after effects of withdrawal, the trauma of the catacombs, but it felt like more. It felt like I'd lost something and had no idea what it was or where to begin looking for it.

All I could do was close my eyes because they stung so badly it was as if someone had tossed a handful of sand into them. I took long drafts of air, sucking in the smells of the tavern, the fresh grass scent leaking through the cracks in the shutters. Crickets sounded outside in a dirge so sweet, my heartbeat finally slowed down to thrum out a nice, languid shuffling beat. It was all so damned confusing, and without the Bloodmist I was a mess of emotion and impotent, unexplained rage.

Hours later, I woke in bed, not in the chair. I didn't remember taking off the gown or putting on a nightgown. I didn't recall climbing into bed or pulling the heavy blankets over me. I just knew I woke that way. And I felt refreshed. As if I'd never set foot in a dank cavern or bitten down into a dozen cheeks or prodding fingers.

Whatever magic the bed possessed, I decided I'd do anything to own it. I gave myself over to a full, arching body stretch, yawned with enough zeal that my jaw cracked. I took mental survey of my body and decided that the residual twistings of my stomach and aching muscles wouldn't kill me. I'd be able to manage travel even if it would be uncomfortable. I had the feeling I'd be aching for days.

Noises from below trickled up through the floorboards like spiders scuttling over a dew-covered web, catching my attention and making me cock my head to the side, listening. I thought I smelled coffee. Roasted meat.

I swung my legs over the edge of the bed and hurried to the door, hoping I wasn't too late to grab a bite of whatever the women had put together down stairs. I stepped onto something soft and thick as I opened the door. Holding my foot aloft, I gazed down at a bundle of clothes sitting squarely beside the threshold, tied into a neat square with a burlap bow. As happy as I was to see a pair of trousers and a buttery yellow tunic shirt, it was the pewter pot of steaming coffee that pulled an excited whoop from me.

I hunkered down to grab the handle of the pot and realized it wasn't alone on the tray. Nestled behind it, sat a wooden plate rounded with a hot buttered roll and cooked bacon. Melted white cheese dripped from the insides of the roll.

It occurred to me as I snatched the tray up and dragged the clothes into the room with my heel, that I should have hollered out a thank you, but I was so hungry I didn't think I could stand waiting that long to bite into the roll. I decided it would be just as polite to express my gratitude as I left.

I ate the bread and cheese while standing in the middle of the room before I even dressed, and then I strapped my karambit onto my thigh and waited for Blade to fetch me. A few hours more and we'd be back at the castle, closer to the finish line.

He came shortly after, and he looked as put out as he'd been when he left the night before. I told myself his state of mind was his own business, and I thanked Sylvia profusely for the breakfast and the clothes. She glowed as she clasped both my hands in hers and wished me well, her partners hovering near the bar, out of range of Blade, darting looks at him that suggested that despite Sylvia's smiling face, they were glad to be rid of us.

We left them to a clean tavern that showed no signs of the horrors Blade had inflicted upon it, and yet the scene burned a path through my mind every time I blinked. For some reason, I saw myself in place of those fae. My limbs. My blood. My beaten and torn body littering the floor, the result of Blade's orders to end me when this was all over.

The images consumed me until I couldn't speak. I couldn't understand why I felt so betrayed. I hadn't expected to live through the task, not really. I just knew it would be worth it. For Kit. For one time in my miserable life, I'd do something good for her. If it meant I had to string myself up from a rafter somewhere and let myself hang till dead, I would have done it.

And that was exactly why I was so damned confused. I'd never been afraid to die. All I'd thought about in those catacombs was vengeance and going down fighting. But now something had shifted. I felt fear. Real fear. It was a vague and terrifying thing, like eyes burning into the back of your neck from a dark shadow.

Chapter 6

The ride was one of tension and shadows that despite the brightness of the morning, seemed to claw striated fingers toward us with every pace along the trail. The forests on either side grew dense in a way they hadn't appeared upon entering. It left me with the feeling that the trail was happy to have us enter it but did not want us getting back out.

No matter how long Nutkin plodded along, I was certain we weren't going the right way. The trees seemed all wrong, skeletal and bare when they'd been lush and laden upon entering.

It was a towering canopy, none the less, with ancient cedars whose mossy foliage hung down in dried fringes of rust. Witch alder frothed beneath the boughs in equally dried bunches of dead leaves sandbar twigs, and through the unearthly lace of that dead fauna, a primordial darkness leaked out into the sunshine.

"Are you sure we're going the right way?" I dared ask when I couldn't stand staying quietly acquiescent to the obviously wrong path anymore. The last thing I wanted was to take a sidetrack down along another horror like the catacombs. I shivered even though the sun was on my arms.

"I'm not lost, I assure you," he said with a note of annoyance. "Not that I'd expect you to trust me."

I bit down on my tongue, struggling not to speak to that comment, since we'd said all we needed to the night before. I just watched the trees grow bigger and thicker, the path less marked. My ears picked up the chatter of unseen animals above the thudding of Nutkin's hooves, a sound that reminded me of bones rattling in the wind of a spectral chime. Once, I muttered to myself that trust was immaterial if the guide was taking us unbeknown into the arms of death.

At length, we arrived at a dead end in the trail. I'd seen it coming for at least ten minutes and mentioned it at least a dozen times to the accompaniment of a host of curses in a language I didn't need to understand to get the gist. I shut up after that and let him take us, waiting for my moment to fling an I told you so in his face. Or more accurately, an I told you so elbow, since I was nestled between those muscled thighs, suffering the movement of them along my own with every determined step of the horse.

Nutkin halted automatically in front of a colossal cedar, its gnarled roots like the fingers of a gargantuan beast clawing through the earth around it. I'd seen the redwoods of California big enough for cars to drive through, but never something as large as this tree. The branches began at least two stories above us and amid a forest of dead foliage, those branches created as lush a canopy as ever I'd seen.

"Well," he said.

"Well, what?" I asked. "Have we gone so far off the edge of the world that we're about to enter the Shire or are you asking me if I'd like to meet an ent?"

"I told you I wasn't lost," he said as he slid down from Nutkin's back, leaving me to climb down the monstrosity on my own.

No problem. I landed as though I had springs in my legs and bounced back into an upright stand, my hand on my karambit. I shot him a wicked grin of victory, which he ignored in favor of striding toward the tree.

He went rigid within a few feet of the trunk and seeing it, I did too. Something was out there. I felt the shift in the air currents, maybe a second later than he did, but it was a change just the same. Fronds of foliage above us rustled. The entire forest went more silent than it had been just a moment earlier.

His shoulders rolled ever so slightly as he swung his head slowly toward me, a sergeant making eye contact with a member of his assault team. We didn't need speech. His eyes said it all. Be alert. To the left, a shape that shouldn't be there.

I immediately went into a fighting stance. Shifting my attention to the hum of air around me, the sounds of the forest, my brain lit up with commands that shot down to every muscle in my body. From the corner of my eye, I caught sight of something brackishly grey. Tall. Wiry.

Without being told, I pivoted sharply, putting my back to Blade's. Detritus on the forest floor moved with my boots, but made no sound. His back was hot on mine, stiff, and powerful. If I lent anything to the fight, I knew he wouldn't need me.

But I'd be damned if I'd let him have all the fun. Even if I was still half weak from withdrawal and still craving the drugs like a mofo.

"Greys," he said, angling his jaw over his shoulder toward me.

"What in the hell are greys?" I scanned the gaps in the trees and foliage and saw a sort of shuffling about. "Zombies?" I'd fought a zombie created by a voodoo priestess as a means to steal bodies for her to use in her ceremonies for a black cult of witches trying to learn the craft. They weren't fun. Stinking and stupid and mere mush by the time you put your fist through one.

"Not far off, Ponytail," he said. "But not quite on, either."

My nose didn't detect the smell of rot. "What does that mean, not quite."

I felt his back relax against mine, a signal that whatever danger he'd sniffed was gone. I wasn't quite so sure. When I looked through the branches and dried brush, I could still see them out there in a sort of stasis, shifting foot to foot.

"I've not seen many in my day," he said. "And that's a hell of a long time, Ponytail. They're a sort of blank entity that can take on the intentions of another. Usually, it's sorcerers who employ them for work they have no taste for. It takes powerful magic to instill them with intention."

"So these are blanks?" I asked, narrowing my gaze as a set of black eyes peered back at me through a weave of branches.

"Seems so," he said. "They are not of the Fae realm," he said. "Their world is altogether different even than your earthly realm." I took a step toward the one looking at us through the branches. It didn't move. Didn't even blink. A closer look proved they didn't even have eyelids, or if they did, they ticked up underneath a fold of skin in their forehead.

I shuddered. Of all the things I'd seen, these creeped me out. "What are you doing?" I growled. "Don't aggravate the damn things. If they're content to stand there, let them stand. Let's get the hell out of here."

With a look of secrecy, he said, "I told you I wasn't lost. I'm here on business."

I spread my arms out to my sides to indicate the forest of ever increasing shadows and death. "Bustling metropolis, this," I said. "Planning to drop a few coin on the stock market?"

He ran his hand over the back of his neck. "I told Mica I'd pick him up a couple of books from the Alexandria Bookshop."

Pinching the bridge of my nose, I cast a glance back at Nutkin, who looked at me with the same sort of look that must have been in my eyes. Swiveling its head toward the grey in the trees, the horse blew a loud fart.

"I feel the same," I said, turning back to Blade and eyeballing him with a look of complete and utter sarcasm. "We call bullshit."

"If you don't have anything useful to add to the conversation," Blade said to Nutkin, and ignoring me. "Best not say anything at all."

Then he strode with purpose through the leaves and twigs toward the cedar. As he got closer, the faint outline of a sign hanging on an ornate frame of blacksteel came into view along with an arched window and a carved door set into the tree trunk at an angle that made it look askew.

Blade pressed his palm against the door and it phased out of existence, leaving in its wake a shuddering, wavering pool of shadow.

He turned to beckon to me. "Would you rather stay outside with the bogey men?"

I cut a glare at him as I strode for the puddle of shadow. "Not because I'm afraid, mind you," I said. "But because my curiosity has got the better of me. His smile was brief but genuine, but as I tried to shoulder past him, he held me back. "Is this how a hunter works?" he asked. "Bluster in and ask questions later?"

I shrugged. "Works most times."

"And the others?"

I lifted my eyebrows at him. "I'm here in Fae aren't I?"

His dark chuckle moved my hair and I pushed him aside, as though I could move that boulder at any regular time, but he did let me and as I stepped over the threshold, the entire interior lit up like a warm Christmas glow at Rockefeller Plaza.

Inside, the bookstore unfurled its wonders like an enchanting tapestry. One large central staircase fashioned as a spiral bookcase wound its way up the middle of the cedar with three wooden platforms offering respites of overstuffed chairs and oil lamps. The staircase and its bookshelves wound downward as well, into an open pit of darkness. Lined both up and down with bookshelves instead of a railing, the spines on the shelves spoke the titles in faded gilt lettering and sometimes in a scrawl that looked more like claw marks dug into the leather than in an elegant hand.

The walls of the bookstore had a rough hewn quality, as though someone had gouged away the guts of the ancient cedar with a melon baller. Blackened pathways of wormwood larvae created a lace work design so intricate, no human hand could have done as well.

There was a smell of an old closet in the place, overridden by that of ink and paper so strong I couldn't even smell the cinnamon that always came off Blade in waves.

One gargantuan hagstone hunkered in a swath of space to the right of the staircase. Two miniature oil lamps hanging from a hook in the middle filled its eye. The light they offered winked in and out, making me feel distinctly dizzy.

It took me several moments to realize those winking lights were actually a set of eyes blinking out at us and I started, grabbing for the hem of Blade's shirt in reflex. His move was fast at my touch, spinning in a blur with his face a rictus mask of warning.

"What do you want?" the owner of those eyes asked in a quaking voice.

"What do you think?" Blade said, striding toward him, his shirt undulating over the powerful muscles of his back. "Books."

The lights blinked off again. A shuffle of movement. Then a head popped up behind the hagstone.

The creature that confronted us was not high Fae, but he did have wings. Tiny bumblebee wings attached to the back of his shoulders in such an awkward spot, I doubted he could fly. His face seemed very frog like, with bulging eyes and warts on top of warts. But in that face, those eyes held a keen intelligence, lids shuttering down over copper colored irises as they panned every inch of our clothes and the way we stood. He was tall and wiry, opposite the toad-like quality of his face.

Neither Blade nor I moved as he came out from behind the counter cautiously and adjusted his waistcoat, a thing made out of silks so fine, it put me in mind of Erachne's shop. Embroidered into the panels, runes and leaves and a few odd lines of script gave the waistcoat a wealthy air.

"My apologies," he said, clearing his throat. "I'm Fraggle," he said, eying me up the way a frog might a fly. "Things in the vale have been off for some time and I never know what's coming in through the door." He shot a harried look toward the pit where the spiral bookcase disappeared. "Or what's coming up."

Blade's jaw ticked to the side. "The greys," he said shortly, and the little fae nodded.

"The portal to the Shadow Bazaar is malfunctioning for some reason. It keeps spitting out all those creatures." He ambled toward us, plucking a sheaf of papers from inside his waistcoat. This, he proffered to Blade. "I've been keeping track as they come. Usually, they are inert, but these last ones I never know what I'll see." He blinked so fast in rapid succession that he seemed to be flirting with Blade, who stepped back, disconcerted.

The fae shoved the papers at Blade, who finally took them from his grasp. As he scanned what was written on them, the owner kept talking, and kept blinking so quickly, I had to turn my gaze to Blade just to keep from blinking at the same rate.

"I never know what they'll do," he said. "Last week one of them tried to rape me." This said with such an affront, it sounded less like he was afraid and more like he was offended it would dare such a thing. "He got a good kick to his nutless groin for all the good it did me." Three blinks this time. Slowing down, it seemed. "Ever since then, they've got even more violent." He jerked his head toward the staircase. "I had to seal off the lower levels, just to sleep at night. But eventually even the inert ones turn." His gaze swept me from head to heel. "Eventually," he said again as though that was important.

"How long?" I asked and he looked very pleased that I'd asked the question. I thought of the greys outside in the bushes.

Blade didn't give him the chance to answer. "My books," he said in a brusque tone. I glared at him for his lack of manners. It was clear the little fae needed help.

The owner clicked his heels together and stiffened his spine. "Oh my manners," he said. "You'll have to excuse me. Bookworms don't often have occasions to fight for their lives." He leaned against the hagstone counter and crossed one ankle over the other. "Fifty serpents a piece," he said extending his hand with a pointed look at the sheaf of papers Blade hadn't even bothered to scan. "Price has gone up." He shot me a wicked grin. "Danger pay."

I was beginning to like the bookstore owner, and when Blade told him the titles of the two books he was interested in, I liked him even more and only because the gleam that came into his eyes indicated he was about to charge far more than Blade thought they were worth. I stood back, crossing my arms over my chest and leaning against the wall to take it all in.

"A God's Guide to Alchemy is a rare edition," he said to Blade. "I believe it is the original printing. I'd have to have two hundred crowns for that. And Diary of an Unnamed Queen resides within the realm of fiction and the subterranean tunnels." His gaze trailed to the bookshelf and where it descended into the shadows.

"Let me guess," said Blade in a drawl that suggested he knew full well the sort of haggling he was in for. "Danger pay."

When the owner grinned again, mischievous dimples appeared amongst the warts. "Any other fae, and I'd refuse altogether," he said. "Fiction isn't worth my little hide no matter how insulting it is to behold. But you." He skimmed Blade with a knowing glance. "I imagine even the vampire greys will quake at the sight of the dark enforcer."

The word vampire got me off the wall and pattering over to the owner. "You have vampires?" Sweet Lord, something familiar. I could have kissed his thin lips.

He nodded. "Indeed. At least three of them. Very strange for a grey to crave blood."

"Maddox is dead," Blade said flatly. "All of the portals in and out of the bazaar are doing strange things."

The owner made a thoughtful sound, his finger tapping his lips. "That explains much."

"Does it?" I asked and he nodded.

"Perhaps not to someone of your earthly predilection," he said. "But to those of us with magic, the bazaar provided so much. Pity it's descended to chaos."

"I'm a hunter," I said. "I've taken out more than the normal woman of earthly predilection."

If he'd have possessed eyebrows, they'd have shot up. Instead, he bowed ever so slightly and in a way that made me feel almost proud. "We'll get rid of the vampires," I blurted before Blade could refuse. He swiveled his head toward me. I didn't need to hear what he was thinking. It was written all over his face. "Danger pay," I said. "What's a bit of violence for the dark enforcer."

"I'll toss in the alchemy text for free," the owner said, hopeful. "It's very valuable and I could ask three hundred crowns for it and no one would bat an eyelash." His own shot off several, rapid fire blinks.

"I thought you said two hundred," Blade said.

The owner canted his head. "Oh, did I? I must have been mistaken. I'm shook, you see." He gestured toward the staircase with the sheaf of papers. "Two hundred is the number of greys I've had to deal with since this all began." He pouted. "You'd know that if you'd looked at my tally."

Blade ran his hand over his hair and huffed. "There's no way the alchemy text is worth three hundred crowns."

"Four."

Blade's shoulders rolled. "What's that now?"

The owner didn't seem afraid of the tension filling the air. "The cost of the alchemy text," he said. "Five hundred crowns." He blinked rapidly again with feigned innocence. "I thought we were discussing the price of it, and I was reminding you. It's six hundred crowns if I have to descend into that pit of hell."

I had to stifle a chuckle beneath my palm. "Sold," I said under my breath but neither fae showed me any attention.

Blade grunted something about that being a ridiculous price and the two of them began the haggling all while I waited to see how long it would take for the inevitable acquiesce or threat from Blade. To my surprise, he agreed.

The owner regarded us thoughtfully before extending his hand with a sly grin. "Deal."

With a heavy, barely tolerant sigh, he turned to me. "Strap on that blade of yours, Ponytail. We're going into the pits of hell."

CHAPTER 7

The pits of hell stank of lavender. Old rushes made with the dried blooms cushioned the walls where they met the floor. Gnarled tree roots created a basket weave of the subterranean walls that surrounded the staircase. All the shelves for the last two stories had been emptied at some point, and now the books that had filled them barred the entrance the way floods were held back by bags of sand. The piles had toppled in multiple places, leaving several openings for creatures to climb through.

"No wonder he's still dealing with them," I said, clambering over a stack of old paper and vellum that moved and slid and fell beneath my knees. "Books aren't exactly a deterrent."

"I guess that depends on whether you like to read."

The look I cut him could have sliced paper. "Stick to violence," I said. "You'd starve as a comic."

A low, rumbling chuckle escaped him and I thought he might follow up the noise with another lame crack, so I pushed forward, aiming for a hole in the stacks large enough to crawl through. The dark enforcer chose a different method of navigating the piles of ephemera, electing to shove through with a force of magic that bowled the books out of his way.

"You might want to save some of that magic," I said. "No telling what we'll face on the other side." I didn't want to say he'd already used a hell of a lot over the last couple of days.

He shrugged and blasted another dozen books out of the way, this time with a crimson light that resembled a laser. "I'm feeling refreshed," he said. "Not to worry, Ponytail. I have a great deal of stamina."

This said with a cloak of innuendo that brought an unbidden image of his magnificent physique and every sinew of muscle in it to mind.

With an irritated fling of several books in his direction, I said, "Well, no one likes a show-off."

"Ask me nicely," he said and I'll get you off too."

Now I knew he was playing with me. I sucked the back of my teeth. "I don't need help to crawl over a few books." Looking sideways, I saw him striding through a path between stacks as though he were Moses parting the seas. His back was taut and straight, and he strode unimpeded through the other side. "But I'm not stupid either."

Several books fell with an echoing thud as I climbed down from the pile and made for the pathway. It was obvious from the earthen floor that we were at the ground floor of the bookstore, and I followed on Blade's heels through the impressive number of tomes the owner had piled into the entrance. Several feet of paper and vellum and cow hide swirled around us until we got to the other side of the barrier.

It was eerie there. Completely dark and silent. I hadn't realized the bottom of the stairwell held any sconces of light until we stepped through and lost it.

"If these things are true vampires," I said. "They won't need to see us to find us."

Although most species of vampires could see in the dark, they all had preternatural hearing and sense of smell. I couldn't see Blade but I could smell him and sense him near. I thought of asking him to cast some light, but before I could do so, something brushed along my shoulder.

On the opposite side of where Blade stood beside me.

A shiver ran down my spine, and I reached slowly and purposefully for my sheathed karambit. Whatever the creature with us was, it knew we were there. It just hadn't decided to attack. Yet. And going on the offensive immediately without knowing exactly what we faced or how many would be foolhardy.

"Blade," I hissed, keeping my voice low and steady as I aimed my blade outward in an attack hold. "We're not alone."

I felt him lean into me, his breath on my cheek. "Five of them, Ponytail. One right next to you, just watching."

My skin crawled at the thought, and I had to fight back the panic, tell myself if it hadn't attacked there was a reason.

"Not vampire," I whispered.

"I don't think so," he said in a normal tone. "It appears to be one of the inert ones. It's just swaying back and forth."

The image that painted in my mind and his seeming calm, buoyed me enough that when I spoke, the words came out in a normal voice. "The others?"

"The same."

At his words, lights blazed here and there along the walls, peppering the tunnel with flakes of illumination that rose up for a full story before it disappeared into the darkness, impeded by the floor above us. As the light came, I found myself back-to-back with Blade, maneuvered away from the grey so expertly I'd barely felt him shifting our direction.

A master of war, this one.

The grey was, indeed, watching me. It stood several feet away, now, the result of Blade moving us along and positioning us in a defensive stance. The thing was eerily reminiscent of the aliens I'd seen depicted in cartoons and old movies, just much taller. They had to be nearly as tall as the dark enforcer at my back.

I didn't see, but I knew the other four were on his side, and though part of me felt slighted that he thought he had to face the brunt of any possible attack, I knew it was the smart move. I also knew we were going to slice through them without provocation and that made my stomach recoil.

"Can't we do this the easy way?" I asked.

"This is the easy way. Both of us are only half-recovered and waiting for them to take on some magical intention would be...harder."

I blew out a long breath. He was right. I nodded my answer, knowing he felt it against his back. "Don't be a hero," I said. "Or get fancy."

He flat out laughed at that, making the grey watching me cant its head to the side. "Monsters don't make good heroes, Ponytail."

And at that his back peeled away from mine. I felt him move somewhere behind me, heard the grunts and squeals like pigs as he scored through the creatures. Wet thuds sounded in my ears, and I imagined I counted to three before I finally pushed through my own hesitation and stepped toward my grey.

It didn't move to defend itself. Just stood there, swaying a hint to the left, a hint to the right, those large black eyes watching me.

"I'm sorry," I said as my hand sliced out and drew back. The angle of the karambit razored through its neck so cleanly, it just sagged to the floor, bleeding out brackish looking blood.

My arms hung to my side as I watched it twitch. Another wet thud from behind me and I knew it was over. My shoulders felt too heavy. A long exhale fled my lungs as I turned around. A small mist of blood peppered Blade's shirt, but other than that, he showed no evidence of having killed anything.

"You wear violence too well," I said and pointed toward the shadows that felt much deeper now that the creatures were dead. "I suppose we have a book to find," I said. "Any ideas on how to do that when we didn't even ask."

He chuckled. "You humans," he said. "You like things the hard way."

At that, he held up his hand, fingers flat and vertical. A pulse of magic moved through the room. I saw it ripple toward a chamber with the same type of door to the bookstore itself.

"It's in there," Blade said, jerking his chin toward the doors. Above it a placard read: Fiction. Fae.

"As opposed to Fiction: human," I suppose and headed forward. "Where do you think the portal is?" I said to break the eerie silence. I wasn't in the mood to kill more blank, befuddled creatures just because I wasn't sure what they'd turn into.

"I imagine Fraggle earns most of his living selling access to the portal so it would be where his costliest tomes are located."

"You say his name like you don't believe he's being truthful."

"Oh, he was truthful at the time," he said."But he made that name up the moment he saw you, Ponytail. I bet you watched Fraggle Rock as a kid."

"What in the hell is Fraggle Rock."

He made a thoughtful sound. "Sometimes I forget how time moves in your world. Never mind. It was a show of fancy."

By then, we'd made it to the door and he scanned it with a thoughtful gaze.

"My guess is the portal is inside. Fae don't lie. It's not like it's criminal to do so, just that it creates a sort of pain between the eyes. The bigger the lie, the greater the pain and even the smallest lie hurts like a bitch."

"What's that got to do with putting the portal in the fiction sections."

"Reading fiction is about as close to living the varnished truth as they can get. So I'm guessing he charges a premium for the risk of reading what could ostensibly be untruthful stories. I imagine he has be-spelled the books to obliterate any pain created by the non truths inside."

I shook my head. "So you read boring old nonfiction all the time?"

He planted his hand on the handles. "I prefer hardcore erotica," he drawled. "Far closer to my truth."Before I could retort, he pushed open the doors and shoved me inside just as a book flew toward me at speeds that would take the head off a horse.

I ducked, but not fast enough, and his hand swiped over my vision to pluck the tome from midair a second before it struck me in the nose.

"You did that on purpose," I growled.

"Just checking to see if the big bad hunter would bluster or duck." His eyes flared with silver at the rims. "You passed. Now let's go."

I rolled my eyes as I advanced into the room, not caring if he saw my reaction or not. "Are you sure it's the porn book you wanted?"

The bristling energy coming off him in waves made me chuckle to myself.

"I told you, this was for Mica."

"Sure, sure," I said. "How bad is the pain between your eyes right now?"

Oh I was enjoying this. He was so stuffy and arrogant and damned brooding all the time. It was fun to see him off his stance for a change. With a roving glance, I took in the chamber and the floor to ceiling bookshelves, the fancy ladders, the cold fireplace and inviting chairs. It would be such a wonderful bookstore if it were in the human realm.

"Maybe we should fix the portal," I said as I walked, running my hands along the spines of books of various ages.

"If you mean put it in working order, that's impossible. But if by fix you mean destroy so no more things crawl through, I'd say it's someone else's problem."

"Spoken like a true hero," I said. "I told you not to do that."

He snuffed on a smothered laugh and I felt him come up behind me, the fragrance of cinnamon a wash that made my stomach clench. "The Ash Gate," he mused aloud. "Would probably be over there." His arm extended, book in hand, toward the fireplace. Telltale signs of footprints, all made of fine ash crisscrossed over each other so often, they'd lost form.

Pivoting, I planted my hands on my hips. "Can't you use your magic to close it," I said. "We can't just leave him to put up with all this chaos."

His eyebrow quirked in protest. "Haven't you done enough fighting, Ponytail? Shouldn't you save some of that for the king?" Crossing his arms over his chest, he regarded me with a commanding air. "Besides, we have things to do."

That rankled. I took a step backward, holding his gaze in challenge. "And this little side hustle to pick up a pornography book counts as things to do, I suppose?" Spinning on my heel, I headed toward the fireplace, feeling him behind me, a glowering, brooding presence.

I didn't get more than three feet before something...hiccuped...in the air around the grate. A pulse of magic rippled out from inside and the next I knew, I was slammed to the floor, Blade on top of my back, pinning me.

CHAPTER 8

At first, I writhed beneath him out of long-ingrained and habitual fight or flight instinct, but his snarl of warning in my ear stopped me dead.

"A dozen of the things just came through," he said. "Stay still."

Meaning lie quietly beneath him like a damn damsel while he assessed if they were more blanks or transformed into something more sinister. But I laid there, because once again, he was right. There would be plenty of time to reprimand him later for treating me like a vacuous mortal woman.

A hiss sounded through the chamber and I heard Blade mutter something that sounded very much like a Fuck Me, comment.

So. Not blanks then. "Let me up," I whispered, a sense of precognition tickling the back of my neck as I lay face down. The coppery tang of old blood and rot swept to my nose. "I know the stink of vampire."

His weight peeled off my back and in a heartbeat, he'd taken hold of my hand and tugged me to my feet. "Not just any vampire, Ponytail," he said.

Not indeed. The inert appearance of the blanks was gone. In its place, snarled a hissing mass of teeth and claws. Not a Twilight sparkle anywhere. No sentience either. Just pure malevolence. It was clear at least five of them had fed on someone or something between the moments it had got caught in the portal and arrived here. Blood dribbled down their chins.

One of them hissed at me as it met my eye, and a spray of viscous liquid misted the air. It struck one of the overstuffed chairs and the fabric melted away with a sizzle of smoke.

"Oh fuck me," I said.

"Maybe later," Blade said. "Over these fuckers dead carcasses." He shifted then. Between one moment and the next the fae became the hellhound. Without a moment's hesitation, he tore for the nearest vampire. I only had time to put a bead on the one I'd go for before another lunged for me.

Karambit held high, I danced away, letting my cell memory move my muscles where they wanted. I spun around at the zenith of the arc to face my opponent, expecting to see a slice through its belly or throat. I'd felt the tug of skin on blade, and I knew I'd done damage, but what confronted me was a shock I wasn't prepared for.

Where it bled, smoke rose. Where the blood touched, things melted away with a sizzle. Several books on the shelf nearby had crackled to near ash.

"Acid," I said loud enough for the dark enforcer to hear. I had no idea where he was, just heard the growl and snarl escaping his throat. "They bleed acid."

If he bit down or tore into any of those things with his teeth or claws, he'd burn. Searching him out, I saw him backing three into the corner, but I knew if he didn't that they were finding a way to ambush him. Two others were already shambling for his back end.

I fought with everything I had, my blade a blur of silver in the dim light. The scent of lavender and the coppery tang of vampire blood filled the air around me as I slashed and danced away, praying I'd get out of range each time.

Every swipe of my karambit that struck home bled out more acid. Soon everything smoked. My sleeve had long burned away into tatters of rags, and I'd taken a hit of droplet that burned like a mother at first on my bare skin, but that evaporated like steam and healed quickly.

Blade, I knew, noticed the hits I was taking and healed me with his magic, giving me more to bring to the fight. It helped but I was far from well enough to last long, and I knew it. Not hours before, I'd been writhing in pain and sweat. A baker's dozen of vampires was too much even for a powerful hellhound Fae and an experienced hunter, both of whom were working on half-cylinders.

Blade showed no weakness even if he was feeling as drained as I was. Healing me instantly on top of all the magic he'd expended over the last few days, had to be taking its toll. When I could, I distracted the vampires to my side, giving him a breath, expecting him to do the same for me when he caught me flagging. But when he noticed me doing that, he redoubled his attacks and the vampires drew themselves to him once again.

It was frustrating. And it was welcome. I was losing my wind easier and part of me wanted to give over the fight to the powerful fae. He was a rampage on legs in hellhound form. He rolled and twisted, a tangle of limbs so fast I could barely make out a single distinct shape as he tore into whichever vampire fell beneath his strikes.

As fast as he was, however, the vampires outnumbered us, and it wasn't long before I was panting from effort. My arm started to drag instead of slashing out with the speed I was used to. My legs quaked and took longer to obey. When I drew back the karambit for another strike, it felt like I was hauling a concrete block through a wall of molasses.

Blade fared better than me. I counted four that he'd taken out with a slash of claws, and they lay sprawled over the floor in pools of hissing blood and steam. I knew I'd delivered a mortal wound to one of them myself and leaped away before the spray of acid blood reached me. If Blade was healing me, he was neglecting himself. I shouted at him to do something about the long line of acid drooling down his hind quarters, sizzling like grease on a hot skillet.

That moment proved my biggest mistake. All five that he was facing flashed their fangs at me, noticing a far less powerful opponent than the one they faced without result, a human with more than enough blood to satisfy their cravings. For an instant that seemed to go on longer than it should have, I stood there, waiting for one of them to act. Their hesitation earned Blade's wrath. He leaped for the nearest one, fangs extended, and struck home so viciously that that one shake lopped off the vampire's head and sprayed more acidic blood over Blade in a wave of liquid.

Seeing him fall did something to me. A scream tore loose from me that made me shrink back. For a split second, I imagined a world without him and I felt strangely desolate.

I'd witnessed his ferocity in the caverns, saw him shred through dozens of fae in that form, high and low Fae alike without exhaustion. But it was clear watching him now, that his magics weren't up to the task. His fur was gathering back together over the gaping wound as I watched, the edges granulating nicely, but the process was slower than before.

I needed to get to him and haul his ass out of there. I told myself that without the dark enforcer, I had no hope of surviving, but there was something else that drove me across the chamber toward him, some tight spot in my chest that formed a lump I could barely breathe past.

I made it about three feet before the room pulsed again. The vampires paused, their attention rooted to the fireplace. Another set of greys popped through the grate.

That moment drew a guttural growl from the depths of Blade's gut, and he heaved himself once more to his feet. His hind legs dragged behind him. The vampires faced him, thinking him easy prey now.

I yelled. I was coming. Hold on. Don't do something stupid.

That was when they turned their attention to me. That was the moment they abandoned the fight with the hellhound and aimed their attack on a mortal human without a lick of magic.

"Come on, then, bastards," I shouted, drawing them further away from Blade. "Come get me."

Everything swam perfectly into focus then. The greys shaking themselves free of the coating of ash they'd gained from traveling the gate, the crimson eyes sliding into place like a top, turning the black to blood red as they transformed into the same monsters coming at me. My hearing tunneled down to the plop plopping sound of blood dripping onto the floor, the hiss of gas rising from the hellhound's skin.

I knew all those things in the recesses of my lizard brain, marking them, as I trod forward to meet them. A laugh escaped me, nervous and resigned. My last stand, I thought. My last stand against a seethe of vampires. It was perfect.

I raised my karambit, bringing it up slowly, heavily, knowing the next instant, those creatures would run for me. I might have had an ounce of strength left, but I was giving them all of it. Behind them, rolling over onto his side the dark enforcer howled. I grinned at him. Fuck you, that smile said. Fuck you and all your damned notions that I'm a damsel.

One second, that's all it took for him to meet my gaze as the hellhound, and then a pulse of magic blew over me like a warm wind. I felt the pulse of energy all around me like an electric fence.

The hellhound collapsed. His head struck the earthen floor with a thud. I was sure my heart stopped.

The vampires drew back as though whatever shield surrounding me was blowing a gale of wind at them. Maybe it was. They staggered. Blade watched, his hound's eyes drooping, his muzzle barely an inch from the floor.

"Sweet Jesus," I blurted out, and the words had no sooner fled my lips than the vampires turned back around. They didn't shamble. They knew victory was in their grasp.

Blade tried to get up. Fury wrapped around me like a heavy shroud. "Fuck you," I yelled, frustrated to be taken out of the fight. I railed against the walls of the shield in vain, kicking, shouldering it. I watched all but helpless as Blade shifted to his fae form, the obviously last bit of his powers, and he got to his knees.

His head low and his arms raised in a blocking posture, his gaze flicked to me. Just once. As it did, the pulse of energy around me seemed slower. Less intense. He wasn't able to keep it up much longer, I knew.

"Drop it," I yelled. "Drop the fucking shield."

Another grey popped into the fireplace. Shook himself. Ashes flew everywhere.

Ash. It was called the Ash Gate. Of course.

I scoured the floor, searching for piles of it. The vampires had reached Blade. One of them had sunk its teeth into his throat. I screamed again, this time a curse filled with panic. The shield wavered.

"The ash, Blade," I yelled. "Gather the ash."

Three more vampires descended on him and the shield fell. A sob wracked its way free of my throat and I raced, staggering and stumbling toward them.

"Gather the ash." I kept saying it, screaming it, flinging myself at one vampire and the next in a frenzy that surprised them. I slashed with my karambit. Ignored the burning of my flesh where the acid struck. "The ash, Blade. Raise it."

And by some miracle, he did. Some part of his magic moved enough to lift ash from the floor, the grate, the furniture. It rose in small clusters at first, then in larger gobs. Clouds of it hovered in the air like floating balls of dust.

I broke free of the seethe, racing for the bellows hanging on the hearth. I had just one thought, and I prayed it was true. If the ash had brought them, the ash should be able to send them back.

Aiming the business end at each cluster, I pumped the bellows. Air gusted through each cloud, and I danced out of the way like a voodoo priestess in herky-jerky movements until the plumes landed on the vampire still clinging to Blade's throat. For a millisecond, the dust coated its back and climbed to its head. I watched it move with my heart in my throat, worried I was wrong.

Then just when I thought I'd wasted time instead of slicing through the vampire, it went rigid. An instant later, it dissipated to dust, swirling within the cloud.

I didn't hesitate then. Blow by blow, pump by pump, I forced the ash onto the vampires one by one. When they came at me, they made it easier. Those ones died looking at me.

Alone, finally, I raced for Blade, who was lying on his back. The holes in his throat were still red and swollen. Wounds showed through his clothes in burnt, blackened, and bloody Technicolor. He wheezed in a breath through swollen lips.

The moment he met my gaze, I knew he wouldn't survive.

CHAPTER 9

"Don't you fucking die on me you bastard," I growled and without thinking about what I was doing, leaped over his hips to straddle him. I wasn't sure what I should do: CPR, bandage, artificial resuscitation. I just knew I had to do something.

I could see him struggling to heal. Several blistered patches on his cheek were twitching and moving as though someone was cloning bits of skin the way they did in digital design. I leaned over him. My hair fell on his face and I swept it back. The serpent of crimson rounded the silver lining in his eyes.

"Blade," I said, sick to hear the worry in my voice. "What can I do?"

Like he'd done for me back at the tavern, I smoothed his cheek with the back of my hand. Comfort. That's what it looked like. I should talk to him in soft tones, rub his hands. I wasn't sure.

He tried and failed to clear his throat. I put my ear to his mouth. Words, garbled and rusty rasped into my ear.

"What's that?" I asked, lifting my head so I could look into his face.

His lips moved. One syllable. Something starting with B. "I don't understand."

With a panicked scan of the room, I tried to find something I could use to haul him out that would increase my chances of getting him out before another vampire came through the portal.

"This place is a fucking mess," I complained. "I don't know what to do."

I was pushing myself off him, pulling my leg back over to one side of his hips when his hand clamped down on my wrist. There was still steel in the grip. I peered down at him.

"Blood," he coughed out. His eyes held mine, flaring with just enough life that I knew if I hesitated, that light would go out.

So I didn't hesitate. I didn't think about what I was doing, I just jammed my wrist against his mouth. I expected a sharp sting as he bit down. I did not expect him to fight me.

"Dammit, Blade. Bite me."

The fingers holding my other hand let go and somehow he managed to find enough strength to push me away. I scrambled back to his side as he tried to roll over. Away from me. I grabbed his shoulders, rolling him onto his back again. Stared down into his face.

"You're dying, Blade," I said. "And if you plan to keep doing so, I'm going to make that death as painful as I can." I jabbed down into one of the sores, poking hard and deep. He winced. That was it. Winced, the bastard, as though it didn't hurt like hell when I knew it did.

To prove my point, I rammed the heel of my hand onto a seeping blister, the greasy fluid smearing beneath my skin and making it hard to hold the grip without sliding away. When he still didn't respond, I used both hands and brought them down in one fist against his chest where a large wound showed through the scorches in his shirt.

"Fuck you, you bastard. Selfish, ungodly, duplicitous bastard."

I hit him again. Again. I was sure I was crying because I couldn't see through the blur of water in my eyes. I didn't know how many times I rained blows down on him, I just knew the moment he blocked me it was with enough force that my teeth clamped down on my tongue.

I tasted the metallic flavor of my own blood. My hands flew up automatically, cradling my mouth. His arm dropped back down to his sides. He sagged, seeming to think he'd won.

"Fuck you," I said and dropped my mouth to his.

I didn't have to force his lips open. They parted with a sigh that made a pulse of longing shoot through me. His tongue ran over my cheeks, lapping up whatever residual blood was there. He sucked on my tongue, drawing forth new fluid, and as he did, a rush of dizziness swept over me.

He wasn't just drinking what minuscule drops I offered him. He was seducing it from me. Each pull of my tongue felt like he was drawing fluid straight from my core. A gasp came to my throat and was swallowed into his own breath. My thighs tightened. My throat ached. God, I thought, to have a moment of joy like this, when nothing else mattered, to be able to savor such pleasure would be a gift and despite myself, that longing saturated me. Guilt flayed the flat back of my mind. This was no time to feel desire of any sort except that he live.

But desire came anyway. Some part of me started to melt like a glacier finding the first rays of sun. Slowly. Drop by drop. It sagged my shoulders, arched my back, drew me down to him as if he was a pool of warm oil that my body needed for lubrication so that each muscle, sinew, and tendon could slide easily over each other. Slide in and out, around and within so that there was no separation between us.

There was a moment when I had to plant my hands on the floor on either side of his head just to keep from collapsing on him. The longer he pulled from me, teasing my tongue, flicking his own over my teeth and cheeks, the drowsier I felt, like a hit of Bloodmist was calling me.

After a time—it could have been seconds or minutes, I had no idea—I sensed a shift in him. Still lost in whatever confusing muddle of emotions he was raising in me, I didn't have a chance to react. One second I was drowning in that sea of fear and desire, and the next I was tossed aside like a discarded buoy.

I landed on my side, my arm flung out to stop me from hitting my head on the floor. He shot me an angry look before he shot up to a sitting position. His face and chest were still riddled with sores and blisters. His throat was still punctured. But he had some magic back. Just not enough to heal.

He dropped his head back and howled in the hound's voice, a sound that rattled my soul for its grief and rage, and I pulled my knees in tight to my chest. Before I could do more, the little bookstore owner was there, a blur of color and flesh.

He dropped to his knees in front of Blade and offered his throat. I watched in horror as Blade drove his fangs into the fae's skin and dug deep. The fae jerked. His legs kicked out. He fought the dark enforcer, twisting and punching, but it was useless. Blade had a good grip. The sound of him swallowing down the fae's lifeblood made my stomach lurch.

A vampire. He was no better than a vampire.

Instinct and training drove me to my feet. Not sure where I found the energy, I pounded over to the two. Fraggle was staring up at me, having managed to twist in the dark enforcer's hold enough to roll to a half prone position. He blinked, numb-minded and empty-eyed.

I couldn't see my karambit, and there was nothing else to hand for a weapon except those damn books, so I grabbed the closest one and started nailing Blade across the head with it.

Pounding once, twice, several more times before he rolled his eyes to mine and snarled beneath the grip he had on the fae.

"Let him the fuck go," I growled. "You've had enough."

I hit him again and this time, he did let go. Without a pause, I grabbed Fraggle's feet and dragged him away to safety. I felt for his pulse, praying he had one in the usual places, and found a faint thrum beat back against the pad of my finger. I sat back on my haunches, relieved.

"Sweet Jesus," I said.

Fraggle's eyes rolled. With a weak hand, he clamped down on the wounds in his throat. A blink. Two. Then he stirred enough to pull a sigh of relief from me.

I was reaching down to help him sit up when I heard Blade's voice behind me.

"I needed too much," he said in a rasp.

I didn't turn around. "So you figured you'd kill him," I said in a ragged voice. My stomach still churned. God. Those moments I wanted him, that I worried he'd die. I was a fool.

"Better him than you," he said in a rasp, and I heard him getting up. In a heartbeat, he'd be standing behind me. I wasn't sure how I felt about that. There was still so much to process.

I moved closer to Fraggle. "Will you be alright?"

He nodded. Slow. His eyes focusing and refocusing. "I have much power," he said. "It was but a trifling." He tried to grin, but I saw the tremor that made his lips quake.

"Let me help you up," I said.

He shook his head. "No need, dear lady. Danger pay, remember?" he said in a tight voice and flicked a glance beyond my shoulder to where I knew Blade was looming over me. I could feel the tension in his body even through the inches that separated us. In my peripheral vision, I could see he held my karambit.

"I'm sorry," Blade said in a ragged voice, but I had the feeling his apology wasn't for Fraggle even if the little fae accepted it as such.

"I'm fine," Fraggle said as he bent to scoop a book from the floor and passed it to Blade. "I knew the risks when I asked you to fetch the book for yourself." He swirled his hand in the air to pluck a vial of something orange from the air. "Strange, is it no? How our powers are restored?" he uncorked the vial and tilted it toward me. "For one, the blood of a fresh kill, for the other a swallow of orange juice. A bit of Vitamin C, a few days of rest, and I'll be right as rain."

I wasn't convinced. My throat ached for entirely different reasons than it had just a few moments before. Without looking back, I headed for the stacks and the entryway I knew the book Fraggle had passed Blade was the bent and bloody diary we'd descended to the fiction level to claim, and now that he had it, we could leave. Somehow, it didn't feel like a victory. Somehow, I felt as if things were left undone.

Blade said nothing as he followed me back to the staircase. I felt the tingle of healing across the injuries I'd sustained in the fight and knew he was projecting his healing magics on me. An effort that would mean more days of healing for him, and maybe more blood. Using up energy he might barely be able to afford. I should be worried, concerned, grateful, even.

But all I could think was that I'd been ready to sacrifice myself so the dark enforcer could live. While taking that risk for humanity was one I faced head-on every day in the earthen realm, it was the first time I'd ever considered doing the same for a monster.

And the truth of that thought tormented me.

Chapter 10

I sat in front of Blade on Nutkin, saying nothing the entire way back to the castle. I was a mess of thoughts and bewildering emotions, not the least of which the complete surrender I'd been willing to offer up so Blade could live.

Certainly, he'd wanted to spare me that price, which was why he'd fought me off when I'd tried to help him, and I understood that now. I might even have warmed to the notion because it meant he cared about me enough to resist, and somehow that loosened a knot in the deep core of my heart.

But it also left me conflicted. Because I couldn't reconcile his willingness to harm the bookstore owner in my stead.

It seemed that the dark enforcer might have a sugary coating over that hide of his, but he was still a hard shell beneath. And I had to remind myself of that. And yet...and yet, I also had to admit to myself that I was drawn to him, wanted him badly, to be exact. I'd realized it the moment my lips laid down on his. Not just lust. Not just the drive to save the innocent, because the dark enforcer was most definitely not an innocent.

And I did not want to be feeling those things. I would not confess the name of the emotion that plagued the back of my tongue like a savory dish, because to do that would be to complicate this whole awful mess even more.

So I kept my mouth tightly sealed and considered other, safer things. Things that would get me the hell out of this realm and remove my sister from the threat of the Shadow Court. Things like the valuable information I'd let slide back in the tavern when he'd offered me the wine. Things that had to do with the mortal woman he'd been ordered to kill, and those he'd saved.

But remaining silent did nothing to ease the tension as we ambled along on Nutkin's back. Instead, it sharpened the edge so acutely, the energy would score a diamond. Blade's body was rigid against mine, lost no doubt in his own contemplations. I held myself so stiffly that by the time Nutkin crossed into the familiar shade of the Shadow Court's spectral property, every one of my muscles was barking.

I couldn't wait to get off the horse's back. I wanted out of Blade's company because having him behind me had made working through it all so much harder. Every so often, when the inside of his arm brushed against my ribs, I had to bite down on the words that threatened to tumble from my lips.

It all set me into a right rage by the time we drew within sight of the Shadow Court's manse and stables.

There was one thing I needed to know that only Blade could tell me before I escaped him and fled to my quarters and found solace in a long, fitful nap, and it was the one question that beat a groove into my mind that I couldn't jump out of no matter how many times the needle in my brain skipped over it.

"I have a question," I said as I slid down from Nutkin's back.

"She speaks," he said in a dry tone. "I was beginning to think I'd ruined your tongue back at the bookshop."

He slid off the horse behind me and landed so neatly he might have been stepping off a short step instead of the massive horse's back. Turning his back to me, he began working on the saddle, his deft fingers unlacing the leathers. Nutkin heaved a bloated sigh as they loosened.

Crossing my arms over my chest, I watched, waiting for him to turn around. I wanted to see him. See his face, his eyes, the entirety of his expression when I asked of him the question burning the brightest in the pyre of my mind. He wasn't obliging me.

"Turn around," I said, and then because I worried he would decide to be spiteful, I added, "Please."

Blade sighed heavily enough that it moved Nutkin's mane before he spun to face me, the saddle held in a slack grip. It was a massive thing with embossing and oiled leather, and yet he held it in front of him as though it weighed as much as a glamored shirt.

"One question," he said, the corners of his eyes tight. "That's all you get."

"What did you give her?" I asked.

His eyelids shuttered to half-mast. Calculating. "What did I give who?"

"Jasmine. In the tavern. What did you give her?"

This above all things was the most important, and I was forgoing my escape from him and my own peace to get it.

It was his turn for his jaw to clench and tick sideways. He didn't want to talk about it, that was clear.

"Not that question," he said and twisted away to show me his back again. His shoulders were bunched up in a knot, the thick length of his neck rigid with corded muscle.

"Don't turn away from me," I said as I grabbed his elbow. "Face me, you coward."

He spun around so fast it made my breath catch, eyes blazing as he regarded me. A waft of cinnamon wrapped thready fingers around my throat, and I should have choked on it, but instead I inhaled, drew courage from it.

"You're brave to call me a coward, Ponytail," he said in a tight voice. "After what you've seen me do."

I flinched at the memory that statement pulled forth, a flash of teeth and blood, the sound of screams as he shredded into each fae in the catacombs. But then, I overlaid on it the image of him lying just as broken as I'd been down in the bookstore cellars, and it gave me courage to stand there in the face of his intense gaze.

"They had it coming," I said as I willed the image of myself digging into Slavin's mouth for a tooth back into its dark pocket.

"Indeed," he said. "Those males deserved to die a thousand times over," he said. "But now you've used up your question." His expression was guarded. As if he didn't trust me.

Not to be deterred, I drew a long breath. "You didn't answer."

A shutter came down over his expression, blocking out even that careful unaffected mask. "I didn't say I'd answer. I said you could ask."

My jaw clenched at his obstinate posture. "You gave her something back at the Velvet Boar," I said. "I heard you."

It was hard to hold his gaze but I was determined not to drop mine, no matter how heated his grew, no matter how tight the corners of his gaze got. "In the restroom," I said. "You gave her something."

I didn't think it was possible for his eyes to narrow more, but they did. "You heard that?"

I swallowed, telling myself I had to push on. It mattered, this detail. Even if holding his gaze made my stomach clench and my throat go so tight I could barely force the words out. He hadn't just screwed her on a sink at the Velvet Boar with me hiding in a stall waiting for them to finish. He'd given her something, and I knew it was important to her. To both of them. And I knew it was connected to our time at Sylvia's tavern.

"I heard everything," I said, gathering courage from the memory of Jasmine's bravery at the end. "I heard every move, thrust, moan, and conversation afterwards." I held his gaze, hard as it was to keep it with the storm clouds moving over his face. Hard as it was with that memory racing through my mind like a flash of images from a movie.

He yanked his arm free of me and tossed the saddle on its stand before picking up a brush from a wooden table nearby. "That matter is private," he growled. "Something between the two of us."

"The same kind of something that you shared with the six women on the Shadow Trail?" I said in challenge. When he didn't answer, I edged into his vision, ignoring the brusque way he was working Nutkin's coat with the brush. The almost too keen eye he skimmed over his coat as he inspected the horseflesh for cuts or bruises.

"Stop using Nutkin to avoid me."

He swept the brush over the horse's coat in a long, graceful arc. "Nutkin is a Pooka. I imagine you don't know what that is, but I assure you, brushing his coat is more about my own neck than avoiding yours."

My fists dug into my thighs. "I know what you gave them," I said. "Sylvia told me. It was a ferryman coin. A coin that could send them home."

His hand paused mid-stroke. "Then if you know that, why are you asking."

He didn't look at me, not so much as a side-eye. Nutkin blew a hot breath through his nostrils that moved my hair. Blade's eye captured the movement, traced it back to my face and for one instant, I thought I saw a glint flash through his eyes.

I had to take a breath to continue. It shuddered through me. "Did you give Jasmine a coin?"

There. It was out in the open. My stomach clenched around the words as I waited for an answer. My mind ran to images of the cellars, the sound of her screams, the way he guarded Jasmine's body after he'd torn it apart. I tried to filter through the images to find one small coin dropped to the floor from a clutched hand. She'd been naked. There was only so many places a woman could hold onto a coin. Wherever she'd hidden it, I'd not seen it fall when she died.

I was still combing through the memory, lost in thought even as I watched his face, when I found myself pressed against the hard wood of a post. He'd moved so fast I hadn't had time to react. Just stood there, my back biting into an area filled with nail heads not fully beaten into the wood. I winced, but I did not cry out even if it hurt like hell.

He strained for me so close I could see the flecks of silver in his eyes. Warmth spread over me as the hot cinnamon smell curled around my throat.

"That's two questions, Ponytail," he growled. "And I'm not sure you're interested in paying the price for a single answer."

Chapter 11

There was heat in the currents of air between us. The kind that suggested the very air would cleave in two with the wrong move. And there was something else too, that memory of me claiming his mouth with my own so I could feed him what he needed to restore his magic, that same energy pulsed around us like a wave.

"You didn't answer," I said through the ache closing off my air in a vise.

"I did answer. I told you that was between the two of us."

I couldn't stop now. If he'd given it to the women at the tavern, then he either must have gotten it back from Jasmine or there were more.

"Did you give Jasmine a ferryman coin?" I asked again, this time, clarifying the question, putting an inflection of urgency in my tone, hoping he'd just answer dammit.

"Did you learn nothing in our dungeons, Ava?" he said in a tight voice, strangled enough that I knew I wasn't just right, but that there was more to the truth than he wanted to face.

"Was all that violence I committed for my father wasted on you?"

The rawness of his tone, the way his gaze roamed my face, taking in everything but my gaze, I knew the question meant more than the words suggested. I was a master of avoiding things I didn't want to face, and I recognized deflection like I recognized my own hand.

"You did give her a coin," I dared breathe, and the awe that sounded in my voice was an echo of the sensation blooming in my chest.

Because I understood as I said the words, by the way his jaw tightened while the narrowed gaze stayed carefully immobile, exactly why he was deflecting. I had only to sort through the memories of him and Jasmine together to see it.

The gentle way he spoke to her in the bathroom, the way he caged her between his arms as he took her, a mark of possession. The way he guarded her body after he'd been ordered to kill her. All those memories made my throat tight. They made the pit of my stomach clench. Because the answer I'd been searching for was so totally unexpected that my mouth gaped open at the realization.

He had given her a ferryman coin. She just didn't have a chance to use it. She didn't have time to. And the reason was the thing that I hated most to say, the thing that had my heart and stomach in such an uproar I would have done anything not to ask it.

"You wanted Jasmine to go home," I said, realizing the breadth of the statement as the words slipped free of me in a whisper. "You wanted to see her safely out of Fae because you loved her."

He drew back sharply at the comment, words that tasted like I'd taken a drink of sweet cream gone off. And that was how I knew I'd been right. Everything inside me sagged like a blown out tire, and yet because of how I felt about him, I couldn't stand to see him hurting.

"I cared about her too," I whispered, feeling the tightening of that energy curl around me, cutting off my air, squeezing the words from me in a trickle like a choked off hose. "I know about blood oaths. I know why you couldn't save her."

Jasmine's face floated up free from the murk of memories. Her smile wavered beneath my eyelids. Her sacrifice enabled three women to go home. But it left her lover bereft and angry. Lost as only a monster can be. The storm riding his expression until he managed to master the fury of it was proof enough. And that proof made my own heart ache.

That gaze flicked upward, captured my eyes. Fierce. Possessive. The memory of his lover pressing between us like a ghost with substance, so painfully there that I could barely breathe.

"Is that what love is to you, Ponytail? A few quick thrusts between the legs of a whore in a bathroom stall?" He dropped his hand on the post behind me, trapping me there as he roamed my face with shuttered eyes.

"Let me tell you what I think love is. For me, it's a most powerful urge to commit violence—terrible, bloody, awful violence—for the sake of an emotion I can't name. A feeling that I'm about to combust inside. It's a want so bad I'd turn my back on every vow I've ever made. I'd wring myself inside out for it, offer the tiniest chunk of soul I might have left somewhere in the blackened tissues of my body."

The muscles of his throat moved almost languidly as he gathered more words, searing, heated syllables that put an ache in the pit of my stomach, choked off my air like a noose.

"I've never known love before this," he said in a pained voice. "Not in all the centuries I've been alive. But even a monster like me knows if it isn't that all-consuming for both parties, it's not worth offering."

I struggled to swallow through a tight throat as he gave me a long look that made me feel like a moth stuck to a board. Heat claimed me, filling my chest and rising to my throat and upward still to my cheeks.

When he lowered his face to mine, brushing his cheek against mine as he whispered into my ear, I wasn't ready for the pain in his voice. It nearly took the legs out from beneath me.

"If you don't think that's what love should be, Ponytail," he said. "Then I pity the male who loves you that way."

He drew away and looked at me. Really looked at me, and I saw in the depths of his gaze all the pain and emotion he'd been hiding behind cruel words, that he soothed with violence. My God. It was a cavernous, dark place inside those eyes.

The bottom of my spine tingled. I should speak, I knew. I should say something to break through this awful tension, but I couldn't allow myself to speak. I was afraid of what I might say.

He leaned closer, his breath a wash of heated cinnamon, sending all sorts of confusing signals along the banks of memory. It was a struggle not to lean into him. Every inch of my body was on fire from the passion in his voice. Those moments we'd spent together in the tavern, the kiss, the agony of watching him fall beneath those vampires and wanting to risk my own life for his...Those moments seared a brand in me.

And all I could think was that Jasmine too had probably felt that same clutch in her throat, known the same desire, and the look he sent me must have been the last thing she'd seen before he tore into her neck. I held my ground, the silence growing tauter until at last he spoke, this time in a low, rasping, angry growl.

"Go away, Mica," he said. "I'm busy."

A movement, subtle and slight, no more than a shadow wavering at the corner of my eye, told me we were no longer alone. I wanted very badly to turn to acknowledge Mica, to use the excuse of his presence to tear myself from Blade's intense gaze, but I felt that if I did, I'd lose something crucial. So, I held the dark enforcer's gaze with my own. Even with my stomach bottoming out, my legs going weak, I held it.

His lips pursed together for an instant as the crimson rode the circumference of his irises, then he slid his gaze to the doorway and I lost sight of his gaze.

"It's not a good time, Mica," he said. "Ava and I are discussing love and violence."

Although the very tone should have sent anyone running, Mica came further inside. I caught sight of his rust colored hair as he sidled along the wall toward Nutkin.

"Father saw you ride in," he said as if Blade hadn't just all but asked him to flee the scene, and I realized he was no more afraid of his brother than a beetle. "He sent Stone to fetch you both."

Blade drew back just slightly, but his palm didn't leave the post. It remained flattened beside my head, caging me there.

I considered dodging out the other side, but I couldn't think of a way to do so without looking like a coward. So I stayed there, but I pushed back, just slightly, forcing him to give me more space, thinking I could brush past him that way.

Nothing doing. He was immovable. When he turned to speak to Mica, he merely glanced to the side, showing me the chiseled jawline.

"And you're here to fetch your books before Stone sees them and knows where they came from," Blade said, jerking his chin toward the saddle bags. "They're wrapped in birch bark and bloody. I doubt our brother will care about them by the time he sees how I feel about being fetched." He put the same note of disdain in the term fetch as he did our brother.

Mica drew up alongside Nutkin and ran his hand absently down the horse's nose before scooping out the books from the saddlebags and slipping them inside his cloak. The beast made a sound that almost came out as a chortle and Mica murmured to him softly. The boy was in full view then, and I noticed he wore the same cloak I'd seen him in the first time I'd met him, but this time, both panels had been slung over his shoulders in a purposefully rakish way until he wrapped them tightly over his torso, hiding the books.

"Thank you, Blade," he said, flashing a grin with two, longer canines than I expected on such a wiry male.

A gruff release of breath moved through Blade's chest as he relinquished his hold on the post, finally, freeing me with a note of displeasure. "Your favors are getting more costly, Mica," he said in an indulgent tone that suggested he would never explain to Mica what that cost was.

I slithered away from the post and was sidling toward the door when Mica shot a look at me. His nostrils flared.

"She's afraid," he said baldly, stopping me short. "Was the discussion more about violence than love?"

His tone was oddly accusatory for a boy facing down the dark enforcer. I was intrigued enough to lurk at an empty stall as he swung that youthful face to me. "Do you need me to defend your honor, dear lady? Sometimes my brother can be a terrible rogue."

The formal manner of his voice, the words all but made me snort in disbelief but for the earnest look on his face. Plus, he was right. I was afraid. I just wasn't sure why. And the dreaded feeling didn't ease even when Blade chuckled in an indulgent tone that had Mica flashing a brief smile of relief toward the dark enforcer.

"Sometimes, Mica," he said. "Love and violence are the same thing."

Mica frowned. "I would never use violence on someone I loved." He looked me over, his nostrils flaring again. "Or someone who loved me." He ran a hand down Nutkin's nose again as he held Blade's eye intently enough that the dark enforcer's mouth twitched.

"Indeed," he said. "I would expect no less from you, brother. Now tell me: why I must have a warning about Stone."

"Maybe because for more cultured fae the idea of love and violence are not the same thing." Stone's voice cut through the stable in a disdainful drawl that indicated he'd aimed his words at Blade and not Mica. A glance toward the door of the stable showed he filled the space with his broad shoulders. He swung his gaze to me. "Are you alright, Ava?"

"She's fine," Mica piped up. "Blade wouldn't hurt her."

Stone swiveled toward his young brother. "You have an inflated belief in the dark enforcer's kind intentions, Mica. One day that will backfire on you."

"But he wouldn't," Mica said. "He just said—"

"Leave it be, Mica," Blade cut in as he turned back toward Nutkin and ran his hand over the horse's flank. "Stone is here now. Our assassin is safe from the likes of this monster."

There. There was the note of disdain and arrogant air I'd come to expect from the dark enforcer. Whatever softness had been in him when I mentioned Jasmine was gone. In its place, settled the underpainting of barely suppressed crimson anger in a masterpiece of somber blue.

I edged sideways, aiming my feet for the door. The air was so thick with animosity and some strange overflowing river of paternal emotion that I could barely make one out over the other. I needed air.

Stone pulled his attention from where Blade had turned away from him to continue grooming Nutkin, showing him his back in a posture that indicated he wasn't just done with Stone, he wasn't afraid of Mica's warning.

"Father wants to see you when you're done, Blade," Stone said, projecting his voice toward the dark enforcer.

Blade muttered his answer, suggesting Stone go do something indecent to himself. Mica chuckled in a sort of shocked and uncomfortable way, and Blade shot him an amused, indulgent look.

Stone, however, went rigid. And Mica, as if sensing the brothers might do violence to one another, flicked his hair over his shoulders and smiled at me. "You look like you could use a drink, my lady. Might I escort you back to the castle?"

I blinked like a stupid lamb. "Surely ladies don't get quite so dirty as this," I said with a grin as I gestured over my dusty clothes and hair. "Or so bloody." I scratched behind my ear where a dried flake came off on my fingers. Mine, I guessed. I supposed I should be grateful it wasn't dried sick after the last few days.

"Then perhaps it's a bath you require," he said, bowing low despite Stone's suppressed snort and Blade's dark, spiteful laugh.

"Oh she doesn't need a bath," the dark enforcer drawled. "She's so squeaky clean she forgets what she is."

Mica canted his head at Blade, then at me. I decided I liked the boy, and I held out my elbow, dusty as it was.

"Not like that," he said and hooked his elbow out toward me, indicating I'd gotten it backwards. "I escort you, not the other way round."

I looped my hand in its crook, smiling despite myself.

That was when Stone decided to nudge Mica out of the way—gently, but firmly. "Father wants to see her," he said. "I'll take her to the castle. Maybe you could ask a couple of chattel women to fill a tub and prepare some food."

"In other words," Blade cut in, and I nearly jumped out of my skin, having mercifully forgotten him for one moment. "Stone here doesn't want to share. Keep in mind what I said, Mica: sometimes violence and love go hand in hand."

Mica dropped his arm to his side, leaving me hanging. Uncertain. His eyes flicked from one brother to the other.

I lifted my chin. "For pity's sake," I said. "Assassin, remember?" I jabbed my chest with my finger. "I'm perfectly capable of traveling the short distance from here to there alone without getting lost."

"I'm sure having an escort isn't really about getting lost, Ponytail. It's about you escaping. We wouldn't want to lose our perfectly capable assassin."

For a lingering moment, his gaze dropped to the rope burn scar on my throat and I knew he was measuring my pulse by the way his own throat bobbed in time with my pulse.

I knew something else, too. He hadn't forgotten what he'd said to me earlier about love and violence. Nor had I forgotten what he'd said about me lasting less than an hour once the job was done.

No matter what we'd shared in the catacombs or in the tavern, he had sworn an oath the same as Stone had, and I heard the promise in his voice of the sorts of things he'd done to those males who had crossed him, and exactly what he'd have to do to me when all was done.

I also couldn't stop hearing his voice in my head, of words he'd used to describe what he thought love must be, and my heart clenched at the desire to be loved that way, with that much depth, to be the sort of woman a man would love enough to promise so coldly to kill for.

I also knew that a woman like me wasn't worthy of anything but the punishment.

Chapter 12

I fled from the stable as though the hellhound was charging my heels. I was aware both Stone and Mica dogged along behind me, but it was Stone who pulled out faster and caught up to me so easily I was left to wonder about the value of my usual daily five kilometer runs.

By the time I spied a cluster of burly looking fae hanging around the entrance to the castle, he was alongside me, albeit a couple of feet away. My heart started clomping in my chest like a frightened mare, and I knew it wasn't because of Stone.

Even so, I side-eyed him, praying he hadn't caught on to the rapid firing of my heart. His strides were purposeful and swift, like mine, but if he noticed me swaying a bit on my feet, he didn't show it.

Blinking as I turned my attention back to the others, I realized they weren't quite so clear anymore. Just blurs and vertical lines, smashes of color.

My skin turned clammy. I tried to drag in a breath and found my lungs would not expand.

Before I knew it, I was clutching for Stone's arm. "I think I'm going to be sick," I said.

He halted and turned, pulling my arm along with him as he made a full arc toward me.

"Ava?" he said.

My mouth flooded with water. I nodded at him because I couldn't do more than that. With a push, I shoved him hard enough that he should have stumbled backward. He held his ground, and I ended up dry heaving while clutching at his sleeves, my fingers a spasm of muscle that must have been giving him a nasty pinch.

I was still heaving up threads of air when he gathered me close, crooning over my hair. I felt the loose strands moving along my temple.

"It's alright, Ava. I've got you." I noticed he'd changed position at some point so that he stood in front of me, blocking me from the guards' view.

My stomach trembled out the last of the warbling, rippling pains, leaving me breathless. I peered up at him through watery eyes. His own aqua ones regarded me calmly, if not concerned.

"I'm OK," I muttered although I wasn't. My brain was rapid firing through the last few hours, trying to figure out if there was any evidence to suggest the Bloodmist might still be throttling my insides. How many hours past the worst of it was I? Not enough to have gone through everything I'd suffered since it, that was for sure.

By then, Mica had reached us. His gentle hand on my shoulder was too much for my skin. "Do you need help?" he asked.

I shook my head and shrugged him off, annoyed at myself, and desperate to gain some space. "I'm fine," I said through clenched teeth. "Just...I don't know. Tired, I guess."

Taking long drafts of air through my nose helped, exhaling through my mouth. I let go of Stone's arms and cricked my neck side to side like a boxer. Blew out another breath. I stood up straighter. Alone.

"I'm good."

Judging by the way Stone was gawking at me, I didn't look it.

"I'm good," I said again because maybe if I repeated it, we'd all believe it. And to be honest, having him there did help. One glance at the guards standing alert at the entrance, and I found myself skirting closer to him. Had I caught a flash of blacksteel in one of those hateful grins?

As if he understood, Stone wrapped his arm around my waist, not pulling me close exactly, just lending support the way one warrior might another, giving me space. I allowed the touch because I wasn't sure I could stand on my own much longer, and the support lent me some dignity.

Mica wasn't so discreet. He stepped in front of us before we had a chance to take another step, barring our progress. Since, like his brothers, he was taller than me, he had to hunch over to look into my face.

"She needs to rest, Stone," he said. "Her face reminds me of clotted cream."

I swatted him away, the words threatening to put my stomach back into full on rebellion. "If clotted cream is half as disgusting as it sounds, I think you need to work on your creative writing skills."

Sweeping him aside, I lifted my chin and forced myself forward. If I didn't look at the entrance, if I kept my eye on the grey stone and the lime green moss climbing the arches in a patchwork, I found I could walk steadily enough that I could extricate myself from Stone's arm. Finally move on my own steam. The blackness at the edges of my vision was receding.

"I'm good," I said with more conviction. "Fuck clotted cream."

I heard Mica behind me asking Stone what fuck meant and Stone trying to explain it, and then things seemed fine again. I could breathe. My pace sped up. Each step grew steadier and with each one, I felt more like myself.

Like peeling off a sticky rubber glove, all the nerves sloughed away. I was even able to realize just how close I'd come to completely losing myself to that moment in the stable with Blade. Stone had saved me from myself.

Exhaustion and confusion had a way of muddling reality, and I was glad for Blade's harshness now that I was out of the stable. Glad for Stone's support. For Mica's kindness. Because the comparison made the stark differences stand out all the more.

And that was a good thing. Letting myself feel anything for the monsters who blackmailed me into this position was a monumental mistake. Feeling anything, even gratitude, would just get me killed. Anything more than gratitude was just plain stupid.

I reached the entrance before either Mica or Stone, who hung back whispering to each other. With shoulders squared, I lifted my gaze to the gang of high Fae watching my every step. A knot gathered in my shoulders, and my hands shook, but it was withdrawal, the last, horrible throes of it, and I knew it. A reminder that Bloodmist had the power to shake me to the core all these hours later. Nothing more.

I pulled in a draft of air, confident that in time it would also slough away. Even so, when Stone came up beside me and glowered at the gang until they stepped aside, I was relieved.

His eye caught mine. I nodded to him, a curt gesture of thanks. He inclined his head, sweeping his arm toward the door, letting me go first like an old world gentleman. I stomped down on the fluttering of my heart as a roguish grin spread over his face. I'd been there already, the moment I'd decided to tumble into the bed with him in that tavern. And that little mistake taught me more about my own weaknesses than anything else. Namely that I didn't really understand Fae if I thought I could simply screw one the same as I would a human man to relieve a bit of pent up energy without consequences.

The fae were just too complex for that. Didn't matter if he'd seemed the right size to fill a hole that had been gaping for years, the same one I'd thought Gideon could fill the first time he'd exploded into a nest of vampires at a blockhouse and saved me.

It took my time in the catacombs to realize I'd been looking in the wrong places all my life, the wringing of Bloodmist and a violent fae with a gentle touch to make me understand the sort of intimacy I needed didn't exist. The kind that came without questions or judgment. The kind where I wasn't the dirtiest piece of the puzzle.

Gideon had been the one man in all my years who could overpower me both in mind and body. I'd mistaken that for love. Despite that, I missed him with a pain that was both sharp and throbbing. I wanted to be home. I wanted all this to be done with.

Catching Stone's eye and my heart and instincts recognized a creature of power. It should have shot up all sorts of flares in warning. It didn't, and I wasn't sure if it was because I was still numb from the events of the last days, or if compared to Blade, he seemed much more manageable.

All I knew right then was that the catacombs had shone a light on the gaping crack in my soul that was so wide now, that nothing could fill it. They hacked away at the dark sarcophagus I hid all those emotions in, exposing the insides to such raw, glaring light, I could barely breathe for the dust wafting out in gusts of ancient spores.

I wasn't sure how I was ever going to close the lid again.

Which was why, when Stone stepped aside to follow me, Mica at his heels, I let him come with me. That solid build of his, that earnest face despite the nefarious power of his background, he was the perfect foil for the tempest of thoughts swirling around my mind. Even if I was pretty damn sure he had some buried motives of his own, it was nice to know he had my back. If only for a moment.

I must have let go a sigh or a soft moan as I crossed the threshold because he sent a look my way with a tilted head. I met his gaze and furrowed brow as he obviously tried to discern from my face what was going on behind my eyes. I shook my head at him.

Nothing. Nothing was going on that hadn't gone on for decades. Just brick by brick, stick by stick, I was walling myself off again because I couldn't bear the heavy weight that was dragging down my insides. My very marrow felt as if it was filled with concrete.

"You look different," he said, running his eyes down the length of my body. If his gaze hitched on the karambit strapped to my thigh, he said nothing.

Neither did I. Instead, I swept through the foyer toward a set of stairs so wide, they required a rail in the middle. Made of oak and polished to a gleam that seemed highly unnatural, the railing led upward in a sweeping curve.

Another set to the right split into two stairwells. One led up and the other went down in a narrow, claustrophobic passage. That was the staircase Stone was guiding me toward with a gentle hand on the small of my back.

I knew the narrow stairs led to the cellar and those dungeons. Three days I'd spent below in those cells, waiting for Terran to release me. Three days that culminated in Stone's betrayal and the realization that he was his father's consul.

I froze and for a second, dark memories tried to sweep over me and seize me, peeling me back from the edge into a receding wave into an ocean of despair. My lungs squeezed. A bat's wings flapped around my heart. I couldn't breathe.

When I didn't move, he pressed just a little more firmly, his fingers splaying out over the curve alongside my spine.

"Are you alright, Ava?" he asked.

I blew out a long breath and nodded. For some reason, despite every intention to, I couldn't pull away from his touch.

"Just tired, is all," I said, meaning it. "I need to rest for a bit." I meant that too. The racing heartbeat, the struggle to breathe. They drained me to the point I thought I'd not make it up the stairs.

"We expected you days ago," he said in a hushed voice from behind me, as though he didn't want Mica to hear. I doubted the young fae would care. He was too busy rearranging the flowers in the foyer's vase. "My father is furious."

I managed to look at him over my shoulder without grimacing. "Is that why you're herding me up the servant's staircase like a hooker?"

That seemed to catch Mica's attention. His fingers paused over a delicate bloom of baby's breath that had begun to shrink. "You need to recover," he said as he waved his hand over the bloom. As it came to life again, his face blanched.

Stone sighed. "Mica is right. You do need some time to recover. Taking you up this way will avoid my father altogether. His wing is at the top of the grand staircase. Let Blade face him first. Any violence that ensues will be perpetrated and run out by the time he comes for you."

"When who comes for me?" I asked too sweetly. "Blade or Terran?"

I took the steps two at a time without waiting for his response, leaving Mica behind to deal with the bouquet, and Stone to think what he liked.

I navigated perfectly to the suite I'd kept before going with Blade on the Trail, and Stone followed behind me at a close pace.

"You have a good memory," he said.

I shrugged as I stopped outside the door to the suite. "I make it my business to remember things. One small detail overlooked can mean someone dies. Likely me."

He looked like he was going to open the door for me, and rather than let him, I held his gaze pointedly before I reached for the handle first. With a twist, the door swung open to show the suite spread out in front of us, looking exactly the same as I'd left it. I almost sobbed at the smell of soap in the air. Combined with the hot butterscotch smell of Stone behind me, I had an almost overwhelming yearning for a warm bath and a cocoon of soft sheets.

Why in the bright blue blazes did he have to smell so much like comfort? Why did this room seem so much like safety right then? I was far from home and security. I just needed to think of the things I'd seen in this castle to remind myself that Stone and Blade were the same sorts of monsters I fought in the human realm. Just...prettier.

"We had some issues on the trail," I said, flicking aside the images that immediately started to spool in my mind, an endless slideshow of horror. With a sort of distant interest, I noted my hand shook enough to rattle the knob.

I let it go quickly, and clenched both hands into fists at my sides, pressing them against my thighs.

"Issues on the trail," he echoed in a voice that held a distinct note of I-told-you-so. "Is that why you look so...strange?" he asked.

I brushed him with a dismissive glance and stepped inside, crossing the threshold like it was the Rubicon.

Even as a prison, the chamber, with its lush interior was a welcome sight. The blankets on the bed called to me. Oil lamps burned low in the corners where the sunlight couldn't reach, lending a warm glow to the room. The wingback chair embraced a plush ottoman, inviting me to cross the room and sit in it, lean way, way back. Someone had left an open book on its seat, as though they'd been waiting for me and were wiling away the time till I returned.

It all felt so damnably cozy.

In contrast, the fireplace stood cold, and all I could think was, good. I needed to feel like I was a prisoner again. I needed to remember what I was here for.

"I really am tired, Stone," I said, pivoting. Once away from him and then back toward him because I had a terrible urge to pull him with me toward the bed and just lie there, soaking in the feel of a warm body next to mine. One that would offer a sweet sort of escape and not the frenzied hedonism I knew I'd find in Blade.

The power of both desires was so intense, I had to force myself to step away from Stone and head for the bed because it was the furthest piece of furniture in the room and I needed to sit down, and I needed to sit down far, far away from him.

But that was a mistake all its own, and I couldn't understand why. I just knew that the closer I got to the bed, the tighter my throat felt, as if a rope was sliding a knot around my neck.

A black sort of dizziness swam over my vision. The bed and its luxurious fabrics, the soft-looking pillows, blurred to a wad of color with fuzzy edges. The back of my neck felt clammy again, the way it had when I'd caught sight of the gang of fae standing outside the castle. I heard him shuffle behind me, a soft sound of movement, deliberate, so I'd know he was coming toward me. So very different from Blade's sudden, stealthy appearances.

In those seconds of overwhelming emotions, my brain raced from suggesting Stone share the bed with me to considering unleashing my karambit and striking out with it, to chasing a squat little hateful fae along a dark cavern.

It was the image of that revolting little male's retreating back streaking along a dark passage that stole the stuffing out of my legs.

I had to reach out for something. That something turned out to be Stone's strong arm. It wrapped around my waist and for a second, I let it take all my weight.

"You're white as pudding," he said as I found the steel in my spine to step away and stand on my own. He blinked at me, concern wearing his features like a dime store mannequin. "What happened there?"

"I suppose white as pudding is a hell of a lot better than clotted cream," I said as I back-stepped away from the bed until my legs met one of the chairs.

"It's nothing." I pinched the bridge of my nose. Hard. The pain grounded me. "Everything. Too much," I said, sitting down on the arm rest.

"Tell me. I'll listen."

He made to sit down on another chair, but I held up my hand. "I will," I said, already deciding I would tell him nothing but the basics because anything more would pull me with it into the oblivion of those waves intent on taking me out to sea.

I wore a dress. I fought wendigos. I got lost in the catacombs. That's what he'd hear.

"I'll tell you," I said. "But not now. Later."

He nodded, but it was wary. I knew he wanted to press me for more but whatever he saw in my face kept him from doing so. "Of course."

A strange look on his face. A note of uncertainty in his voice. He didn't want to wait. Maybe he couldn't. Maybe neither of us had the luxury of time on our side. Don Sidhe or whatever the hell he was called was waiting.

Stone's long look in my direction was one I had to endure with a tight smile before he turned and headed for the door.

Dammit, I did not see myself as a Patty Hearst, but there I'd gone and formed some sort of bond that made me feel safe in this room. Safe in a castle that just a handful of days earlier, I'd been beaten in and nearly starved. This was no safer than the catacombs and yet the familiarity of Stone's face, the kindness in his voice—a kindness that was likely more rooted in some motive I didn't understand, all that made me realize why Ms. Hearst had swung over to her captive's side.

The devil you know and all that.

Trusting anyone here was a risk, no matter how much I needed to feel like I wasn't alone. They were liabilities, those things: Stone's attempts to regain my trust. Blade's seemingly selfless kindness. Illusions, all.

For all I knew this damned attraction to them both was no more than Patty Hearst's affliction resonating in me after all the horrors of the catacombs. I couldn't trust my own emotions. Not right then. Everything was still far too raw.

I'd let go of my hunter's instincts because the monster within was too damn exhausted to resist.

Gideon would be so hideously disappointed in me.

I considered all those things with a hunter's eye once more. A killer's eye. I knew I couldn't trust what I saw in Fae. It was all just a realm of illusion. A shirt became a corset. A gown transformed scarred killer into a woman of beauty.

"Stone?" I said, catching him as he laid his hand on the door.

He looked back at me over his shoulder. "Yes?"

"It's time you told me everything too," I said. "I can't be kept in the dark any longer. I don't care why your father wants the king dead. That's none of my business. But if I'm to do the job, I need to know everything."

They could either trust me or not. I was done playing. Done trying to see through the gauze of magic to the reality beneath.

"I will," he said, and I waved him back toward the door when it looked like he planned to come inside again.

"Later, though," I said. "If you can hold your father off for an hour or so. Right now, I'm beyond exhausted." A thin smile that I could barely manage as I regarded him.

His smile came easily and with such genuine emotion that my heart squeezed out a series of rapid butterfly flutters. I wanted to trust him. Part of me insisted I could.

With a start, I realized he would be hard to kill. And not because he was strong, fast, or possessed magic.

But I'd kill him if I had to. If it came down to him and me, I'd do my best to take him out and I'd die trying, because I hadn't let the catacombs take me down without a fight and I'd not let him either.

Because if the Fae Mafia was anything like the human mafia, they wouldn't leave a single loose end.

And they would send the one I trusted most to finish the job.

Chapter 13

Exhaustion filled all the cracks in my body like molten gold repairing ancient pottery. Hours after I returned to the Iron City, days after I'd been assaulted and attacked in the Catacombs of Dread, hours after I'd suffered the worst withdrawal of my life, I lay like the dead on a luxurious mattress and stared at the ceiling. Because I knew I'd been dodging truth the way a shadow dodges light.

Panic dogged those cracks and found new ways to flay them open again. I felt real fear for the first time since my parents died. In those days, I'd thought I could outrun the sharp, splintering steps of emotion with the warm haven of drugs. I'd believed my sister was a threat to my self-mediation ritual with her constant mothering, her warm meals and questions about where I was going, who I spent my time with.

I didn't have time or inclination to accept those kindnesses, and when she'd finally given up on me, I'd thought: there. It was what I deserved. She'd finally got her senses back and relieved me of all that unease I felt every time she looked at me.

Now, I knew the true fullness of terror. I was alive because of Kit, she was the reason I hunted and killed, the reason I'd forged into Fae without looking back. To save her. To keep her alive one more day.

But I knew I couldn't do that any longer, and that was the real truth of it. I'd blustered my way here, made everyone think I could do the impossible. My time in the catacombs, my moments with Stone and Blade, even Terran and his guards in the cellars, all those moments proved I wasn't capable. She had lived half a life because of me, and now she would die because of me.

I was expected to kill a king. A fae king. Someone so powerful that even the Fae Mafia wanted to cover their tracks by using a mortal assassin to do the deed. Magic was out of the question since I didn't possess it. I'd barely survived the catacombs, and even then, I'd had Bloodmist on my side. A few hits took me through the worst of the violence done there, but the drug was gone. The vape empty.

Arrogant I'd been in those first days. You need a killer? Sure, I take life on a regular basis. I'm your gal.

But I wasn't. I wasn't that gal and now I knew it with a painfully acute awareness. I was weak in the face of Fae magic. I could take down an ogre, maybe two if the day was good, but here in Fae, even the basest of them had overwhelmed me. It had taken the aid of the dark enforcer to level the playing field, and even then, the battleground was choppy and uneven.

Who was I next to a powerful king? And if I was nothing and no one, then what would happen to Kit when I failed?

My stomach twisted into a thousand knots just thinking about it.

No matter how hard I worked to reclaim my earlier bravado, my confidence that I could handle anything because I didn't care if I lived or died, that thread of self-esteem fled with my every grasp. And so I lay on the mattress and prayed for some intervention that I knew would never come.

But there was no one else. Terran had ordered his own son to shadow my sister close enough that a whisper would end her life, and I could do nothing but lie here on a cushioned mattress atop a velvety bedspread and steep in my own dread.

No. That wasn't quite all I could do was it? I'd certainly found a way to stare blindly at the ceiling, searching for webbings of cracks in the surface of the plaster as if it was some sort of metaphor for the problem I was facing. I hoped for cracks. I prayed for them. I thought if I could find just one, there might be hope for me.

I found none.

Good as his word, Stone won me not just one hour, but several, and I wasted each one on thoughts that got me nowhere.

At one point, my gaze roamed as far as the armoire and over to the fireplace. The room was cold, I noted. Whatever fire had been built inside the hearth had long ago died, leaving gray ash in a pile. Nothing of interest there unless I wanted to get up and try to build a fire myself.

I discarded that notion as quickly as it rose to mind. Instead, I yanked on the blanket beneath me and coiled it over my torso and shoulders, crossing my arms over my belly and hugging my waist. Every muscle felt like it had been boiled until it was a tangled mess of mushy pasta.

Closing my eyes against the sights of the room, the ceiling, of my own failures, I snuffled through a clogged nose and tried to center my breathing. Not that I'd cried at any point while I stared at the ceiling. Just that my body was still reprimanding me most heartily for abandoning the Bloodmist.

I tried for several moments to ignore the pounding of my heart, a loud and insistent thudding in the back of my ears. It could have been hours before I realized it wasn't my heartbeat at all, but a soft but determined rapping on the door.

My feet slid to the floor in one more heartbeat, touching down in time with my pulse. All fear slid away, replaced by the catlike focus of a hunter. I slid my karambit from its place beneath my pillow and held it out. Let them come. Even if I couldn't hold my own for long, they'd have to work to get to me.

The boots I'd not bothered to take off scuffed in whispers along the floor as I held my karambit snug in a reverse grip. My index finger threaded through the hole in a solid but loose enough hold that I barely felt my thumb resting along the back of the blade. Ten seconds, that's all it took for me to reach the door. I counted them with my breath.

The rap came again. I stared at the wood, gaze narrowed, mind racing. Surely if someone wanted to attack me, they'd have rushed the room, not knocked.

But here in Fae nothing was what it seemed. Maybe even the sense of privacy. My gaze flicked up at the ceiling, looking for some spectral, if not magical gaze witnessing my every move in lieu of spy-tech.

"Who is it?" I said, deciding on the direct approach. If I didn't like the sound of the voice, I'd slice my way through the first bit of skin that showed through the door.

"Mica, my lady."

My shoulders relaxed on their own even as I aimed a suspicious look at the door.

"Are you alone?"

A short pause. Then a rustling, breathy sound. Was he out there laughing?

Before I could rethink what I was doing, I pulled the door open. Mica did indeed stand there. Alone. And he was laughing. A soft chuckle that he smothered with the back of his hand. A glint of fine points showed through his lips when he tucked the hand into his pocket, pushing aside the cloak in a casual, but entirely model-like pose.

My knife dropped to my side. "What's so funny?"

One shoulder moved ever so slightly. "You sounded afraid," he said. "No one has ever been afraid of me."

At that, he pulled a tiny bouquet of baby's breath from his pocket. It went from looking crushed and broken from being stuffed into the tight confines of a small pouch to lush and lacy in one flourish of movement. He held it out to me in a rounded bunch that had all the appearance of a mound of ice cream in his fist. Vanilla ice cream on a pistachio flavored waffle cone.

"These remind me of you," he said.

Despite my efforts not to smile, I felt the corner of my mouth tug upward.

"No one has ever given me flowers," I said. "Or said I brought flowers to mind."

He tilted his head to the side, so boyish. "Never?" he asked sweetly. "Then I suppose it's a day of firsts for us both." This time he shoved the bouquet awkwardly at me and I realized I'd not reached out for it when he'd proffered it at first.

They ended up smashed against my chest and I had to do my best to sheath my karambit without him noticing, while trying not to mash the flowers too much.

I failed. Sprinkles of white blossoms cascaded over the floor and immediately dried to tiny buds on the wooden boards.

"Oh, I'm sorry," I said and made to sweep the errant stems back into my arms. Thankfully, the motion distracted him and I was able to slide the karambit back into its sheath before I ended up slicing him with the thing as he ducked low, the same time I did. I was left with one hand hovering over the sheath on my thigh while the other clutched the remaining bouquet to my chest. I knew I should just reach out and grab the dead and dried stems but I wasn't sure if I should touch them.

He frowned down at the floor as he hunched over, staring at the way they lay scattered beside his boots. "They shouldn't have done that," he said absently, then peered up at me with a confused look. "Are you actually afraid of me?"

The earnestness of his voice took me aback. And I realized that yes, I was afraid. Now that I was alone in the room, with the fragrances of the bed, the fireplace with its ash in the grate, the undercoating smell of burned sugar, no one watching me from dark corners, I didn't want it invaded in any way.

I actually stuttered as I answered.

"Are you here to hurt me?"

I could have sworn at the question his lower lip trembled, just a bit. Then he squared his shoulders in a gesture so reminiscent of Stone and Blade that in that second, I saw the familial resemblance.

"I would never hurt you," he said and a swirl of energy seemed to move throughout the room, so much that I caught the flutter of the curtains from the side of my eye.

I smiled at him. Genuinely this time, and without holding back. He grinned, sheepish, awkward in return. The two of us stood there for several moments before I realized he wanted to be invited in but was too nervous to ask.

It took a monumental effort to stand aside, but I forced myself to do it. I didn't like the feeling of clamminess on the back of my neck.

"Would you like to come inside?" I said, forcing the words from my tongue.

He toed the floor with soft leather boots. "I really shouldn't. You need to rest."

At first, I was relieved and almost shut the door so I could flee back to the bed, where it seemed the safest, but the way he was fidgeting, his gaze darting from my face to the floor and over my shoulder, I knew he was just being polite. I told myself it was ridiculous to leave him standing there.

Despite the haggard way my shoulders pulled on my neck, I found myself saying, "I've had plenty of time to recuperate."

It was a lie, and I wondered if he knew it, but when he pursed his lips ever so delicately and dipped his head at me, I knew even if he did sense my hesitation, he wouldn't mention it.

He crossed the threshold and into the room as though it was the entrance to some sacred tomb. I gestured toward the wingback chair and the fireplace as I held the bouquet aloft in the other hand.

"I'll put these in water," I said although the moment I did, I wondered where in the heavens I find a vase in the room. I ended up standing beside the door, gawking around the room in numb bewilderment.

"It smells of her in here," he said in a musing tone. "I was never allowed in here when she was here," he said, turning on those soft boots, the heels making barely a sound as he did so. His gaze fell on the dried and crumbled flowers that we'd missed and that still littered the floor at my feet. "Oh bother," he said. "I wasn't thinking."

At that, the tiny buds flushed to white again. With my eyebrows climbing an inch to my hairline, I stooped to retrieve the now lively blooms and stems and tucked them into the bouquet

"Do you like them?" he asked. "I've been practicing."

"I do like them, Mica."

He blushed. "Mica isn't my true name," he said. "But I like how you say it. May I use your name as well?" he asked.

I nodded, some warning in the back of my mind tugging at my tongue. "You may call me Ava," I said.

"Is Ava the whole of it?" he asked. "Your true name?" He smiled with such warmth I felt as if the room had grown warmer, like a rolling bit of heat against chilled cheeks. I wasn't sure, but I sensed that I could trust the boy.

"It is," I answered. "To both questions."

That seemed to please him even more. His cloak fell back into place over his chest and he fiddled with it as he watched me, his face, throat, and chest all growing so red my own face must be doing the same thing. Then, with a start, he enacted a bit of a hop before he raced for the bathroom. I heard water running for a long moment and then he came back with a gilded cup made of basalt that was hollowed out in three places.

With great tenderness he plucked the flowers from my grasp and arranged them inside each hole. He sent a flirty, furtive grin in my direction before setting it down on the table beside the fireplace.

"Lovely," I said and clapped my hands together, dusting off any debris, and so that I would have something to do with my hands that had now gone all clumsy. "I wouldn't have thought of using the toothbrush holder."

I closed the door quietly, looking him over just as silently.

He tilted his head, looking at me pensively. "You want to know why I'm here," he said, and in his tone, there was none of the shy, awkward youth. In fact, I very nearly heard Blade's voice in the words.

"To be frank," I said. "Yes."

He nodded and sent a questioning look toward the chair. I shrugged my consent but he waited, his own eyebrows raised until I realized he was expecting me to sit first. Like a gentleman would do before he took a seat.

I was beginning to realize why Terran showed such disappointment with the boy. He was far too sweet and gentle for the likes of the Shadow Court. No doubt Terran was discouraged at the lack of brutality the boy possessed. I imagined he'd want every one of his sons to be as ruthless as he was. Like there was no profit in holding prisoners indefinitely, there couldn't be much use for a gentleman in the brutality of the Shadow Court.

But I was relieved to see the boy's gentle spirit. Something in me responded to it, and the hot electric wires of my nerves cooled in his presence. He was as good as a tonic, and if that was an illusion too, I'd take it.

I plucked the open book off the seat and set it onto the hearth, then settled on the chair, legs crossed, and he watched my every movement. Only when I seemed comfortable, did he sit down opposite me. Sighed. Planted both hands on the armrests as he faced me. We watched each other for a few moments, and I let the silence stretch out between us because I had the sense he was gathering his thoughts.

Tough as it was to remain silent, I held my tongue.

When he'd finally got his fill of looking me over, he said, "I want to know what my brothers have done to you to make you so afraid."

I shifted in the seat, fidgeting. "What makes you think I'm afraid?"

His fingers tapped against the fabric of the chair. "Do you realize emotion has a smell?" he asked as though it was the perfect response to my question.

"I know predators can scent fear," I said, my gaze shuttering, my own nostrils flaring as I tried to pull in the boy's scent. Blade had come to me before as Stone. I'd not realized the difference in their pheromones until then.

Was he doing the same thing now as his brother, trying to throw me off balance?

"Are you a predator, Mica?" I asked when my senses failed to inform me of any aroma at all coming from the boy.

His eyebrows shot up as his torso jerked in surprise. "Hardly," he said, with a hand to his heart. "Quite the opposite."

I uncrossed my legs and leaned forward. I saw his nostrils flare.

"Now you're angry," he said.

"Confused," I corrected.

"No," he said. "Confusion smells like peppermint. You smell like peppers."

I noted he'd shrank into the back of chair. "Are you afraid, Mica?" I asked, deciding he wasn't Blade after all. I couldn't imagine the dark enforcer backing off even if it was an act.

"I don't like the smell of anger," he said. "It gives me a headache. I sensed anger in the stables with you and Blade. And your fear. I can only assume you're afraid of my brothers because they did something to you. I want to know what it is."

It was such a surprising statement, one so loaded with command, that for the second time in a few moments, I was left speechless. Was he that innocent that he had no idea what sort of business his brothers— his father—was into here in Fae?

I leaned forward, steepling my fingers between my knees as I regarded him just as soberly as he was me. Innocent and naive he might be now, but he had steel in him. He'd be an adult fae to reckon with some day.

"You know I'm not here voluntarily," I said. I didn't form it as a question. If he was old enough to ask, he was old enough to hear.

Surprisingly, he nodded. "I'm not blind or stupid," he said. "I see many things." Still that steely posture to his shoulders, to his gaze. "I know what my father is. I also know my brothers."

"If you know your brothers, then you know how ruthless they are, and yet you have to ask why I'm afraid of them."

He shrugged. "They can be cold and calculated when need be, but they are good fae."

I almost barked out a laugh, but then I realized that maybe that was true for him. I decided to take a gentler tack.

"In the whole time I've been in Fae, I've not met many good ones. I've been forced to come here to do a task I do not want to do, and I know nothing about your world that will help me do it."

"You mean the king," he said and I all but gasped. The brief ghost of a smile played over his mouth and then disappeared. "I know about the king," he said. "They think I don't hear, but I do."

"Indeed," I said, thinking I might be inclined to think his shyness was an act except he was still blushing beneath his cloak. His neck bobbed with nervous muscle each time he swallowed.

"Yes, indeed," he murmured. "What I don't know, though, is why my brothers would risk a woman they love to the bastard who sits the throne."

CHAPTER 14

I wasn't shocked to hear Mica say the Brothers Fae were in love with me. From one so young as Mica, so sweet and naïve, I imagine he saw love in a secretive glance or a courtly bow. And yet my stomach ached at the words just the same. I thought there was some truth to the words. Even if Blade had confessed in the stables that he'd never been in love, I knew he cared about me. Those days on the trail, in the tavern, the bookstore, those all revealed what had to be as confusing and distressing an emotion as it was to me.

I certainly felt that magnetic pull between us. It was getting harder and harder to resist, but resist I must. Trust and love had never shown me any quarter. With Kit's life at stake, I couldn't give them any either. Not with Blade and not with Stone. Not while both males were enslaved to a blood oath that might demand at any time that they slash through any ties of emotion they felt for anyone.

Emotions were a complex thing, so full of uncertainty and muddled nonverbal cues that I doubted even a keen sense of smell could untangle all the motivation behind them.

"You scented anger in the stables," I said. "And fear."

He nodded, waiting for me to continue.

"Well, both of those emotions are as complex as any other. Fear isn't always a fast-rising or fast-dissipating response. Sometimes it lingers. And sometimes fear creates anger. What I felt, what you sensed, came from many different stimulus."

"Is that why you and Blade spoke of violence and love?" he said. "Were you angry and afraid because you love him?"

I started. "I was angry and afraid because of things that happened to me here in Fae, things that are far from over."

He widened his nostrils, scenting for truth no doubt. He'd find the air filled with it, but I didn't want to revisit those things, truthful as they might be.

"Let's talk instead of other smells," I said. "You told me when you came in here that the room smells of the woman who used these rooms," I said, recalling my own thoughts on her and the fragrance she left behind, one even I could smell all these years later clinging to spaces like an oil. "Did you know the woman who stayed here well?"

He shook his head and those ashen locks moved like liquid. "I was a child," he said. "And I had my own mother to love me so I didn't know her well."

"Stone said he kept all of his mistresses here," I said. "How long ago did she leave?" Even though the scent permeated the undercurrents of air in the chamber, it wasn't so strong that it should have caused him to react so strongly. Unless she had recently vacated the suite.

"How long?" he asked, confused. "It's been a century since she graced the manse. I barely remember her face, but her fragrance? I can't forget it, not so long as Blade holds onto it."

I grappled with the thought that a woman could be gone for centuries and still be remembered by a child. But then, Mica was no normal youth.

"Did he spend much time with her?" I asked, thinking maybe Blade's comment about never having fallen in love might have been just one more deflection. That he'd shared Terran's mistress if he still clung to her scent that way.

Mica blinked. Not once but twice. "I would think he'd spend as much time with her as he could," he said. "The same as I did with my mother."

"What was her name?" I asked, thinking maybe some insight into the woman Terran found interesting enough to introduce her to his sons might help me to understand him.

"It's impolite to ask for a fae's true name," he said, crossing one leg over the other. "But we called Blade's mother Aoife."

It was my turn to blink. Not once, but three times in rapid succession as I reeled the information onto a spool so fast it puddled on the other end into a tangle of tape. Blade's mother. Not a mistress he was cuckolding Terran with. Interesting.

"Blade's mother?"

He canted his head at me. "Yes. His mother. That's who held these suites before you. My father allowed her to remain here while Blade came into his full magics. So she could train him." He straightened his spine and cast me a glance that suggested he was pretty damned impressed with his older brother. "I've heard my father say to Stone that she was necessary. That no one but she or a mate would be able to control him or his magics."

I felt like a landed fish, mouth gaping open. "Blade's mother was Terran's mistress."

"Of course," he said. "I thought you knew he's our half-brother."

My head dropped back in comprehension. The hatred. The animosity. The reason for Terran's disdain over his dark enforcer's nature, one he obviously didn't understand because no doubt it came from his mother's side.

"My God," I said.

He grinned. "Well," he said. "Half right. Maybe not your god, but rumor has it Aoife was one of ours."

"Are you telling me Blade is a bastard in more ways than a figurative one?"

He frowned and I hastened to apologize so I wouldn't offend him and choke off the stream of information. "I'm sorry," I said. "But he has been a bit of a prick."

He had the grace to look uncomfortable. "My father puts him in impossible situations," he said. "I imagine to mortals like you, he looks very much like a cold-hearted bastard."

The temptation to paint a picture for the boy in a story of blood, gore, and clammy fear was only smothered by my own reluctance to revisit the events in the catacombs. And even that was over-shadowed by those in the tavern.

No one deserved to witness that sort of horror, not even in recollection. I certainly wasn't going to detail it for a young male who obviously adored his brother, and who seemed far too gentle to hear such things.

I chose instead to work at uncovering more about the dark enforcer. The son of a Fae god didn't bode well for my chances to overwhelm him when he came for me finally, but perhaps a bit of armor wouldn't be a bad idea. So informed by his own nature, I might well be able to hold my own if not call on that information to aid me in an escape.

"Do tell me more," I said.

I fully expected him to protest, but to my surprise, he actually got giddy, as if he'd been dying to talk to someone about it for years. His voice grew hushed, a sort of reverent whisper that I had to strain to hear.

"Blade is the eldest," he said. "But my father has kept it no secret that he sired Blade out of the bonding-ritual."

"Bonding ritual?" I asked. "Is that like human marriage."

He snorted. "Nothing so crass as that. Human marriage can be broken. Our bonding rituals are eternal. Our mates are either born for us and fated, or we perform a ritual that makes them so."

"And your father performed this for your mother?"

Mica's lips pressed together tightly for a moment, a sign he wasn't sure if he should divulge the information. But I waited patiently, sure he would continue. With an even softer voice, he said, "He tells everyone he did, but I have evidence to suggest what he did with my mother was not quite so respectable as that."

"Really," I mused aloud, trying for the least amount of words I could in an effort to keep him talking.

He looked over his shoulder. "I've seen a book of sacred gems in my father's study," he said. "I thought it strange he kept it under lock and magical key, so I broke the spell."

Impressed, I made a small sound of encouragement and he glowed with pride. "My magic tutelage includes many such things, but magic is complex here in Fae. The harnessing of it depends on so many things: natal magic, which we all have that is unique to each of us. Mine includes empathetic magic and affinity for growing things." He put a finger to his lip. "I suppose they do go hand in hand, do they not? I'd never thought of that before." A sound of comprehension slipped from him even as I was dying to hurry him on.

He leveled his gaze at me. "Our natal magics are a sort of blend of our parents, the timing of our birth, and the lineage we spring from. But there are different types of magic. While all fae possess magic, some of the baser fae cannot access the power in their blood. Some say it wasn't always so, but it has been as long as our history books say."

"And your tutor is helping you with your natal magics?" I asked, pinning the note about the gem stone to the bulletin board in the back of my mind.

His grin was slight. "Not exactly. He's helping me with borrowed magic. Borrowed magic is power given or grant-ed or bought. Or being able to transfer power to another fae or object or living thing."

I guessed borrowed magic was more complicated if it needed tutoring. "Can anyone purchase this magic?" My mind was already reeling with possibilities. I was willing to bet that pouch of cursed objects held such power.

His hand seesawed in front of his chest. "Technically, yes. But most fae don't have the ability to wield it even if they could marshal the resources to purchase it. There are far more who sell it than buy it."

The way he phrased it reminded me very much of the gangster movies I'd watched and the thugs offering to provide protection for a price to humble merchants. I was beginning to realize just what the Shadow Court dealt with here in Fae. What magic they didn't possess, they bought or stole.

"So your tutor," I started because I found the explanation intriguing. "Can she utilize borrowed magic? Is that what she's teaching you?"

"He," he said, correcting me. "And yes. He is of the order of Fae who can use borrowed magic. The king is too."

And Terran, I was willing to bet. I thought of the City of the Dead and the no man's land in the dungeons of this very castle and gathered that's what was happening between Terran and the entity who provided a space for the Don to feed it the suffering of others. But then I looked at Mica and I realized why he was being tutored in the magic.

"You can wield borrowed magic too," I guessed.

He grinned broadly. Proud. He didn't have to answer for me to know I was right. "Does Stone have the ability?" I asked somewhat tentatively. This was rocky ground. One misstep and sinkholes would appear quickly. If Terran had the capability and Mica was his son, did the talent get passed down?

Mica's brow furrowed in thought. "I don't know," he admitted. "I've never seen a transference between him and any other, but I know Blade does." He canted his head sideways, thoughtful. "I guess that's why he's paying for my tutor. He understands how difficult it is to wield, even for those who possess the ability."

Blade was sponsoring his brother's training? How odd it wasn't Terran. I would have thought he'd want to use such a tool and know exactly how strong the skill was. Dictators like the leader of the Shadow Court didn't like too many things going on that they didn't control.

Unless he didn't know.

My fingers trailed to the delicate blooms sitting beside me in the makeshift vase and brushed them thoughtfully. I could feel the magic vibrating against my skin, and for a second, the crisp white of the flowers dulled.

"Drat," Mica said. "I guess I need more practice. Father won't like that I can't hold the magic longer than a few moments." He stood and gathered the flowers from beneath my touch and clutched them against his chest. "I'm sorry, Ava," he said shyly. "I really thought I could keep them fresh for you longer."

I stood with him, touched him gently on the shoulder. "It's alright, Mica," I said. "You've given me a greater gift."

His obsidian eyes flashed to silver for an instant. "I have?"

I nodded. "You've told me more about Fae in a few moments than anyone else has, and that is a great gift indeed."

He looked down at the blooms against his chest and they flared to life once again. Raising his eyes to mine, he flashed me a bright smile. "Maybe I can be your tutor," he said. "You know, while you're here. I could come every morning before my lessons and teach you all kinds of things about fae."

The poor soul. He obviously knew nothing about my ultimate fate or that his sweet brother would be the one to take me out. I supposed I couldn't blame Terran and Blade for keeping that from him. But he looked so earnest, so naïve, I couldn't help returning his smile.

"That would be lovely," I said. "I'd like that."

He hesitated, his smile faltering for a second and I realized he was probably reading my emotions and finding the sadness beneath the smile, so I plastered on an even brighter smile, and forced myself to think about how fun it was to have a young fae with a crush on me. That warmed my heart and his smile returned.

"Maybe next time you can tell me about the book of sacred gems. You've got me on pins and needles to hear what you learned."

His gaze flicked toward the book on the hearth before he poked the stems of the flowers back into each hole in the toothbrush holder with such care, I thought he was rethinking his offer, maybe regretting telling me so much. When he stood back and surveyed the makeshift vase and the clutch of tiny blooms, he sighed.

"Maybe it would be best if we spend the time learning about the king," he said in a far away voice, distracted, maybe preoccupied trying to keep the blooms fresh, I thought.

At least until he swiveled to face me, tossing his cloak back over his shoulders again. "I can teach you how to control him."

My heart stuttered in my chest. "Control him? That's possible?"

But he was already heading for the door and I had to race to catch him. I was about to hook his elbow, when he spun on his heel. He faced me with such a blank expression I wondered if he had somehow forgotten everything he'd just said to me.

"Mica?"

Too late, I realized he had gone to the door to lock it.

Chapter 15

There was no time to duck because I had no idea what he planned to do until a blast of magic came at me. I had time to think that his magic was purple, just like Flint's. Belatedly, knowing I couldn't get out of the way, I braced myself for the hit. I expected it to slam into me, knocking me off my feet. I expected violence. Pain.

None of that happened.

The magic washed over me like a cascade of warm air and as it moved over my skin, it...tickled. Like a whisper on the back of an ear. The vibration eddied over me, coaxing me to melt into it. I would never be sure why I let it take me, but I did.

It was a delicious abandon, not unlike Bloodmist. I wondered for the breadth of a heart's pump if I'd find myself on the floor waking from a near comatose sleep. Then, I surrendered whole heartedly, dropping my head back, savoring the sensation. I might have spread my arms out. I might have arched my chest as I laid back on the currents of magic that held me aloft even as it swirled around me.

For a moment, I thought I could hear Mica's voice from outside of me, a chattering, almost fearful sound, companioned by a stronger voice, one filled with chastisement.

I didn't care. Whatever he was saying, it was nothing to the things I saw in the swirl of magic. It was nothing to the feeling of my entire body being coaxed apart molecule by molecule by the softest of feather brushes. Like a painter sweeping away dust from a canvas, my cells shifted and moved and...slid toward and away from each other.

And oh the visions that played out in the spaces between rational thought. Like a waking dream, the images moved so swiftly, resonating on a deep level that went beyond language. I felt the images. One moment I was angry, the next grieving. From second to second, I heard the pictures and felt the emotions as though they were my own and not some strangers flitting through my mind in a page corner animation.

When it was over, I found myself in strong arms. The familiar scent of caramel enveloped me. Stone. Somehow, sometime, Stone had come into my room.

"How long?" I asked as I opened my eyes to see him peering down at me. I'd collapsed, it seemed, because we were sitting on the floor. Draped across his lap with my legs splayed wide open.

"How long have you been out or how long have I been holding you?" he asked.

I craned my neck toward where I thought the door was. Mica was gone. A quick scan around me proved he'd blasted me and left.

"I suppose both," I said as I tried to sit up. Stone's hold on me tightened enough that I shot him a scolding look.

He immediately relaxed. "Sorry," he said. "Reflex."

Little by little, as if he was afraid to let me go too suddenly, his arms peeled away. My core picked up where his support left off and I was able to slide off his lap onto the floor. The boards felt too hard beneath my bottom. The room seemed too dark. I could barely detect a fragrance of caramel.

I pulled my legs in and crossed them one over the other like the Buddha, facing him. For a long moment, I just watched him. He remained silent as I did, both of us sussing out exactly what might be said to fill the heaviness in the air.

My mind was racing as it tried to assemble and reassemble the images Mica sent me, but they were like droplets of gassy air dancing out of reach on the currents each time I so much as crept up on them.

"Where is Mica?" was the best I could do.

His lips pressed together. "I sent him to his rooms."

My eyebrows climbed upward. "Like a child? How very parental of you."

I was sure he heard the note of disapproval in my voice. I didn't try to disguise it. "Why?" I asked.

"You were out for about an hour," Stone said.

"That's not what I asked."

He cocked his head at me. "You did."

I waved the comment away. "I don't care about that now. I want to know why you sent Mica away."

He pulled his legs beneath him, tucking his feet in and rising as though he'd been pulled upright by some invisible force. I thought I'd never get used to the fluidity of Fae movements, but at the same time was awed by it. He stood peering down at me, his gaze shuttered as though he thought I would refuse the hand he extended me.

He was right. I had no intention of asking for help. He wasn't the only one in spectacular shape. I might have been exhausted from the catacombs but I still had a good core. I got up and shook out my hands, a boxer readying for a fight.

"Mica was giving me information you all seem to have decided I don't need."

"Mica has been forbidden to use that mode of magic," he said.

"Oh? And just who forbids him?" I realized I was probably a bristling mess as I stood there, but dammit, a hell of a lot of visions had blasted through me, and I had the feeling Stone was not going to be useful in figuring them out.

His face softened. "Ava," he said in an entreating tone. "You don't understand."

"Then help me, dammit," I said, my fists clenching at my sides. "Stop keeping stuff from me. I need to know these things."

In reply, he gestured toward the wingback chair by the fireplace. I noticed the fire was crackling along merrily. So in my semi-coma, someone had lit the thing. I heaved an irritated sigh.

"I'll sit," I said, "But only if you tell me what the heck is going on."

He waited until I was perched on the seat, with my head resting against the back of the chair because, boy, did I have a headache all of a sudden. And my mouth felt like someone had just taken a huge wad of cotton out of it. A bit of queasiness in my stomach, too. If I didn't know better, I'd say I'd just enjoyed an all night bender.

Stone settled on the hearth instead of the seat opposite me. His long legs bent at odd angles to gather himself into the small space and I couldn't understand at first why he'd take such an awkward position until he jammed a skinny stick of wood into the fire and then turned to face me. A decidedly nonthreatening position, I thought was entirely on purpose. He was working me. Just like the fire.

"I didn't send Mica away," Stone said in a patient voice. "He left. He had to. I suggested the best place for him was his rooms."

"I don't understand."

He nodded. "I know. What he used on you was very complex magic. It takes centuries of training and practice to wield and well..."

"He's still a boy," I said, guessing that the blast of magic had likely drained him the way I'd seen Blade drained after the catacombs. A shade of discomfort sent a shiver over me at the thought of the dark caverns, and I hugged myself as I did my best to shove the unwanted thoughts to the back where they belonged.

I felt Stone's hand on my knee and was surprised to realize that even though he was sitting on the hearth he was still the same height as me. "Mica is a boy in looks," he said in a gentle tone. "But he's not really a boy. He's two centuries old."

"If I'd known..."

"You still couldn't have stopped him from wielding it," Stone said. "But you might have been prepared for the blast. Braced yourself."

I shook my head, still trying to worm my way around all the images and emotions that had come at me. "I wouldn't have had time," I said, not enjoying the confession because it didn't bode well, considering I'd be facing a Fae king.

I sighed, frustrated. "And none of it made sense anyway." My brow furrowed in thought as I stared past Stone's face to the stones of the fireplace. "I don't know why he'd do that to me. It was all just..."

"It's never just," he said. "It's always intentional. It takes as much practice to understand what you see as it does to send the images. That's why it's so peculiar he did that to you. He must have had a reason to use that magic."

My skin was still tingling, far more than Bloodmist ever made it feel. "I suppose we could just ask him." I twisted so that I could see the door, thinking maybe we should do just that.

Stone exerted a bit of pressure on my leg, not a lot. Just enough to keep me from rising. "If he could have used his words, he would have."

I pinched the bridge of my nose. "Maybe he could at least explain why he did that to me without asking." My chin started to quake and I mastered it with great effort. It wasn't as if what he'd done had reminded me of the catacombs, but for some reason, the thought that I'd been violated in some way wouldn't go away. Even if my gut told me the boy didn't have the least intention of causing me ill. "It's not pleasant to have your mind invaded that way."

Stone watched me carefully. "I doubt he understood what he was doing to you." He pulled his hand back and leaned on his knees. "He's never been to the human realm. He has no idea what you are or aren't capable of."

"So he's ignorant," I said, a note of bitterness creeping in to my voice. How many misdeeds had been done and forgiven in the name of ignorance, I didn't want to contemplate. And yet...I knew I could find forgiveness for Mica.

"Let's call it naïve," Stone said.

"If that's the right word, then I'd say the boy should be educated. He just left me here." I swept my hand in a gesture that would encompass the floor beside the fireplace. "Like a landed haddock. Deaf. Blind. Helpless." The breath sucked out of me at the thought of what might have happened had he done it to me outside or within reach of some of the more nefarious fae. My breath hitched as I imagined someone finding me and dragging me back off to the catacombs.

Stone's response was a dark chuckle that drew my attention. My face must have looked like a storm cloud because he said, "Really, Ava. I can't imagine you being completely incapacitated and helpless."

For some reason, though I knew he meant to honor me, the comment ground into my psyche like shards of glass. He'd not seen me helpless. He had no idea what befell me in those caverns or how badly I'd had to fight just to stay alive. How close I'd come to something worse than death.

But Blade had. He'd hunted me down and made those who'd hurt me pay when I couldn't do it for myself. And then he let me have my vengeance. Without judgment.

What would Stone have done, or Terran? I eyed the fae in front of me and tried to imagine him tearing through those catacombs to find me, and I realized I couldn't imagine it. Some part of me was relieved that I couldn't think of him in such a violent way, and part of me felt disappointed.

It was only when Stone's hand touched my shoulder that I realized he'd been speaking to me, and I'd been lost in those thoughts. I blinked. Turned my gaze to his.

"Guess I'm not myself yet," I said, and his gaze softened from the sharp, concerned look of a moment earlier.

"It's alright," he said. "I understand. I bet Mica is in a similar state in his rooms. I don't have intimate knowledge of that sort of magic, but I know it takes a lot out of both parties."

He ran his hand over the top of his hair. "Even so," he said. "I do think it's important that you tell me what you saw. If he sent you the vision, he had to do so because he thought he should. It might mean something."

I shrugged, helpless to recall much more than scraps of color and shapes. "The last thing he said to me before it happened was that I needed to know more about the King."

Stone's eyes narrowed. The blue color deepened. "Did he?" he said and a hard edge cut through his voice. "I suppose he thinks I've been keeping you in the dark."

My brow rolled into a dozen furrows at that inference that he was as innocent in all this as Mica. That he'd dare feel affronted.

"You have been keeping me in the dark," I growled. "I'm dragged here to kill a king, and I haven't the faintest information about him or what his weaknesses are. I'm just supposed to accept that I'm to go to some harem and seduce him with my less than stellar female wiles enough to get close to him. Then I'm supposed to what? Shove a homemade shiv past his ribs? Him? The most powerful fae in your realm?" I sucked the back of my teeth in frustration. "Ridiculous."

"Not the whole realm," he said and I shot him a cutting glare.

"What's that supposed to mean?"

"Not the whole realm," he repeated. "Ferranus is the most powerful in the Iron Kingdom, but Fae is much bigger than what you've seen. The earth doesn't just belong to humans. You've not seen nearly a hundredth of it. There are other 'areas' of Fae and other 'king's.'" He pulled air quotes around the words.

I huffed loudly and rose from my chair. "Brilliant," I muttered in a tone that indicated I thought the information was anything but. "Why don't you go blackmail one of those powerful fae and leave me and my sister in peace."

He rose with me. "I wish it was that easy, Ava, I really do."

My arms folded over my chest so tightly I had a hard time inhaling. "Then at least tell me what a mortal can do that you all can't, because I'm struggling to reason all that out."

The desperation in my voice, I decided, had more to do with frustration than fear, but I didn't care what Stone thought of it.

"It's not what we can't do," he said as he lifted his hand to hover in the air beside my cheek. "It's what you don't have."

I had the horrible feeling he was going to touch me, and I didn't want that. I was in no mood to feel that electric touch that always seemed to move between us. Not then. Maybe not ever again.

So I jerked away and his hand fell to his side. He stared at his fingers as he spoke, instead of looking me in the eye. "Tell me what you saw. Maybe I can help interpret. And we'll go from there."

"I'd rather you tell me what the hell you all are so afraid of if you won't bring all your magic to bear yourselves. Why am I here?"

His lips pressed together and I swore he was counting in his mind, trying to put enough time in that I'd change the subject. Well I wouldn't.

"A trade, then," I said. "You tell me why your cartel won't touch the king and I'll tell you what I saw."

He sighed. "Fair enough," he said. "But it must be between us." He lifted his hand toward me as if he was going to make some sacred vow and I grabbed his fingers, squeezing them together.

"No vows," I said. "Just words between friends."

He canted his head to the side as his eyes flashed. "I suppose if that's all we are, then it will have to be enough," he said and blew out a long draft of air. The equivalent, I thought, of a fighter shaking out their hands.

"My father will no doubt tell you most of this anyway this evening, so I suppose it's not breaking any confidences anyway, so it should be fine."

I waited, smart enough not to interject and get him off track. But it was hard. Damnably hard not to flog the information out of him. Especially when it seemed he was so reluctant to divulge. Especially when, at first, he planted his hands on his hips and started to prowl the room, picking up one thing after another and scanning it like it was interesting.

They were not. A copper goblet. A candle with wax threads tangled over its sides in knots. The same open book I'd found on my seat when I'd arrived. This, he scowled at when he picked it up and closed with a snap before tossing it on the fireplace hearth.

It was a test of my patience if ever there was one, but I held on and finally, he rewarded me by spinning in place and shoving his hands into his pockets. A long-suffering sigh fled his lungs.

"I'm not sure what Mica showed you about the king...if it's possible for him to show you why he's called the Iron

King, but I would think that would be the thing he'd want to show you the most." He paced back and forth in front of the fireplace. "I believe you've realized iron and fae don't mix well. For some of us, it hurts, others' magics are blunted by it. For some it's lethal or painful. It's not natural in Fae, and fae need natural order for their magics to work well. It's why so few of us stay long in the mortal realm."

I thought of his aversion to getting on my motorcycle and refusing to use a cab. "Technology," I guessed.

He nodded. "Something like that. But Ferranus is unique in that he can wield iron in any shape or size. I've seen him hold the blade end of a cold steel knife as if it was as harmless as blacksteel. Watched him heat it to red hot molten metal till it dripped down his arm, and he remained unharmed."

I found myself thinking of the way I'd lain on the bed in the tavern sweating and swearing as Blade kept his cool, watching, tending me, and I shoved the image stubbornly aside. It occurred to me that he'd handed me my karambit in the catacombs, and that made me wonder exactly how he'd carried it in those moments he'd melded into his hell hound form. Unless the karambit, like many other things in the realm, were not real.

I realized I was squinting at Stone as the thoughts played with my natural inclination to suspicion.

"Do you know of any other fae who are immune to iron?" I asked, not really expecting an answer, but he shook his head.

"As far as we know, it's an affinity unique to the king's line."

He halted and his gaze returned again to the book as it sat open on the hearth. I considered reaching for it but I was afraid to move until he did. I'd already interrupted enough.

But I did clear my throat, a tip I'd learned from Gideon in the early days, to catch someone's attention. I knew if I didn't follow it up with anything, he'd start to speak.

Which he looked like he would, but he also returned to the chair by the fireplace and sat down opposite me before he decided to. And I waited patiently, struggling not to prod him as he gathered his thoughts or his courage or whatever else had his attention in those moments. By the time I was about ready to cough again to force him to continue, he sighed heavily.

"Trying to explain why we need a mortal assassin is harder to put into words than I thought," he said. "I almost wish I had Mica's ability to inject information magically."

"Trust me," I said, thinking of the lushness of the experience partnered with the sense of violation and guilt. "You do not want to try that with me again."

He shot me an uncertain smile. "Even if I could, I wouldn't do that to you."

I slung my leg over the armrest, leaning back in the chair in as casual and trusting a posture as I could manage when my whole being was screaming internally for him to just get on with it.

"I'm sure you can manage if you try," I said, my patience running out finally.

"Fine," he said and stretched his legs, eliciting a popping sound that made me wince. "When I said we needed a mortal more because of what we don't have, I meant it literally." He propped his arm on his chest and stuck his elbow on top of that, running two fingers over his brow thoughtfully before he spoke again. This time, more confidently.

"While it's true that other fae don't have this affinity Ferranus does, we do share the magic of Fae itself. We are not mortal, but we do share the same things that mortals do: breath, heart, blood."

He waited, for what seemed an interesting amount of time before I realized he was waiting for me to interject. That the point he was making meant something. I guessed this was probably territory that might be tricky for that oath he'd taken. That he wanted me to point out what he didn't want to say. A cunning strategy, I thought, providing I knew what the hell he was on about.

"So what mortals share with the fae is also something that will give me an edge," I guessed and he touched his nose with his finger.

"Plants thrive via different mechanisms," he said. "Just like in your world. But here, those things all possess some sort of magic. Just as most living things possess blood."

That was important, I guessed, judging by how he stressed it.

"Blood," I echoed, leaning forward as the realization moved through me like liquid metal. "Blood has iron in it."

His face lit up and I knew I had hit the crux of the issue. I was so excited, I grabbed his knee and squeezed. A zing of energy moved up my arm, warm, and fragrant in a way that the nose can't smell, a pheromone, I supposed.

"Does fae blood contain iron?" I asked him, careful to ask the question in a personal way, in a manner that might not encompass a group of beings he might be sworn to.

His smile told me I'd done well. "Fae blood, though mixed with gold and silver, and some modicum of magic and other elements we don't understand, indeed, has iron in it. What is human blood made of, Ava?"

"Well, certainly not gold and silver," I said. "But I imagine the more important thing is that we have no magic in our blood," I said aloud, talking to capture the thoughts as they raced along to catch up to what he was saying, doing my best to remember my biology when I knew damn well I'd been stoned for most of my classes.

"True mortals," he said carefully. "Those who are fully human do not have magic in their blood. You have other substances, all components that are necessary to keep you alive, all bound by a protein that uses iron."

"But yours is not bound to protein, I'm guessing," I said, my eyes narrowing thoughtfully.

His eyebrows rose a considerable distance from their original spot, an indication of how pleased he was that I was catching on. I wasn't. Not entirely, but I was getting there.

"You said you needed me because of something I didn't have. I don't have magic." I all but stood up in excitement as the realization shot through me. I didn't have magic.

"Sweet Jesus, your blood is not bound to protein but to magic." I blinked like there was too much light in my eyes as I looked at him. He seemed to glow all of a sudden, the pleasure written all over his face.

"You need me because Ferranus can control your magic," I said. "Because if he can wield iron, he can control your magic and so control you."

I almost fell back down onto the chair, because the very thing that made me useful also put me at risk.

Because if Ferranus could control the iron in Fae blood, he could surely control mine, and with more iron in it than Fae blood, I was pretty sure I was risking more than a bit of control.

In fact, I knew I'd rather die than lose control to anyone ever again.

CHAPTER 16

I was used to having my life on the line, but every hunt, every kill, every trophy I took, I was the one in control. I took the chances. I made the choices. Me. If the decision was a bad one, at least I knew it had been mine to make.

Gideon and I argued about his lack of control over me so often, he'd found another version of me that was more amenable. So the thought of putting myself in a position where a powerful fae could control me tossed me straight back into memories of the catacombs. That didn't just make my palms sweat. It made my skin itch like a rash was spreading beneath its layers.

I needed air. I needed a drink. Something.

I wasn't aware I was crossing the room toward the bathroom until Stone touched me ever so gently on the shoulder. I spun around so fast I surprised myself. My fists were up and already swinging. He caught them easily and a sob escaped me.

"Ava," he murmured in a soft voice that was so achingly tender my breath hitched in back of my throat.

"Don't," I said, shaking my head. "Just...don't."

His hand dropped away but I felt him there behind me, close enough that his breath brushed the back of my shoulders and neck. I pulled my hair back, scooping it into a ponytail and twisting it on top of my head. My eyes closed. The scent of him curled around me and I had to blow out a long slow breath just to find my composure.

"You do realize what you're asking of me," I said, forming the words as a statement and not a question because I knew the truth as well as he did. "The king's magic must really be something if your father isn't willing to risk him reaching in and manipulating it. Imagine what he can do if he can access your powers. Imagine what he can do to my blood if he can access mine." I swallowed hard at the thought. "Imagine it," I said again. "Except you don't have to. You probably already know and that's why you brought me here because all of you are damn cowards."

This last said with enough venom that it burned my tongue. My voice rose to a pitch that should have had me flinching. When I thought I could turn around and look at him without losing my shit, I squared my shoulders and spun around.

He was watching me closely.

"I didn't know you when this started," he said calmly, but his throat bobbed as though he too was struggling. "I didn't know how much I'd care about you. I just did what I was tasked to do. Find an assassin. Threaten him if I had to. Buy his consent."

"But you chose me. Not Gideon."

"I did. I wish to the gods I hadn't. But we're here now, so..."

"So you would have 'schooled' Gideon on the inner workings of Fae and the Iron King, would you?" I asked. "But you wouldn't give me the same courtesy until I begged you."

I was sure he heard the bitterness in my voice the same as I did, but I didn't care. In fact, I hoped he did hear it. I hoped he felt shame over keeping me in the dark. I reached out for the door frame and ran my palm along the wood, absently checking to see if it could support me, I supposed. Or maybe because I didn't trust my legs to carry me the last few feet to lean on it. This was one bloody cluster fuck of awfulness.

His sigh filled the air with regret and shame. "I was hoping I could convince my father to find someone else. I thought maybe if you didn't know too much, he'd let you go. He'd release your sister. No harm done."

"Let me guess," I said, leaning against the frame. "He refused."

His mouth twitched but he didn't argue. I appreciated his silence in that moment because I was sure I would try to choke the life out of him if he tried to argue.

I took a beat. Just one. And then I heaved a sigh. "I think you had better start schooling me the way you would have any other assassin, because it's not just my life on the line, Stone."

"I know, Ava."

I snorted. "Do you?" The door frame seemed too unyielding all of a sudden, and I wanted to hurt something. Pushing off the wood, I scanned the room for a path that might put objects in my way. Pitchers. Books. Candles. Anything I could throw or smash.

I spied the book on the hearth and headed for it. The damn thing was open again. Well, it would be minus a few pages in several more seconds. I stooped to grab it by the back cover. It flapped closed in my grip like a nun's legs. I yanked it open, began leafing through the pages because I fully planned to yank every single one of them out. Except I couldn't get hold of a decent grouping before they slid free of my grasp.

"If I'm still on the docket," I growled. "Then the least you can do is tell me why your father wants him dead. I think I deserve that. And don't tell me it's about power. Terran seems to have plenty of it already."

I wrenched at the book, trying to rip it in half but it remained crisp and solid. I pulled and tore and twisted and the damn thing wouldn't give.

By the time I had resorted to tearing at the pages one by one and balling them in my fist to throw across the room, Stone was in front of me. A mere blur of color one moment and a solid, anxious one the next.

He took the book from me and set it on the chair. It fell open, exposing creamy pages that held my attention for several long moments.

"Tell me what Mica showed you," he said.

I dragged my gaze from the pages to glare at him. "I don't know."

"You do know," he said. "It doesn't matter if it's coherent sentences. Just tell me."

His voice was too soothing. Like a hypnotist. I backed up, shaking my head.

"You agreed to trade information, Ava," he said. "I held up my part of the bargain, as bad as it made me look. Now it's your turn."

"Don't treat me like a child," I said and he gave me a grim smile that suggested I got what I asked for. A growl tore through me and I threw up my hands in surrender because, really, I knew he was right. Even saying nothing, I knew he was right.

"Fuck it," I said. "You want to know, here's what I remember: none of it made sense. It was all just a mess of color and shapes and emotion."

I was barely aware that he was guiding me onto the chair until I touched down on it.

"That's a start," he murmured. "You can do it."

The fight and frustration sagged through me like rice falling from an open bag. I dropped my head back, feeling as though closing my eyes might be the only way I could reclaim those images. Doing so was a measure of how much I trusted him, despite the things he'd done to me, despite dragging me here.

"Three figures," I said as a blast of color and shape finally moved behind my eyelids. "I remember seeing three figures. Anger. Lust. A sense of betrayal. That was the strongest. I know the feeling, I suppose, so that one I know for sure. The others?" I shrugged. "Who knows?"

Emotions could be complex and without any reference, it was difficult to know what they meant. Sadness could manifest as anger; fear as excitement. But betrayal? I knew the gut-wrenching weight of it well.

"I don't know for sure what the other emotions were. They could have been anything. But I know what betrayal feels like."

I paused, and opened my eyes, mulling over the rest of it, trying to recall the sensations if not the images, and as I watched him I realized he was avoiding my gaze. He'd settled onto the other chair opposite me and was staring down at his pants, running a finger over some flaw only he saw.

"I wasn't accusing you," I said as I realized the effect my words had on him.

His gaze flicked to mine for an instant before it trailed off again. This time to his hands. They were tucked neatly in his lap as though he was trying not to move them.

"It's alright," he said. "I did betray you. "It's a great shame for me."

I had a nearly irresistible urge to reach for his fingers and tangle mine into his. He seemed so forlorn sitting there and despite my own reluctance to get involved, I wanted to comfort him.

But he scrubbed them through his hair, dropping his head back. I sat frozen, unsure what to do. I ended up just sitting there, waiting for him to address me again. Waiting for him to get up. Growl. Do something.

When he leveled his gaze to mine again, all evidence of the sad fae was gone. All that remained was a haunted look behind his eyes, but the face was a mask of careful neutrality.

"I told you what I could, Ava," he said. "And I swear I will give you the rest as I am able in whatever form I'm able, but you're asking me to trust you when you won't trust me."

I fidgeted, my hands twitching in my lap. "Trust doesn't come to me easily, Stone."

Even as I said the words, an image of Blade kneeling at my side in the forests of dark Fae, telling me he would stay by my side came unbidden to my mind. I'd slept, then, with him on guard, believing no harm would come to me while he was there. Perhaps fitfully, but I'd slept. That had to mean something.

I swallowed down the emotions that rose from that memory. They were useless to me here, a risk if anything.

His lips pressed together and he rose from the chair, a subconscious power move or maybe an intentional one. I crossed my arms over my chest. Let him make of that reaction to his power stance as he would.

"You have to trust someone, sometime," he said. "Here in Fae you need that more than anywhere else."

"And you're looking to be that trustworthy someone?"

He canted his head at me, his eyes flashing with real surprise. "I thought you knew that. I thought I was clear about my intentions."

Before I had a chance to protest, he was on his knees in front of me. He grabbed my hands and held them tightly in his own. That careful mask was gone, replaced by a different sort of emotion, and he looked so much like Blade that my breath hitched.

Half of me wanted to pull my hands away and the other half couldn't bring myself to do it. I left them in his warm grip as he looked up at me.

"Let me be all you need here, Ava."

My jaw ached too much to speak for a moment. "I'm not sure what I need here, Stone," I said. "I'm so far out of my depth I don't even know what to ask for."

"Anything."

"You say anything, but there are things you can't do, Stone." I pulled my hands away, finally. "You just proved that anything doesn't include things that go against that vow."

He shoved his hands beneath his armpits. "I told you why those vows are so binding, Ava. Think about what I said, and realize just how much I care about you if I'm afraid to break them. "

The admission threw me. So much that I couldn't speak for a moment, and by the time I had the words to say, he cut me off, as though he knew full well that it would be a protest of some sort, and wanted to head it off at the pass.

"You don't have to tell me how you feel," he said in a soft voice as he pushed himself to his feet again. "Just tell me what you saw. It may help, and I want to help, Ava. I'll do everything I can."

He turned his gaze to the fireplace and the book that somehow was sitting back on the hearth. We both stared at it for several moments, and I found myself trying to remember where I'd put it when I'd tried to rip out the pages. A furtive, curious scan of the room showed the crinkled balls of pages still littering the floor. I reached for one and bounced it back and forth in my hands, thinking, trying to pull the moments to me once again.

"It wasn't just people...fae," I corrected. "Definitely fae. I got a sense of power and authority. But there was also a flash of blue."

"Like magic?"

I shook my head. "No, I don't think so. It had substance. Like a rock or a gem of some sort."

"That's helpful," he said.

"I don't see how."

"And the fae," he said, not quite a question. Almost a suspicion. I squinted at him, wondering what he thought I saw in those images and tried harder to see through the foggy glasses of memory to the very blurry pages of the story and make sense of them. "Tell me about them. What impressions do you get of them?"

"I think two were women." I pursed my lips, thinking, and realized something more. "Old Fae. The images came one after the other, not altogether. Like a slideshow."

I squeezed the paper in my hand, making a tighter ball. "I don't have more," I said. "I'm sorry it isn't much."

I thought long and hard about what I would say next, because I did remember something else. I remembered that being struck by that magic was like being wrapped in warm oil and cushioned by velvet. I remembered that it was as saturating as Bloodmist ever was, that I would happily let the magic take me again if I had the chance.

But I knew better than to mention that, because I knew it wasn't something he'd understand. I didn't know anyone in the realm who might understand except for Blade, and I had the feeling he'd disapprove. The feeling of that magic was too sweet. Too warm. Too much of every good thing for a woman who possessed no willpower to resist such pleasure.

So, I said nothing of how I'd give anything to taste that magic again. The feeling of the power I sensed either behind the magic or behind the images of those fae was indescribable. Best kept out of the way of prying eyes. Best kept out of my eyes as Stone sought to capture my gaze with his own, and so I fiddled with the arm rest to give myself an excuse not to meet the deep blue going cold as it regarded me.

Only after I was able to focus on the way my fingers tapped against the armrest, and slow the movements down to a steady rhythm was I able to look at him again, and I had the feeling he'd noted every touch down of my fingers to the fabric.

Noted it and measured it, and knew it had matched the rapid staccato of my heart.

"I'm not sure I even remember that much accurately," I said. "I mean, maybe there was more. It's kind of like chasing a dream you feel strongly about but can't grab the tail of, you know?"

He reached over and patted my knee. "I do know."

His touch felt reassuring. It felt accommodating, but something squirmed in my gut, telling me he was just letting it go for the moment. We'd return to this moment again, I was sure of it.

"Maybe if I give it a rest it will come back in the same sorts of snatches as a dream does."

Sitting back, he gripped the arms of the chair. "If you can't remember more, I'll check with Mica later. Maybe once he's recovered, he can offer some insight on why he chose injecture instead of words."

My gaze fell to the book again, feeling chagrined now at my outburst in light of the discomfort Mica might be feeling at that moment. "Do you really think he wore himself out that badly?"

"There aren't many who have that natal magic," he said. "And it takes many generations to master the power. I imagine he used up more stores than he expected."

"Can we check on him?" I asked, deciding I couldn't rest until I knew he was alright. It was a simple enough question, I thought, and yet something in Stone's face suggested not as simple as all that after all, and so I waited till he'd schooled his features into the neutral mask I knew he wanted me to see.

Only then did he speak, and it was in a voice thick with regret. "Maybe we can check on him later," he said.

"Meaning we have other business," I said in a flat voice because I knew what he was going to say even before he said it.

"Yes," he said. "My father wants you to explain where you've been."

As though I could. The mere thought of verbally walking through everything that had happened from the time I'd climbed atop Nutkin with Blade till now made me want to curl up on the bed—and I wasn't a shrinking violet by any stretch. But because I wasn't a shrinking violet, I shook out my hands and straightened my spine. The hunter resolve settling around me like a cloak.

"Then let's crack on," I said and when he gave me a peculiar look, I shrugged. "I want this over with."

"Keep that in mind, Ava," he said as he gestured for me to go ahead of him. "And remember I'm on your side."

A strange thing to say, I thought, until after several moments of walking silently with him behind me, urging me with a gentle touch now and again to guide me, we passed several of glowering, sober-looking males. I knew we were close to Terran's wing when the clusters of guards grew more knotted and surly looking.

And by the time we reached a massive oak door with a blacksteel knocker in the very center, a shiver of precognition coiled around my throat like a rope.

"What's waiting in there for me, Stone?" I asked without turning around.

"I'll be with you," he said quietly.

The feel of dozens of eyes on my back grew so strong, my fists clenched at my sides. The edge of my fist brushed the sheath and the karambit that lay against my thigh. At least he'd not taken it from me. That had to mean something, right?

I eyeballed the intricate scroll work on the door. Runes, they looked like, but nothing I'd ever seen before. They curled among leaves and wolf jowls and forested trees so subtly only a keen eye would notice.

I wondered what they meant. If they were spells of protection or avarice or if they merely told a story the way pharaohs of Egypt proved their prowess in stone. Then I decided it didn't matter what the reasoning was behind the artwork. I had to go in there whether the symbols were spells or not.

"I'll be right with you," Stone said. "Standing at your side."

I looked over my shoulder at him and the way his jaw was clenched, I knew even he was afraid of what I'd face inside.

"If I tell you more of what Mica showed me, will you go first?" I asked. I wasn't afraid and I didn't know more, but only a fool walked into an ambush and trusted the man behind her to have her back.

His jaw softened and the color of his eyes deepened to cerulean. "You don't have any more to tell me, and we both know it. But I will go first."

At that, he slid so smoothly in front of me, easing me so gently backward, that I was barely aware he'd moved at all until I found myself staring at his back. He flashed me an encouraging smile over his shoulder, one that crinkled his eyes and made my throat ache.

Then he was opening the door in a blustering movement that had to be for the benefit of those who waited inside.

And it didn't take me but three seconds to realize why he was so careful to prepare me for the worst.

CHAPTER 17

Terran's apartments possessed the richness of dark, sumptuous colors predominated by a deep midnight blue that gave off the sensation of stepping into the velvet of midnight. A sort of dark chill even permeated the room and gave off the unmistakable fragrance of hot wax. Another aroma hunkered beneath, too, something that held the snap of metal striking stone, as though someone had knapped two pieces of firestone together.

Everything within me wanted to back out, but I forced myself to step over the threshold and into the sitting room. My every sense was on high alert, but it wasn't enough, because like the catacombs, this room held the whiff of threat and I needed to be on my toes.

I wished I had a blast of Bloodmist so my subconscious could pick up things my mind was too busy to register. Just thinking about why I didn't have any made my skin itch. In that moment, I wanted to see Blade. I wanted to catch his eye and hear him telling me it was going to be alright. And then I hated myself for the weakness.

Stone halted several paces in front of me, and pivoted on his heel to face me. Confusion rode his expression.

"No one is here," I said, answering that bewilderment as I scanned the sitting room, taking in plush chairs, the crackling fire in the firebox. The whole room smelled of butterscotch and cloves, and a hint of an aroma that tugged at my memory with spectral hands. The room was empty, but hadn't been long.

Emboldened, I crossed the room to where two columns rose to the ceiling and beyond on either side of the fireplace. Made of some sort of twisted wood, they were carved with more runes and symbols. I knew better than to touch them, but they drew my hands to them close enough to hover over the surface. Static moved between the wood and my palms.

Definitely spelled.

Stone moved closer, his gaze on where my hands were roaming the air over the symbols. "They must be in the antechamber," he said, brushing my hand away so that he clasped my fingers in his. "They do more than protect," he said. "Don't give them any of your energy."

My jaw ticked and I nodded. Several moments passed before I decided to withdraw my hand from his, but he didn't move away. Instead, he took a step even closer. When he laid his mouth against the back of my ear, a conspiratorial move rather than a sexual one, I angled my head toward him.

"Remember I'll be with you. No matter what."

My mouth twitched. "Sure," I said. "Just like the last time." I didn't mention the dungeons below, but I was sure he'd understand the inference.

He pressed his lips into a white line, and I had the feeling he wanted to protest, but then a sound from beyond the fireplace took my attention away from him altogether. Like the dinner I'd been invited to the first night I was released, a seam of purple threaded itself into a rectangle in the wall.

"It's time," Stone said in a breathless voice that had my head snapping to him. If he was nervous just how bad was this going to be? He inclined his head toward the door that appeared, showing a warm glow beyond that flickered as though a cozy fire kept the space warmly lit.

"Why do I feel like I'm about to step into Narnia?" I asked.

He canted his head at me curiously, and I muttered that it didn't matter. And it didn't. Not once I crossed the room with him on my heels like a collie herding me into a pen.

I expected many things. I imagined Terran would be sitting in some massive and expensive looking chair surrounded by several thugs—which he was. My skin prickled as I panned the room with every expectation that those thugs would be plentiful—and they were. I wouldn't have been surprised to see the fae from the dinner party who jabbed me with a prod made of wood or all of the under-bosses.

None of those were present in the room.

I half expected to see Blade standing with his back in the corner, his arms crossed, glowering at me as I entered, curling his lip at the sight of Stone on my tail.

Some of those things greeted me, and I marked them subconsciously, but each one of them was overshadowed by the way my stomach dropped to my feet as I caught sight of Flint standing behind Terran's chair as though they were posing for a family portrait. And as horrible as that feeling was, it was nothing to what happened to me when my eyes ran to a familiar form standing so tightly against Flint's side that my fists curled of their own accord.

"Kit," I said in a flat voice. My mind reeled with possibilities and scenarios. I wanted to drill Stone with a nasty glare because he'd known what I'd see here and didn't prepare me. All I could do was stand there, frozen, my hands clenching and unclenching as they fought the instinct to pull my karambit free and start slicing.

"Ava," she said, her voice electric with shock. "What's going on? Why are you here?"

The sound of her voice put a strangle-hold on my throat. She looked thinner than I remembered. Her hair was a different shade, lusher, I thought, with low lights placed just perfectly here and there, creating a chestnut sheen when she moved. Her simple button up shirt was in her favorite shade of pink. The narrow-legged jeans and ankle boots suggested she'd taken some care in dressing. The bright red lipstick was the dead giveaway.

When her eyes narrowed at me in suspicion, I almost sobbed, but I managed to hold it together. I had to say something, but what? How much did she know? What if I said too much and she too became a loose end?

I needed to sit down so badly I had to fight not to ask for a chair. As if Stone understood, he moved closer to me, leaning into my shoulder in invitation. I swallowed, straightened my shoulders and took a step away.

There was no way I was going to look weak.

Despite the way my stomach was squeezing its way down through my intestines, I lifted my chin. Defiant. Determined.

"I think the question is what are you doing here?" I asked her, and Flint casually draped his arm over Kit's shoulder. She looked up at him and shot him a fleeting smile.

"I'm fine," she said and damn if he didn't display the most charming of smiles right back at her.

Fine, she said. Fine. As if she was so blind to everything around her that she couldn't see this wasn't home. This wasn't even Earth as we knew it.

I found the courage to head toward her and noted from the corner of my eye, several of the thugs suddenly straightening their backs. I told myself that at least there was no fear in her voice. She wasn't hurt. Things just might be alright.

"You've changed your hair," I said in a tight voice.

Her hand went to the bottom of her bob and smoothed out the strands. Not shaking, I noticed. Just casual, almost thoughtless.

"You haven't changed a thing," she said and I flinched at the tone. I knew it well. Knew the hard glint in her eye behind the well of disappointed tears. A reel of images raced through my mind in the seconds I saw her, so many nights where she confronted me in the wee hours of the morning in her nightdress and robe while I swayed on my feet, high and completely unable to answer to her accusations. A montage of memories flitted in and out of my mind as I held her gaze. I felt like the same, stupid teenager in those moments.

I was aware that my hand had gone to my throat only when her gaze followed it and pinned itself there.

"What have you got yourself into now, Ava?" she said.

Shock gone, she reverted to accusation. It was alright. I could handle accusation. It meant that while her hair and weight had changed, not much else had. I took hope from that. What she thought of this place, I had no idea, but she certainly didn't see any danger here for her. But the way Flint loomed, the way Terran's fingers tapped the armrest, the way the thug in the corner angled his feet ever so purposefully toward Kit, I knew differently. The moment Flint's hand left her shoulder, something broke in me.

I felt fingers hook my elbow, and realized I'd been well on my way to run for her. Somewhere in the back of my mind, instinct had taken over. Save the innocent. Get her out of there. I might have overplayed my card, then. Terran all but smirked at me.

Swinging my head to the side, I saw Stone holding me back, his eyes blasting a warning shot toward me. Don't do anything foolish, that look said. It was a look I knew well. I swallowed because I totally had been about to do something foolish, I realized. I had to be smarter than that. I could feel my lungs doing their best to find a natural rhythm.

"What is she doing here," I demanded. "This wasn't part of the deal."

"What deal?" he said. "The last I knew you agreed to complete a task for me but you disappeared."

"I didn't disappear," I said. "I was—" My eyes cut a path to Kit whose head had tilted to the side in bewilderment. Her eyes were narrowed anxiously. I didn't think I could go on with what I was going to say. I didn't want to admit what I'd been through out loud.

"It wasn't intentional," I said, correcting myself.

Terran's hand slid over the armrest, back and forth as though he was charging his skin with static. "You agreed to kill the king," he said, not bothering to use a euphemism. That couldn't be good. Not at all.

I stole another look at Kit. Alarm had started to rise in her gaze. She'd no doubt caught the words kill and king, and now she was probably running through all the horrible things I'd done and adding them into one gigantically impossible algebraic formula that meant I'd finally crossed the line from petty crimes to murder.

She wouldn't be wrong. She just didn't know the whole of it, and I had the feeling it was too late now to try to hide the truth from her. If she didn't know she was in Fae, and that magic, supernatural, and all kinds of baddies out there worse than me, she would know it soon.

With a tight voice, I turned my attention back to Terran, avoiding Kit's eye.

"Nothing has changed," I said, careful not to admit too much or be too specific. Just in case.

"I don't imagine it has," he said. "But just to be sure..." He flicked his hand toward Kit in a gesture so subtle, it might have gone unnoticed except she let go a mouse-like squeak.

It wasn't much magic, I knew, but enough to send me a message. Kit was craning her head to look behind herself as if someone had pinched her from behind.

What I noted was the way Flint's hand tightened on her shoulder. Not so subtle.

"Don't," I said, starting forward again and getting yanked back by Stone's grip. I shrugged him off without looking in his direction. I kept my eye on Terran. "You said you wouldn't hurt her."

At my words, Kit's hand flew to her throat and a look of betrayal came over her face, one the likes of which I'd seen many times in our lives together. Once again, I'd disappointed her in the worst way.

"What did you do?" she demanded of me, even as Terran rolled his eyes at the drama unfolding. I tried to ignore him as he rose from the chair, but Kit had begun to struggle. She wanted at me. The docile, motherly sister gone along with the mousey hair and thin layer of fat.

"I tried to warn you," I said, my attention divided between what the powerful fae boss might do and what the one standing beside her with his hand on her shoulder might if she got free of his grasp. "I tried, Kit. But you hung up on me. Just like always." The bitterness in my voice overrode any sense of desperation, and I realized with a fullness of emotion that I was pissed at her.

This wasn't my fault. It was hers.

"You hang up on me every damn time," I said. "You have no idea if I'm in trouble or if I'm calling to tell you I miss you. You don't care to hear one second of my voice. We're fucking sisters, Kit. We shouldn't be fighting like this—"

"Sisters?" she shrieked, and this time she tore from Flint's grip and he let her go. "Let me tell you about sisters, Ava."

The whole of the chamber watched as she stormed the room toward me. The flush of her face spoke of rage and exertion, and I knew when she reached me, she was going to hit me.

I stood still, expecting it, wanting it even. And when it came, the crack of the blow reached my ears before the sting of it registered in my skin. I didn't move to rub my cheek. It had been a flat-palmed slap with enough force that it must have hurt her palm, but my heart ached far more than my face did.

She stood back, chest heaving. Every inch of her face was contorted with emotion, so many of them that they warred for control of her features. It took everything I had to remain stoic in the face of it.

"Sisters don't put sisters in situations that make them race out in the middle of the night in their god damn slippers and housecoat because some kid—a kid, Ava—A kid saw you getting beaten by a god damn crack dealer outside an old gymnasium," she yelled. "But were you outside the gym when I arrived? Oh, hell no. This sister had to find you hanging by a rafter with your legs kicking the air and piss running down your leg. She had to believe, really believe that you were dead. That this time, you'd gone too far and now I'd have to bury you."

She gagged on the last words and still I stood there, too afraid to reach out to her or say a single word. It was all true. I deserved her wrath and more. I'd spent a lifetime trying to make up for it.

But now here we were, with her life on the line once again. She dragged in a long breath, but I wasn't fooled into believing it was because she was finished. That breath was fuel. I waited, fingers scrabbling over my thighs in an effort to keep my legs still despite the overwhelming urge to run back the way I'd come. I waited, core trembling, and when they came, they felt as much like a blow as her slap had.

"Sisters don't fucking have to blow a disgusting drug dealer who hadn't washed in God knows how long, they don't have to gag on his seed just so he'd consider letting you go. I thought you were dead even then," she said with her lips curled back. "Did you know that? I thought you were fucking dead and I still blew that cocksucker because I was sure he wouldn't let me have your body when he was done with it. I wasn't even sure he'd let me live."

I staggered backward and fetched up against Stone's shoulder. Behind her, I saw Terran's eyebrows flicker upward. Flint lowered his chin at me. I felt Stone beside me stiffen. Oh the shame of it all as it echoed through the chamber. There was no escaping it, no shoving it down, no jamming it into a dark closet and holding the door closed.

My eyes closed against the weight of it, like the junkie I was, savoring the pain like a thousand tiny cuts scoring my flesh. When I opened them again, she was backing away from me. Done. She was so done with me.

I so badly wanted to say something, not to warn her of the dangers present right here in this room, but words of apology, pleading, self-revilement. But my throat ached so badly that my jaw hurt like someone was ramming splinters into the muscles and zapping them with electric shocks. Whatever needed to be said escaped me. The time for them to be spoken was long gone. And we both knew it.

Through some miracle of will, I managed to keep the tears from spilling. I managed to stand there while her chest heaved. While her lip curled back. While her eyes were so dry I wondered if she'd somehow lost all ability to cry.

"Don't call me sister ever again," she said in an even voice, then she looked back over her shoulder. Flint was smiling at her. Smiling, the bastard, as though he'd encouraged exactly this speech from her, as though he'd somehow known about my secret shame and manipulated it out of her just so it could hurt me right at this moment.

Rage flooded me then. Rage that he'd tricked this intimate information out of her, that he made her feel as though he could be trusted, as though he was the one protecting her.

I might have torn through the entire room with my karambit raised, my fury slashing along with the blade for anything that got in my way, but Stone grabbed for my hand just as it was moving toward the sheath on my thigh.

I whirled on him with every intention to strike out, but the sight of his face made the blur of tears finally slide free. My chin trembled. My legs went to water. And despite my best efforts, I couldn't keep my face from screwing into a horrible, gut-wrenching ugly cry.

He gathered me in, and I fell against his chest, burying my face in his shirt. His palm ran down my back, stroking, brushing away all the shuddering unshed sobs that I was struggling so hard to contain. I heard the vibration of his voice in my chest as he spoke.

"Are we done here?" he asked and I knew the question wasn't for Kit but for his father.

"Done?" Terran said. "We've only just begun."

My spine went ramrod straight at the words and I shoved myself back from the comfort of Stone's embrace.

Because I knew by the tone of Terran's voice, that whatever was coming, it would be far far worse than a bit of emotional violence.

CHAPTER 18

I steeled myself for the worst. Fists clenched against my thighs, I turned toward Terran, fully expecting some violence to erupt. From the corner of my eye, I noted Flint gathering Kit into his arms. She was as ramrod straight as I was, even when she slid beneath his arm and turned to face the room. There was no softness in her.

The thugs were all rigid as well, but for different reasons, I knew. Beside me, Stone had edged closer. The fragrance of caramel was sharper, I realized, tinged with something that might be brine or sea air.

I smelled my own pheromones, that tangy acid of sweat leaking from my pores, but I willed myself to keep my attention on the boss. As if high on Bloodmist, I spread my senses out over the room, noting the way Flint held Kit. She might think it was protective, defensive.

I knew better.

Some part of me soared above it all, scoping the chamber, my spirit alight with the knowledge that in seconds things would change. Stone's presence beside me was the only thing that grounded me. No matter what he'd done to me before, now was all that mattered.

Terran stood a few feet from his chair, holding his hand out toward the grate in the fireplace as if he was cold. The shadows of the room seemed to grow lighter, or maybe they were slithering off the velvet covered walls and tapestries toward him, I couldn't be sure. I just knew Stone was gritting his teeth so hard I could hear them grinding.

There was enough electricity in the air to light a spark. My fingers whispered their way to the sheath on my thigh.

"Get out," Terran said in a soft voice, as though he didn't want any ears to actually hear it.

In a sudden movement, and as one, all the guards started and shuffled in my direction. It seemed Kit believed she was supposed to leave as well because she made a move to leave. Flint tightened his grip on her shoulder and my lips curled back. He caught my eye and held it. Challenging me.

Long, shallow breaths moved through my lungs as without a word, and without touching me or Stone, the guards passed us.

Only Stone and I remained to face Terran, Flint, and Kit.

"Let her go," I said without looking at her. "She has nothing to do with this."

Kit snorted and Stone swiveled his gaze toward her. I didn't need to see his face to know the sort of glare he'd shot her. I only had to see her shift deeper into Flint's embrace. Her green eyes roamed my face in the same sort of challenge I'd seen in his.

Terran watched it all with interest. He even angled his body ever so slightly toward her. He inclined his head toward her in a gentlemanly gesture.

I near went rabid.

"Leave her the fuck alone," I said. If things were going to go down, let them. The time for play was over.

In response, Terran strolled toward me and it took all I had in me to hold still as that preternatural gait took its agonizingly deliberate time eating up the distance between us.

"I thought you learned your lesson down below," he said, his gaze narrowing. "I thought you agreed to do as I asked."

"I've not done anything but," I said.

"Where were you?" he asked so gently it might have been a mother calling on an errant child.

"I was with your damn enforcer," I said, aware that Flint had taken to stroking Kit's shoulder. My throat tightened. "Why don't you ask him."

"I did," he said. "He said there was trouble on the road."

"There was."

His jaw ticked to the side. "You don't care to elaborate?"

I said nothing. I had no idea how much Blade had told him, but I wasn't about to revisit those horrors for anyone. I'd rather he kill me right there.

Terran sighed. "I see," he said. "Well, I suppose it doesn't matter now. She's here. There isn't much we can do about that now."

My gaze shuttered. "What does that mean?"

He gestured toward Flint, and in a flash, the bastard had wrangled Kit to the center of the room. Her surprise made her stupid, like most women about to be harmed by a man. That ages old expectation of safety overriding her intuition.

I almost bolted for her, to yank her out of Flint's grip, but Stone's quiet warning whispered over me. Stay still. I stayed still. Even when Kit struggled in Flint's hold, confusion and irritation warring for first place in her features.

"What it means," Terran said as Flint got her under control. She glared up at him, chiding him with her eyes as though she were a lover. "What it means is she knows about us."

I felt Stone's anxiety slide over me and up my spine. I knew what both of those things meant: Terran's words and Stone's worry. I took a deep breath.

"If you hurt her, you'll have nothing left to bargain with," I said, clenching my fists. "If you hurt her, I won't care if I live or die when I come for you."

"Ava?" Kit's voice, shaking, pregnant with the dread that I'd gone and made things worse. That this was all my fault. "What's going on?"

Despite her anger, my sister was afraid. I heard the fear threading each syllable she spoke. Whatever sense of safety she'd clung to upon entering the room, it was being stripped away bit by bit.

I was still struggling for the answer, one that would extend both warning and comfort when Terran took the opportunity from me.

He turned to face her and a calm, almost beatific smile lit his face. He was mad, I realized. Calculatingly, preternaturally mad. "What's going on, my dear, is that your sister made a vow."

"I kept it," I ground out.

He didn't turn to me when he went on. "Your sister bargained your life for the life of another. We are holding her to that."

Kit's face blanched. "My life?"

Images flashed behind my eyelids so fast I couldn't keep up with them, but I knew they were snippets of those moments in the dungeons. I smelled the tang of blood. Heard the shrieks of pain and the silence of death.

"Where is Blade?" I said, taking a step toward Terran. He had no guards here. No way to protect himself. Just Flint and Stone and I reasoned I could take out one with the help of the other.

To my surprise, Terran laughed. A wave in my direction that, if it was anywhere else, at any other time, might mean he wanted me to have a seat and a cup of tea.

"Don't worry, Assassin," he said. "I'm not going to kill her."

Kit sucked breath in with a hiss.

"What then?" I asked.

He strolled to the fireplace and jabbed at the flaming logs with a blacksteel poker. "You see," he said. "We have a problem. Most mortals don't know about Fae and we like to keep it that way. When you and Blade didn't return, I presumed you'd escaped. I worried my enforcer wouldn't find you before you warned your sister. So I had Flint collect her."

"Meaning you were going to kill her."

He shrugged as he looked over his shoulder at her. "If you must be so crass, yes. I keep my vows."

A furtive glance at Kit showed she was blinking owlishly, a vapid, stunned look on her face. It made my heart hurt to see her struggling to make sense of it all.

"Don't worry, Kit," I said, holding my hands out, supplicating toward Terran. "He's not going to hurt you. I won't let him."

Terran snorted at the emptiness of the threat, but my words weren't for him. They were for Kit.

He dropped the poker onto the hearth and crossed his arms over his chest. "Despite the ridiculous bravado, we are both in agreement there," he said. "I am not going to hurt her. Since you are here, there is no need. But her presence here is still a problem."

I could feel my shoulders sagging. Stone's hand ran over the small of my back. I wanted so badly to touch his fingers, to feel the warmth of touch. I resisted because I knew even if Terran had suggested Kit was safe, the smell of threat still lingered in the air.

"What then?" I asked.

A heavy, long-suffering sigh fled the boss's lungs. "Since we can't have her wandering around in the mortal realm talking about faeries and magic, then I suppose she'll have to stay."

I'd seen enough mortal women in Fae to figure out what staying meant without asking.

"But she doesn't know anything about faeries and magic," I protested. "All she knows is that I'm standing in front of another prick who wants to screw her because of me."

His eyebrows climbed upward at the comparison. "I'm afraid her being privy to this conversation has changed things somewhat."

A swift look at Kit proved she was already beginning to filter through all the information to piece together the truth. She might not believe it, she might fight it, but she'd sense it, and that was going to change everything.

"There's only one remedy that will serve us both," he said.

I was afraid to ask.

"You will take her with you to meet the king. He likes mortal women with a bit of flesh on them." His scan of Kit drew a glower from Flint but he ignored it or didn't notice it. "That way, she becomes useful to me and I don't have to break my vow."

CHAPTER 19

I didn't have a chance to protest that he was breaking his promise by putting Kit in harm's way. I didn't have a chance to do much as he gestured at Flint, who immediately started herding Kit away. I yelled her name, and she turned around to look at me over her shoulder. In her face I read all the confusion and fear I'd expected when I'd seen her there upon entry.

The barriers were coming down and she was beginning to realize just how serious this was.

"Don't worry," I said as she started to struggle in Flint's grip. "I won't let anyting happen to you."

Her chestnut eyebrows arched downward and she gave one more twist, almost breaking free of Flint's hold, but with a word in her ear that made her face go white, she submitted. I watched her go with my heart dancing in my stomach.

"Leave her," Terran said in a command that drew my attention to him. He'd sat down again, and this time, for the first time since I'd entered with Stone, he gestured at us to sit. "We have much to discuss."

Stone sat. I didn't. I stood there with my chest barely rising and falling as I fought to control my temper and the sense of helplessness overwhelming me.

"I prefer to stand," I said.

"I didn't ask your preference." He swiveled his gaze to Stone, who was perched on the edge of an old fashioned settee, its brocade pattern and fabric making him seem so much thicker and out of place than he might have been in the plain wooden chair on the other side of the room.

"You seem to have some influence on your assassin," he said. "Do ask her to sit or she will find she can't stand."

"Don't bother to threaten me," I said to Stone, not Terran. "I'll sit."

Stone's throat bobbed as he swallowed and inclined his head to the spot next to him. I guessed he wanted me close, and I didn't question why. I didn't need to.

But it would mark me as weak if I sat there, and it was time I showed myself as what I really was. A killer. Blade had called me that in the days we'd first met. Stone had said it the same night he'd procured me. It was why I'd been 'hired'.

I elected to take the ladder-back wooden chair and pulled it, scraping, from its spot beneath a large tapestry that hung on the wall. Rather than sit on it like a prim lady, I turned it around, much as he had in the dungeons when he'd ordered me beaten. I turned that bad boy around and I straddled it like a male, because for some reason, some males only saw power when they beheld another that looked like them.

And when I 'discussed' things with Terran, I wanted him to know, really know, what kind of woman sat in front of him.

"I'm listening," I said. No hint of pleading. Not an iota of concern for my sister. If a speck of uncertainty laced my voice, I didn't hear it. I was certain when I heard a low chuckle escape Stone, that I'd managed to sound confident. Some small part of me was gratified that he appreciated it. Even so, I didn't flinch when Terran's eyebrow quirked in response to the command in my voice and his lips turned down in a prim line.

Laying both elbows on the back of the chair, I swept away all thoughts of Kit. I shoved down the look of anxiety on her face, the thought that she was in more danger now than she had been hours ago. Those things had no place here. All that existed was this damnable fae and the job he wanted me to do and how I was going to disguise the fact of how badly I wanted to see him dead.

I pulled all my hunter background to me, gathering it like a storm as I held Terran's gaze boldly. "Start discussing."

This time the sound Stone made was nothing like a laugh, but I ignored him. He wasn't the important one here.

All my attention was on Terran and the way he crossed one leg over the other. The careful, purposeful way he pinched the crease at his knee as he regarded me.

"There she is," he said. "Finally. The killer has come out to play."

I schooled my expression into one of careful neutrality. "I'm glad you recognize her," was all I said.

"Indeed." He leaned back, a show of how unafraid he was in the face of my very mortal power. "Dare I ask if she came out to play at any time during her hiatus from Fae?"

This again. I leaned forward. "I wasn't on hiatus, but yes. She enjoyed a little freedom."

"So Blade tells me," he said. "Trust me when I tell you I know everything. My Blade, like my Stone and my Flint are the hard places between the rocks. They are blood-sworn to me. When I ask them for answers, they give them to me."

"Bully for you," I said. A blink. Only because I had to. I had no intention of revisiting those events even if pressed. They belonged to me. I owned them. I refused to feel betrayed by Blade's dishing on my pain. "But what I did to protect myself on the Shadow Trail has no bearing on what happens here and now. It has nothing to do with Kit. You overplayed your pawn when you brought her here."

"Your tone is dangerously close to impudent."

"Fuck my tone," I said and leaned so far forward that the back legs of the chair came off the polished wooden floor. "If you wanted to punish me, you'd have done so already." I didn't say that I understood as well as he did that if something happened to Kit, he'd lose my cooperation, and because he hadn't, it meant he desperately needed it.

"Things are about to get hairy," I said, guessing at the reason, but not showing surprise when his brief flinch proved me correct.

"I prefer to say things are about to get real." He uncrossed his legs and leaned forward as well, his hands steepled between his knees. "The days of Endowment are about to commence, and we need you in place."

"And these days," I said. "What happens during them?"

Stone started to answer, but Terran cut him a glare that made him push back in his chair. I almost pitied him except he didn't look the least bit quailed. Surprised, maybe, but not weak. I was glad of that.

But I couldn't hold his gaze too long, either. I needed to focus, and focus meant keeping every ounce of attention on the fae who could and would do my sister harm. "You were about to explain the days," I said.

"The Days of Endowment come once a century. I know you have discovered our magics aren't limitless," he said. "Blade confirmed that for me when we spoke."

"So you said," I replied. "But that doesn't answer my question."

His eyebrow quirked. "Yet another impudent comment," he said. "But I'll ignore this one as well for the sake of brevity because we are on a time crunch."

He rubbed at the armrest again, the way he'd done before he'd blasted Kit, and when he looked at me, I swear I could see electricity in his gaze.

"I mention Blade's confession about your knowing of our very limited power because it cuts short on what I need to explain to you." The overt chiding in his voice rankled but I kept silent, and because I did, he kept talking.

"The base and demi Fae haven't the skill or longevity to use their magics that high Fae have. They possess plenty for the inane things like encouraging plants to grow or general healing and in some cases, glamor. Simple things. Things that don't take generations of practice."

"So their natal magics are powers they can wield without so much tutelage."

He cocked his head at me, curious. "Not all natal magics are as base as those ones most fae possess. It's just that without the longevity of lifespan that the high Fae own, the lesser Fae can't access anything stronger. Some can't access even that, depending on their order. That's where Ferranus comes in.

"Ferranus's powers are rare in that he can grant and receive magic. As king, once a century, Ferranus claims the magic of the base Fae for his own, and they grant it to him."

I squinted at him. "Why would they do that?."

"Ah, there's the question that should be asked, finally. They might want protection from a greater, more powerful fae. They might feel threatened into giving it. They might even hope for some greater world where all fae are treated equally." At this, he smiled such a greasy smile I was immediately put in mind of a human mafioso offering protection, but I knew this wasn't the reason as surely as that smile was greased by cunning.

"They get something they want more than protection," I said.

He touched his finger to the tip of his nose. "One hundred gilded tokens are distributed to the realm during this festival."

I thought of the token Jasmine had given me and my fingers twitched so much on the back of the chair that I had to pull them down to my lap. "I'm guessing these tokens contain a spell of some sort."

He shook his head. "Nothing so crass as that. We are fae. We do love glamor. We must fete and dance and sing and glut ourselves on all manner of wondrous cuisine and other more hedonistic rituals." His smile left his face as the tone turned bitter. He found the whole thing distasteful, and I doubted it had anything to do with a reluctance to dance and sing. "Ferranus offers a transfer of power to the holders of these tokens. One year of full access to their powers."

"And in return, he gathers an entire realm's worth of magic," I said, breathless at the breadth of it all. "Brilliant."

My jaw ticked sideways as I stole a glance at Stone who was rigid as he sat there. His eyes were on mine, his fists clenched at his sides. I tried to figure out what was bothering him so much. I found my answer in what he'd told me already.

"Once the king has all that power to hand, he's the most powerful he'll be for the entire century," I said. "And that means if he discovers a plot to assassinate him, he will be less inclined to look away from those who would steal the power of those tokens."

It was growing more clear as we talked, that Terran had been planning the hit for decades, perhaps centuries. I thought of Jasmine's comment that Seamus's son had won a gilded token and been murdered for it. A glance at Terran, and I realized exactly who had ordered the hit. It didn't take much imagination to realize that Terran and his Shadow Court had been acquiring tokens for centuries, gaining more and more power.

What I didn't understand was his motive. Why bump off a king who would ignorantly procure power for one faction of the realm who would eventually rival him?

It had nothing to do with power, I decided. Exactly what it had to do with, I didn't know. Not yet.

"So if he's granted all this magic, and becomes even more powerful, how will a mere mortal assassin be able to take him out?"

He stood up then, moved by the question, it seemed, enough to have him nearly charge me with excitement. I held my position by the barest threads of will.

"You forget the most important thing, mortal assassin," he said in a darkly rich voice.

Not to be left to sit while he loomed over me, I got to my feet. "Your powers wane," I said. "When you use them too much."

"Not just when we overuse them," he said with a glint in his eye. "It's a great conundrum in that we must use them to hone them, but in doing so, we drain them. Our king does not transfer power often. Just once a century."

I staggered backward at the insinuation. "So he's not practiced in it," I said, thinking suddenly of Mica and how he had to return to his chambers when he'd used the injecture on me. "That means he must expend a lot to transfer it."

Terran smiled. "You are a smart killer," he said. "Yes. During the climax of the Days of Endowment, when the good king doles out all that magic to one hundred random lesser Fae, he will be at the weakest he will be for an entire century."

And in so being, give me a chance—just one chance—to slip in and deliver the hit.

Providing the king didn't see me coming first. Providing his magic didn't seek out the iron in my blood and turn the instrument of his death into something far worse.

Chapter 20

The logistics of the hit set my teeth on edge. "Just what sort of time frame are we talking about here?" I asked. "Minutes, hours, weeks? And when exactly does he get the transfer of power? Because if we get the order wrong--"

"You won't get the order wrong," Terran cut me off. "There is a specific ritual."

"What if the order gets changed?"

"It won't. The lesser Fae will not grant him their power until the one hundred have been selected and given their year's worth of magic. That distribution alone takes several hours, and in order to make it fair to all, a Fae sorceress is invoked to make time stand still while it occurs. That way no one is shorted a day of their year and Ferranus can complete the transfer of what remains of his power in one day. We are not a trusting sort, which is why every one in the Iron Kingdom is welcome to the festivities. It needs to be very clear that the king has fulfilled his part of the bargain, and in several centuries, Ferranus had not failed to complete his part of the bargain."

"Bully for him," I said, thinking I might at some point want to know just how many centuries we were talking about. "So when does this transfer happen?" I cracked my knuckles. "I'm guessing it's right away?"

He shook his head. "Quite the contrary. For many, this is the most interesting thing that will happen in their entire lifetime. It takes them days and for some, weeks, to make the journey from all over the realm."

I was aghast. "We're talking hundreds?"

"Thousands. And all of them stuffed inside the ballroom."

I glanced at Stone in disbelief as he picked up the thread. "The sorceress casts a spell to make the chamber as big as it needs to be to contain everyone. It's very difficult magic."

I thought of the pouch Lilah had shoved all those cursed objects in without it changing size or shape, then Erachne's gown and the way it hid my karambit so beautifully. Complex magic, indeed. If those two had been able to cast such magic and yet only manage to contain it to small objects, then just how powerful was this sorceress to be able to alter an entire room?

Pretty bad ass, I was thinking.

I was beginning to understand why none of the cartel wanted to take the chance of committing the hit to another fae. It wasn't just the iron in their blood attached to their magic, it was for the sheer show of power the king had at his bidding. A power that could turn on an enemy.

It also explained why Stone and Blade insisted the usefulness of that damned itchy corset and why they assured me it would be important to be able to disguise myself. I wanted it back very badly in that moment.

Too bad some evil little fae had stolen it from Blade. I finally understood what all the panic was over its disappearance.

I dropped the chair back down onto its four legs, feeling suddenly very tired. "What else?" I asked, noting the way Stone was picking at his trousers and knowing there was more.

He waggled his head back and forth, his gaze running to his father, who rolled his eyes. "I doubt she'll need to know all that," Terran said.

"I need to know everything," I said, slicing a look toward Terran. "You want the king dead or not?"

With a barely suppressed growl, Terran crossed the room to the ceiling high bookshelf filled with tomes of various widths and bindings. I thought more than a few looked to be bound with skin.

He held his hand out toward the shelves and a narrow book dislodged from the very top and sailed into his hand. It struck with a solid thwack that sounded impressive given the size of the book. I eyed the book suspiciously.

"The transfer of power is very ritualistic," he said as he flipped the book open and held it out to me. "See for yourself if you're so curious. It's all in there."

I took the book from him, expecting something light but felt my shoulder twinge with the weight. "What's this?" I clutched the edge of the book against my chest in order to hold it, covers splayed open in my hands to show pages made of vellum.

"It's A History of Endowments," Terran said. "Written by Ferranus's own tutor, who was said to be the dynasty's tutor from the very bud of the tree."

"So this has been going on for a while, then?" I said. "Not just with Ferranus."

He rolled his eyes. "The Iron line is a long one," he said and reached out to tap the pages forcefully enough that it felt like he was pushing me backwards with each strike. "You said you wanted to know everything. Here everything is."

I glanced down at the book in my hands. "What does it say?"

"Oh for fuck's sake," he grumbled. "Did I pick the one assassin in the mortal realm who can't read?" He tapped the book again. "It's not written in runes or elvish." His brow furrowed as he pushed the book at me. "And it has pictures. Surely you can see for yourself."

I sucked the back of my teeth. "It's fucking blank," I said as I slammed the book against his chest the same as he'd done to me. "There are no pictures. And for your information, I can read elvish."

He looked down at the covers splayed over his chest and plucked it away as I pulled my hand back, feeling as though my fingers were sticky. "Blank?" he said in voice laced with confusion. "I wonder why it's doing that."

I exchanged a glance with Stone, who seemed as confused as I did. He lifted his hands in befuddlement. I rubbed my palms along my trousers to get rid of the tackiness from the book. "Just tell me what's in there," I said.

The look the two of them exchanged suggested to me that neither of them could see what was on the pages, and that both of them thought they should be able to.

I groaned at the thought of having to sit there while Terran filled me in.

"Why don't we start with the important details. Like how long these Days of Endowment go on."

With an irritated flick of his wrist, Terran bid both of us sit again. I guessed he was about as happy spending time with me as I was with him.

"You might as well get comfortable," he grumbled and snapped his fingers above his head. The same boy I'd seen during my stay at the beginning appeared.

"Gather us some drinks," Terran said to him, and the boy was gone in a flash. The stink of acetone clung to the air as he leveled his gaze at me. "This is going to take some time." He all but flopped onto his chair and waited until both Stone and I had sat again.

"The grand ball is the first of the events, meant to keep all Orders entertained and out of mischief. And since it's so large, and the king will be surrounded, he'll feel safe. That's where we originally wanted you to strike."

I couldn't help a sniff of disdain. "You expected me to slit his throat in front of a room full of fae with enough power to wink me out of existence with a flick of their wrist?"

"Not in front of everyone," he said, shaking his head as he dragged his gaze a bit too familiarly along my assets.

"You know I have all the skills Gideon has," I said in a tight voice. "I can easily just slit his throat and be done." I crossed one arm over the other, laying one palm on my shoulder. "I don't need to act like a whore to kill him."

He snorted. "Yes, well that doesn't matter anyway," he said, waving the comment away. "Once we discovered the ballroom was to be spelled, we had to change tactics." He peered at me thoughtfully as I waved my hand in the air in the universal 'get on with it' gesture. "But you know this already."

The boy returned in a puff of acrid smoke, holding a tray with a pottery jug and several goblets. Terran did no more than raise his eyebrows at him, and the boy poured the pitcher into a glass and drank deeply.

"Clean," he said, then snapped his fingers and the goblet he'd drank from was replaced with a sheer glass one. For Terran, I supposed.

What happened then was a drawn out process where Terran sniffed and inspected the liquid poured inside each goblet. He passed one to Stone, then one to me, and finally poured one for himself into the glass. The boy disappeared and I looked down into the depths of my goblet. Red, this time, the liquid did not fizz or bubble. It appeared to be no more than wine.

I waited until Stone drank. Terran waited until I did. Only then did he deign to take a sip, and with a long sigh, laid back in his chair with the glass sitting atop a muscled thigh.

After that, he and Stone both took their turns explaining the details. The gala, location of the castle, that we'd arrive by horse-drawn coach, that Stone would escort me and present me to the king.

Basically, a Cinderella type affair just much more stabby.

"So," I said. "How long do I have, exactly? You said the bestowing of magic to the token owners could take days, so once that's accomplished, how long before he's back up to full power? Surely that's more important than the pumpkin I'll arrive in."

Terran's mouth twitched. A tell I'd realized indicated he was less than pleased with what he was hearing.

"What aren't you telling me?" I asked with a narrowed gaze.

Stone's gaze skirted toward his father, who said nothing, leaving the answer to his son.

"Stone?" I said. "What are you holding back?"

"We don't know how long it takes to recharge that much power. There aren't many powerful enough to wield all the magic granted to a single fae, let alone one who possesses the magic that allows him to instill it in others. All we know is that he can't accept the grants of the others' magic until he does." He ran both hands over his hair. "We do know he needs to recharge before he can accept the magic."

"So you're saying he's a big battery the likes of which you've never seen. Great."

"Oh we've seen it," Terran said, rising from his chair. "What we haven't seen is the duration of time it takes him to recover. He is careful never to take the same amount of time. So he could be recharged in an hour, in a day, or a week."

"You aren't seriously telling me you've all waited around for a full week for the king to deign to return to the affair."

He rolled his eyes. "You haven't been listening."

My teeth ground together. "It's all the fuck I've been doing."

He sighed, peevish. "In the 1500s, your world enjoyed a three day affair called the Field of Cloth of Gold, held between the English and French monarchs. During those days, there was jousting, drinking, eating, dancing, and much more. It is the same for the Days of Endowments." He shrugged. "People and fae find ways to entertain themselves. What the king doesn't provide, they'll find for themselves."

"And while you all are drowning yourselves on booze and food and sex, where is the king? Or is that the one little detail you both are afraid to tell me because I see the looks you keep sending each other, and I know there's a 'but' attached to every damn thing you're telling me."

"We do, in fact, know this," Stone said. "He retires to his harem to recharge."

"See?" I said. "There's another but." Knowing I'd get nowhere with him, I faced Terran. "You're saying he gluts himself on sex until he feels right as rain again?"

Terran's snort caught my attention, and he lifted one shoulder. "In a manner of speaking, yes."

I raised an eyebrow, catching the meaning, finally. "And I'm to be part of this harem, and why I needed the fancy dress, and why I needed to demonstrate my less than feminine wiles on your dark enforcer."

He tilted his head, suggesting he wasn't willing to revisit that but that I'd nailed it.

"By its very nature, the harem cannot be spelled against magic, lest he be unable to recharge."

I nodded. "Then I'll finish him there."

"Ah, there's the quicksilver mind Stone assured me we would find useful." He eyeballed me with a less than impressive look. "That is exactly correct. But there is a catch, and we're aware it's less than perfect since you'd need to catch his attention long enough to get close. He receives many gifts from the High Fae and his harem is already fairly large."

Instead of answering to that insult, I swiped at my pants.

Terran seemed unimpressed. "That is why I sent Blade to you. Because he knows what it takes for a mortal woman to catch the eye of a fae like Ferranus."

I refused to let him assess me that way. "Don't worry," I said. "I don't need to be pretty to get close enough to kill."

He crossed his arms over his chest. "I don't worry, Ms. Ashe. I plan. Ferranus likes his mortal women in all flavors. Chunky is one of his favorites." The look on his face suggested I was still missing some point, and it took me several long moments of switching between Stone's rigid, blanched face and Terran's stoic one to realize what it was.

"You're sending Kit to the harem with me."

His smile came slowly, but it was broad enough to show the points of his teeth. "Consider her your incentive to make sure pretty has no bearing on how close you get."

CHAPTER 21

I stared at the male in front of me, barely aware I'd stood and was clutching my karambit in an attack hold. Stone had risen along with me and stood a breath away. My chest rose and fell in time with the heart pounding in my ears. Terran was not moved.

"I will kill you where you stand," I said. "If you so much as suggest she'll be going anywhere near that damn festival."

"Stone," Terran said. It was barely a murmur, but the command in the tone was unmistakable.

I danced away before Stone could take hold of me. The karambit slashed sideways to ensure my retreat was solitary. In a heartbeat, I was backed against the wall because I didn't know if Terran would strike along with Stone, but I needed to have at least one of my sides protected, and I had nothing but solid wood to do that.

Too late, I realized I'd just cornered myself.

Stone's expression was aggrieved. "It's alright, Ava," he murmured as he held his hands out. "No one is going to hurt you. Don Sidhe understands you're just upset."

A flicker of movement beyond his shoulder. Terran. Sitting down of all things. Sitting the fuck down like he was not the least bit concerned.

My throat went tight. "Try me, Stone," I said. "Just fucking try me. I'll see just how hard you fae fall."

"Don't, Ava," he said. "It's not worth it."

"For who?" I said. "You or me?"

His lips pressed themselves into a thin line. "For anyone. Just let me take you back to your suite. We'll work it out."

"She's not going," I said.

"She'll be safe with you," he said.

Terran took to checking his nails in the midst of pouring himself another drink.

"You knew," I said. "You fucking knew what he was planning. How he wanted to use my sister." Though my voice was even and calm, I felt the shrillness deep in my chest. "You knew she was here and what he planned to do with her."

Terran lifted his glass, tilting it in my direction as he stood, and then turned on his heel. I watched him stroll through the chamber toward that part of the room where he'd arrived. The purple seam outlined the door and it swung open.

He glanced at me. "You seem upset that your sister will be in your care instead of ours," he said. "I would think you'd rather her be with you than my Flint." He lifted his glass again and drained it, then tossed it on the floor where it smashed into shards.

Then he stepped through the door and was gone, leaving me with my chest heaving in impotent rage at the fact that he wasn't just right, he had probably done me a favor. And that made me pissed. Before I even realized what I was doing, I'd charged Stone.

Karambit high, chin down, legs pumping. I went for him. And when I collided with him full force, hard enough to knock him over, I was sure he was as surprised at my reaction as I was.

He tumbled backward onto the overstuffed chair, taking me with him. The wind went out of me at the contact. Somehow the karambit flew from my grip to the floor and my hands were wrangled in his.

The maneuver was swift and expert, a testament to how long he'd been a warrior. But I was no slouch either.

We twisted and writhed together on the chair, both of us gaining and losing ground until we finally tumbled to the floor in a knot of limbs.

At first, I thought I fell on top of him, but a breath later and I was pinned on my back, with him straddling me. My chest was heaving. His was not, but the pulse in his throat was a rapid thing that drew my gaze like a cobra's eyes to a charmer.

"You let me knock you over," I said flatly.

The bright light in his gaze suggested it was true. "You needed a win," he said.

"Fuck you."

He leaned forward, his face, that gaze, that mouth, coming within a whisper of mine. My entire body cried out for some sort of release. The pent up energy. The anger. The adrenaline. I was trembling with it all.

"Maybe that's what you need, Ava," he said. "I could take you right now so easily, I think you'd be surprised."

"Surely not as easy as that?" said a voice from the doorway that froze Stone's body above mine into a rigid block of granite. The lust in his eyes hardened to anger as he sliced his gaze toward the door.

All of me sagged into the floor as I recognized the voice, and I tilted my head to the side. Blade filled the doorway like a shadow. If the sound of his voice scored a small chunk from me, then the way his eyes glinted with red as the green lost its color to the serpent coiling around his irises, was enough to slice its way straight through my stomach.

"What are you doing here?" Stone asked without making a single move to heave himself off me.

I bucked from below, twisting at the same time, and he rolled away and onto his feet long before I'd even got to my knees.

Blade's gaze flicked to me then to Stone. "I would have asked the same thing, but it seemed pretty obvious."

He prowled into the room, his eyes never leaving my face. "It seems the security here has gotten pretty lax if just anyone can rut about on the floor of the don's sitting room." He leaned against the door frame. "I'm surprised at you Stone. I thought you were strictly a missionary style beneath-the-sheets kind of male."

A muscle in Stone's jaw tightened and didn't let go. "You didn't answer my question," he said. "I thought father sent you off on business."

"I finished that business. Now my business brings me here."

His demeanor was all casual, but the flexing of his shoulders as they bunched beneath his shirt belied a barely concealed and rising temper.

"And what business is that, exactly?" Stone asked. "I happen to know father is done with you."

Blade tilted his head. "You make it sound so final, brother," he said and casually, ever so casually, strolled toward where I stood, bristling at the two of them. "Has she been informed?" he asked.

Stone nodded. "She has."

He crossed his arms over his chest and shot a heated look in my direction. "I'm guessing by your reaction that you don't know all of it or you wouldn't be rolling around on the floor with my brother."

"They filled me in."

"So you know you'll be a present to his majesty."

I sucked the back of my teeth. "You're not adding to the data pool."

His head swung my way, the green eyes mere chunks of lake ice as he caught my gaze. "Really?" he asked. "So you have no problem being a Blood Gift."

Chapter 22

At the words Blood Gift, Stone choked, and my gaze sliced over to his face. It had gone pale. I might have deluded myself into believing he was as surprised at the term as I was, but the color was still in his ears, those damned delicately pointed things, and I knew his look of shock was more about being discovered than discovering.

I pivoted sharply toward him. "What is a blood gift, Stone?" I asked in a low voice. "I'm guessing that's the insignificant thing you and your father were holding back from me."

Stone glared at his brother, whose eyebrow had lifted a good distance from its normal spot.

"I would have gotten to it," he said.

"Would that be before or after you tried to screw me?" I lifted my chin. A challenge. "I think you best crack on with it," I said. "Before I lose my shit."

He bobbed his head and gestured to the chairs. "Might we sit?"

"We might," I said. "Except I don't want to sit. I want to throttle you for keeping information from me."

Blade snorted and I glared at him. He was so not in my good graces right then either. "You need to leave," I said.

He was nonplussed. "The poor messenger," he said, putting his hand to his chest.

"You are not a messenger. You are a harbinger." I turned to Stone because even if I didn't have a single card in my hand, at least I could control some part of the game. "Don't you have some power over rabid beasts?" I asked. "Can't you command him to leave like you did at Gideon's house?"

At that, Blade laughed out loud. "Is that what you told her?" He strode toward the chair and sat down on the seat, crossing one leg over the other. A definite signal that he wasn't going to be leaving anytime soon no matter who asked nicely or nastily. "I left because it was his turn at bat. I was just the pinch hitter. Isn't that right, Stone?"

"I hate baseball," I said between clenched teeth. "And I hate baseball analogies even more, so someone had best tell me and tell me right now or I'm going to start tearing to shreds anything that blinks wrong."

I dropped my gaze to Stone's crotch in a pointed look.

Both of his hands moved to cover his groin.

"You are not in danger, Ava," he said. "Not from me or the king even if you are a blood gift."

Blade sucked the back of his teeth. "Coward," he said. "She deserves the truth. Get on with it or I will."

Stone glared at him before turning his gaze to mine.

"We told you the king retired to his harem for a while after he transferred some magic to the gilded token holders."

I nodded. "What's with the abstract? You're not writing an essay. Get to the point."

He swallowed. "Ferranus is old fae. Very old."

I huffed in irritation, and he hurried on. "Remember the joke I made outside your suite about fae eating their lovers?"

There was a long moment where my mind did exactly that, racing to the memory and examining it, and as it came forth, the blood drained from my face, leaving me feeling distinctly clammy. "He's not glutting himself on sex, is he?"

Stone's jaw ticked to the side and he had the grace to look chagrined. "I'm sure he does indulge in hedonistic acts while he recovers," he said. "It's just that afterwards--"

"Afterwards, he eats his lovers," Blade snapped, cutting him off. "Or rather, he gluts himself on their blood. All very iron-rich and docile, provided by the very ones who want him dead." He cut an eye at Stone, who stood and turned to face him.

He scrubbed his hands over his hair. Back and forth. Twice before he spoke again, this time to Blade, and this time in a voice that didn't sound a bit like his own. "I won't put her in harm's way, Blade."

"And how will you ensure that, brother? How can you once she's behind the veil?"

I saw the struggle in Stone's back, the tightness in Blade's features and I knew both of them were upset.

"What is this veil?" I asked.

Blade stood rigid. "Just what you think. A veil of magic with a threshold only those who are sanctioned can cross."

I felt weak suddenly. "So the king's power is recharged by blood and only the diner and the dinner can get in or out."

Stone nodded as he looked back at me. Blade pressed his lips so tightly together they turned white. The serpent in his irises flared to crimson.

"Jesus," I said. "So if it had been Gideon you sent to kill him, what then?"

Blade laid his hand on Stone's shoulder, a strangely comforting gesture, considering how much they hated each other, and that made my stomach clench.

"Ferranus can be one hell of a raunchy male, Ponytail," he said. "Any time other than the Endowments, he takes as many mortal men as women to rut. But with a mortal man, there is less chance of having a wayward seed sprout to a comely stem."

Stone moved away, letting Blade's hand fall to his side. "He has no children," he said, shaking his head. "Without another of the sort of lineage he is...well, with him goes the endowments, and the lesser Fae will not lose that one in a hundred chance once a century to own the magics they were blessed with."

I thought of the French and Russian revolutions. "And there are far more lesser Fae than high, I'm guessing. But why then assassinate him? Without a battery, won't they revolt?"

Stone's eye flicked away from me. "How will they know?" he asked quietly. "Once they gain their powers, who will care for another century?"

"Pretty damn short-sighted for such a long-lived species," I ground out, knowing there was more to it he wasn't saying. "Then what about this damn veil? Can you at least tell me more about that?

Even as I asked the question, I started to realize why Erachne's dress was so important, and why no simple dressmaker would do. "My karambit," I said. "I can smuggle it in beneath the dress. Erachne has the same powers the sorceress has to spell objects."

Blade nodded. "Get close to him, Ponytail. Do it before he sets his eye on your sister. Spill his blood before he can spill yours. Then get the hell out of there before the veil disintegrates."

My eyebrows climbed to my hairline. "Disintegrates?"

Blade sent a glower in Stone's direction. "I thought you told her everything."

Stone threw up his hands. "I didn't know," he said and gestured at the book. "Father gave her that book to read but—"

"Sweet Gods, Stone," Blade spat. "Read the damn book. That veil will start to dissolve the moment Ferranus is dead. It has about sixty earthly minutes before it's gone and everyone trapped inside goes with it."

I gawked at Blade. The veil would be the thing to kill me. Not him. Something in my chest flared to life even as I realized the omission was no doubt a purposeful one. Terran's way of tying up that loose end, the bastard. How many mortal men and women would die for his greed?

I didn't have much chance to ask Stone what he'd had planned to get me the hell out again, because he stormed out, swearing more than I'd heard him do, presumably to hunt down his father. I was left to stare at the door, with Blade standing so painfully close that I could barely breathe.

"You weren't kidding when you told me I had an hour to live after the assassination," I muttered.

"You think I would lie to you, Ponytail?"

I stared at him. "I don't know anything anymore."

There was a moment when his eyes flared and I thought I'd see that serpent moving about his irises again, but then he cleared his throat and the moment was gone.

"There is one thing you can know for sure. Come with me," he said. "Stone might be ill prepared, but I'm not."

I followed him from the room, taking in the way he moved, the long stride that was both purposeful and powerful. He spoke as we walked, mostly carefully chosen words and topics that seemed so banal I might have pulled my hair if I hadn't realized he was doing so to keep prying ears from listening in on what was being said.

"I told you I would watch over your sister. I meant it," he said when we stood in front of the door to the suite

I swallowed down the tightness in my throat because as much as I wanted to tell myself it was relief that the dark enforcer had my sister's back as well as mine, I knew when it came down to it, I was all she had. The weight of her soul and untold others' put a knot in my stomach.

"There are many things you can't trust here in Fae, Alathir," he said. "But I am not one of them." He gestured toward the door, inferring I should open it.

Once I'd swung the door open, I took in the room with a careful eye. It was exactly as I'd left it hours earlier...except for one thing. The table was laden with a silver tray holding a tall bottle and two crystal flutes. I recalled it as the same tray from days earlier.

"Go in," he said. "I'll follow you."

The words held a shiver of promise not of threat. He waited, his body still and calm, as though he was doing his best to school it into a state of comfortable and unassuming pressure. I had the feeling he wasn't sure if I'd decide to trust him or not.

To be honest, I wasn't sure either, but one look at his face and the composed look in his eye, and I forced myself to remember those moments on the Shadow Trail, and then beyond it to the horrors of the catacombs. Maybe he'd had my back right from the beginning and I'd just been too stubborn to see it.

With a sigh, I crossed the threshold, him on my heels, and I headed directly to the table. As the door clicked behind me, I squared my shoulders and settled into the prim chair behind the table. I laid my hands on my lap. I lifted my chin, and watched him prowl toward me, the muscles of his arms bunching beneath the shirt, his shoulders knotting and letting go. Moisture flooded my mouth the way it might at the sight of a salted caramel cheesecake.

"Fae have already begun to arrive," he said in a low voice that hummed with something far deeper than lust. "The grounds around the castle are teeming with carts and carriages and horses. I wouldn't be surprised if tomorrow morning we receive word that the Days are upon us. This may be the last moment we speak," he said as he lifted the bottle and tilted it toward me.

I inclined my head in acceptance and he poured a sparkling green liquid into each glass. The rims fizzed for a split second, and I thought I heard a sigh coming from inside each glass.

He held one out to me. "I want you to understand something very crucial."

I leaned back, sliding my feet under the table. "And that is?"

"Double-crossing the Shadow Court means so much worse than death."

My mouth twitched. "Strange comment to make after you said I could trust you. But you and your father already made that fact abundantly clear back in the cellar with Jasmine," I said.

The light flared crimson in his eyes again before he pulled down the hooded shades and gave his attention to the glasses. "We are the same, Ponytail. I don't trust easily and neither do you. What I'm trying to say is that I am trusting you."

He inclined his head toward the glass he held out to me. I took it from him and held it close to my chest. There was no way I was taking a drink before he did.

"We've been here before," he said, his eyes shuttering, and I nodded. We had indeed. And he'd stormed out on me when I refused to drink with him. Probably this very same drink.

"You wouldn't trust me then," he said. "But I'm telling you. Of all things in this realm, Alathir, you can trust me. All you have to do is believe it."

I said nothing and he lifted his glass, tilting it in my direction. Then he upended the glass and swallowed deeply till it was drained. When the last of the liquid had disappeared, he eyed me meaningfully.

I'd not drank then because I'd been waiting for him. Well, this time, he'd drained the glass without having to be asked. I couldn't very well refuse.

The liquid tasted unexpectedly like cinnamon sticks and cloves but with a hit of latent whiskey.

"I assumed that would taste like mint," I said, feeling decidedly warm.

He eyed me over the rim of his glass before placing it beside the bottle. "It's from my own stock," he said. "I have a brewer who includes a few choice, and unique ingredients in the wort."

At that, his eyes found mine and for a second, my heart hiccuped. "What ingredients?" I asked as my vision went blurry.

CHAPTER 23

I thought for a moment I was going to faint. Then my vision cleared and I merely felt tired, all the wash of the events coming at me at once.

"You can take him, you know," he said and I looked up sharply, realizing I'd been lost in my thoughts. I had the strange feeling I'd been floundering about in them for several moments.

I blinked, clearing away the cobwebs from my vision, and sighed. "A few weeks ago, I'd have agreed with you," I said. Pushing away from the table, I sighed as I thought of all that had gone on from the moment I'd brashly informed Stone he could go to hell for suggesting I kill an innocent. "Now, knowing all the things I don't know, I'm just not sure."

It was a painful admission.

He got up too, standing in front of me with a sort of pained look on his face. His shoulders were tense, two powerful knots of muscle that held his corded neck aloft as he gazed down at me. I had the feeling the room had suddenly grown smaller.

When he laid his hand on my shoulder, I felt a buzz of electricity so strong I almost bolted but for the warmth that followed it, coursing a trail to my neck and throat that had me melting.

"When I first saw you, I thought you were just one more arrogant hunter. Cocky. Stepping into cow patties you might never get clean from your boots." He scanned my face with a heated gaze. "But you stood against Flint. You tricked me and escaped Lilah's cottage. I had to backtrack for several long moments before I caught your scent again and found your clothes discarded in the cul-de-sac. I knew then you were different."

He shifted foot to foot, his hand never leaving my shoulder, and I felt pinned there. "I had to stay in hellhound form to find you, did you know that?" His voice was painfully low. "And I wanted to find you. Your blood called to mine in such a shrill, keening note that it ached deep inside my ears. And when I saw you fawning over Stone at your mentor's, I wanted to tear his throat out and feed it to you."

Such violence in that jealousy; my knees quaked at the notion of it, but I snorted because every inch of my body was straining for his and I was so afraid of what might happen if I let go the tension in my spine. My whole body was hot. Too hot. I couldn't protest. Not one word. Just stood there, letting him go on as though I needed to hear every word in order to breathe again.

By the time I regained the power over my tongue, all I could say was, "I didn't fawn over him."

"It's alright to be attracted to him, Ponytail. He is the better male when it comes right down to it. He has qualities my kind find repulsive and your kind favors. There is humanity in

Stone, something uncommon in the Fae world." He said this in a thoughtful voice as he canted his head at me. "So many of us are selfish, violent things. But much as I hate to admit it, Stone is not one of them. He sees the good in you and he wants to protect it. The problem is his protection puts you at risk because he doesn't want you to know the true horrors of the realm. Ignorance is not your friend here."

With a movement so fast I couldn't see but a blur of color, he was behind me. I might have dropped and prepared to sweep out his legs from some muscle memory trained into me by long hours of fighting, but there was no time for the brain signals to travel to my muscles. By the time I realized I'd even considered it, something warm and solid fell between my breasts as he burrowed beneath my hair from behind with both fists, fixing something there.

"I want you to have this," he murmured. "When you're afraid you don't have the courage to do what needs to be done, touch this and remember what you are."

My fingers went to the stone at my neck, a long, irregular thing that felt heated against my skin as though something alive lay curled up inside it.

"It will look like part of Erachne's dress," he said in a haunted, far off voice. "And when you change out of that, the stone will look like anything you wish. Even your own skin. Or it may not be glamored at all if you so desire."

I turned to face him and stared up at his face, so guarded, so carefully schooled. A gift? From the dark enforcer? My throat started to close up, and if he noticed the way I was struggling to master my expression, he chose to hold my gaze from an expression so tightly shrouded I couldn't read it.

"It's not much," he said. "But it might help."

"Thank you," I managed to say through a tight throat.

The serpent of crimson started its march through the silver in his irises and a flicker of emotion, strangled and hopeful all at the same time stole over his face for a split second before he mastered it. My own chest fluttered like bats had taken residence and were protesting a spark of light. I fought to inhale, to send a gust of wind below to force them back into the shadows but he closed the small space between us so tightly I lost all train of thought.

"Stone pays attention to the wrong things," he said in a hoarse voice. "All he can see is the fragile human beneath the façade you show the world. I see the grit and edge that kept you alive in the catacombs. And that's what will get you through, Alathir." His breath swept over the top of my hair, carrying with it the fragrance of cinnamon and spices. The space between us charged itself with energy, a magic all its own that made my throat ache even as I chided myself for feeling it.

"You're fierce, Ava. And so fucking stubborn."

I had a feeling we weren't talking about the king anymore. And despite the way my skin sizzled at the heat in his voice, I lifted my chin, determined to hold my composure, to keep things on track lest I lose myself when I could least afford to do so.

"It isn't stubbornness that keeps a snake charmer from teasing the snake," I said.

His smile came slowly, with a knowing curve that in itself made my stomach flutter.

"There it is," he growled. "That determination to ignore how fucking badly you want to try me on just because you have some sort of aversion to surrendering to the monster within."

"I don't want to—"

"No?" he said as his hands moved around my waist and splayed over the small of my back. "You don't back away from running that smart ass mouth of yours when you want to look tough, but you can't admit to yourself that you want to fuck me."

"You're an arrogant ass."

His hands slid lower, cupping my backside and eliciting a small hiccup of breath as I drew in a sharp inhale.

"You're taking a chance," I said through clenched teeth.

"Am I?" he asked, dragging me up and forward so I could feel the press of him against me. The room felt far too small and cloistered. I swallowed hard as he dropped his nose to my neck. "I can smell you," he said. "All that frustrated arousal and nowhere to put it."

Those fingers crept between the mounds of my cheeks and I hissed, dropping my head back and looking up at him, easing my neck out of reach of his too-accurate nose.

He looked down at me with a hooded gaze filled with a drowsy sort of lust. "I don't mind being your punching bag if all you need is a bit of release. Want to prove to this monster that you can walk away without a scratch?" His body molded to mine. "Fight me, Ponytail," he said. "Let's see how hard you strike."

His grip tightened, pulling me closer, a hair's breadth away from his massive chest. He drew back with a hooded, lust-filled gaze that made me feel drunk just to look at it. A tingling started behind my ears, ringing like a craving.

Before I could even decide if I wanted to resist, those lips claimed mine, sealing off my air, taking what they wanted and forcing me to taste the cinnamon and clove flavor of him as I sucked in threads of oxygen from his lungs.

That was when all resistance left me, but it didn't go quietly into the dark night. No. It left fire in its wake, and a pit of rage because dammit, he was right. I did want him. I wanted all those things: his body, his surrender. I was weak in the face of my own desire and it had taken more from me to fight it than I wanted, than I could afford to lose. And I was pissed at myself for all of that.

I abandoned myself to the craving coiled in my stomach the way I surrendered to Bloodmist over and over again, knowing it was bad for me. Knowing I'd pay the piper sometime, but wanting it so badly I was willing to face it. Later. All of it. Later.

For now, I let my arms coil about his neck, using the leverage of my weight to tug him closer still. A long hiss of desire fled his lungs, and I thought I heard him swear, but that was smothered by the sound of my own moan as I released the last of resistance from my lungs.

"Fuck, Ponytail," he murmured into my mouth. "I don't know whether to throttle you or fuck you."

"Pick one," I said in a rasp. "I'll match you, you bastard."

That was all it took, that one taunt and that was all I got out before he bowled me backward, his hands scooping me by the backside and lifting me just enough from the floor that I could hook my legs around his waist.

But I had no intentions of letting him carry me like a supplicant lover. I bit down on his shoulder, raising a growl from him that lifted the hairs on the back of my neck.

"Hellcat," he rasped. "I hope those claws are sharp because it's going to get rough."

"Bring it," I said.

One moment more...just one deliciously delayed bit of tension, before I was pressed against the fireplace. The stone façade dug into my back. I felt the lines of grout seaming my spine as he strained against me.

It wasn't the least bit comfortable. It was gritty and hard and punishing, and I reveled in it. This was what I deserved, this and no more. Not gentle, accepting compassion that made me feel like I could never measure up, never be worthy. What I could take, what was right for me was a good hard screw without an ounce of pity or love. I could take his lust and feel as if that was just and right. It was the other, the worming, casual way he'd found to burrow beneath my skin and into my marrow, to ride along in the blood cells and capture my heart. That was terrifying.

But sex. Just sex. Just hard-boiled, rough sex. Primitive. Beastly. Punishing. That asked nothing of me but the moment and release and I dug my nails into his neck. He growled beneath his breath as he ground me deeper into the bricks. A cry of pain fled my lungs and he cut it off with a harsh kiss.

I was vaguely aware that he was tearing at my clothes even as he leveraged me against the hearth. My own breath came in harsh rasps, fast and short. I couldn't drag in enough air.

When his fingers slid into the moistness of me, I almost moaned aloud, and the rasping, aching way he responded with his own low-throated groan drove me to the edge. I clung there, my breath in gasps, my head dropped back. Eyes closed. I would tumble over. One second more.

That was when someone coughed. A harsh, angry bark of sound that slammed me back into my body.

"I suppose this is how you show how worried you are about your sister," the owner of that voice said in a tight voice.

CHAPTER 24

It took me several seconds to catch my breath and find my awareness. In a rush of shame, I realized how far past sanity I'd slipped. My mouth was wet, my thighs, slathered in my own juices. My pants were hauled down past my knees and my hands, my damn hands were shoving Blade's against my sex, forcing two fingers inside. I was wet there too. So wet I felt like vomiting at the thought of what I must look like.

"Mica is sick," the voice said in a flat voice.

Stone, I realized. It was Stone standing there in the maw of my wide open door, a witness to my shame. Stone with that horrible news still clinging to his lips while I tried to punish myself with his brother.

I felt Blade withdraw from me. His hand slid free of mine, still slick with my juices. A smear of it oiled my belly as he drew his hand away. My head sagged back onto the stones of the hearth, and I knew that wasn't enough. I cracked it backwards, letting the pain shoot stars behind my lids because where the hell had I gone in those moments.

Mica. Dear God.

The glazed look of a beast in rut slowly receded from Blade's face, and I saw him fight to school it into something neutral. He lost the fight for a brief moment as his features crumbled, but then he mastered it. Took a deep, shuddering breath. I caught his throat bobbing with the struggle to speak.

This battle, too, he lost. His chest was heaving at the same rate as mine, two partners pumping like pistons to rev an engine back into control.

"Mica," I said in a rasp, doing my best to shake off the rush of lust.

The stone of my necklace swung free of my breasts. Blade's gaze fell to it before it sought mine.

"Mica," he said in a gravelly voice, seeking ground with the name the way an electrical current strains for the earth.

"Mica," Stone said.

Blade swallowed, and I saw the serpent in his eyes shrink into a thin line of crimson and hide behind the silver limning his irises. With great care, he cradled my legs in both hands and lowered my feet to the floor. My thighs quivered with strain until my soles met the wooden floorboards and then the trembling ran to my insoles and finally calmed. I was able to take a breath.

But Blade. He wasn't nearly as in control as he should have been. Wherever it was I'd gone, he'd tipped over the edge of it when he'd taken me there. I could see that the journey back was a tough one. Every muscle in his body was rigid as it fought for control as he placed both hands on either side of my head, caging me between them.

I started to duck down, thinking to slide out of the cage and edge sideways, out of the way. Putting some space between us.

He growled. Growled. Lips curled back, a possessive wolf demanding its mate remain pinned for its own pleasure.

I froze, realizing how close to a beast he really was in that moment. My hands went to my throat instinctively, seeking the feel of the rope scar, an assertion that I was still alive. At the thought that I'd stepped into the lair of a monster naked and unarmed and come away with only minor damage.

Except, I didn't think that was true. Not by a long shot.

"Mica needs you, Blade," Stone said, and there was no recrimination in his tone. He sounded almost...sympathetic. "Come back, brother."

Blade lowered his head to his hands and one by one, he dropped them. He blinked once. Twice.

"Mica," he said.

Stone advanced into the room, catching my eye and shooting me a pointed look. There was no recrimination in that either. Just concern.

"He's asking for you," he said to Blade. "He needs you, brother. Come back."

Blade's shoulders sagged. He dragged his head up to look at Stone, and in his entire posture was the shadow of the hellhound. When he swung his gaze back my way, my breath caught at the naked look of violent possession I saw in his face.

Stone gestured at me subtly. Move, it said. Get out of the way.

I didn't question, just slid away, pulling my shirt over my bare chest, hauling up my pants even if I couldn't button them. As I found some space away from Blade, I felt the lust peel away like a dirty glove.

I found myself staggering toward the chair because I wasn't sure my legs could hold me. I fell into it as Blade began buttoning his trousers.

"What happened?" Blade said. His voice had regained that arrogant note even if there was a hint of quiver in the undertones.

Stone put himself between Blade and where I sat in the chair. "He used his magics," he said.

Blade's head snapped up. "Which magics?"

Stone's cheeks blanched. "He tried to show Ava something about the king," he said. "We don't know what it is and he is wasting from the use."

"What do you mean, wasting, Stone?" Blade all but yelled. "Tell him to recharge it."

"You don't think I've tried," Stone yelled back. "For fuck's sake, Blade, you think I'd let him lie in waste without trying to get him to refresh."

Blade shoved his sleeves up, exposing several of the silver scars lining his skin. "If he won't take a woman, then I will have to force feed the boy."

Stone inclined his head. "I tried that too," he said. "I don't have the power he needs."

Blade's jaw ticked sideways. "You did that for him?"

"He's my brother too."

For a moment, I watched the two, with Blade's gaze softening, Stone's shoulders remaining rigid. I could swear I saw time moving as they stood there staring at each other, taking the measurement of the other.

"Go to him," Stone said softly. "I'll see to what needs to be done here."

A curt nod from Blade, a mere dip of his head as though he was ashamed, except the dark enforcer couldn't know the emotion. Then, as if he wanted to show me he did indeed have mastery over his instincts, he offered me a lingering touch of his lips to the corner of mine before he laid his cheek against mine, his mouth whispering along my cheek to my ear.

"I know what you're made of, Ava," he said in a hoarse voice. "You can't fool me any more."

He took a step backward then, the corners of his eyes tight. His gaze lingered on my throat for so long, I thought he might have forgotten Mica's need for him. My breath caught and held under that gaze, and then he sighed and pivoted toward the door. He left without closing it, with Stone still standing just inside.

I put my hand to my forehead, feeling slightly dizzy.

I had to fan my face to keep the heat at bay. With his mouth pressed into a thin line, Stone passed me his shirt and I pulled it on over my torn clothes and buttoned it. As if he knew how awkward it was for me for him to be standing there bare chested, he crossed his arms, those muscles bulging.

The long moments of tension in the room drew out so taut I had to get up just so I wasn't sitting there like a dolt beneath the weight of it.

Standing on quivering legs in front of the table, I reached for the bottle. Empty. Both glasses drained.

"I don't know what the hell was in that wine," I said, tilting a glass forward for inspection and setting it back down when it refused to show even a drop of liquid. "But it just kicked my ass."

"Seems it did more than that to your ass," Stone said in a tight voice.

I cut him a glare. "How bad is Mica?" I asked because I didn't need any reminders of my behavior. "What do you mean he's refusing to recharge."

He sighed and ran his hand over his hair, worry seaming his features. "It's not good, Ava," he said.

Damn, but my knees really did feel weak. I had to touch down on the back of the chair to keep from swaying side to side. Even Bloodmist didn't do that to me. I drew in a sharp breath, shook my head side to side. That seemed to help.

"So," I said as I focused my attention on Stone. "What can I do to help?"

"Nothing," he said. "At least, not if you want to live." He waited for me to narrow my gaze at him before he offered an explanation. "Mica is the same as Ferranus."

"That boy?" I said, surprise putting a shrillness into my tone that didn't sound normal. "He consumes blood to recharge?"

I thought back to the needs Blade had, and while I had no problem equating the dark enforcer having the same types of needs as Ferranus, I couldn't reconcile the gentle Mica. I imagined sips of lilac tea and twinkling starlight as his battery source.

"So if he doesn't recharge his magic what will happen?"

"He won't die, if that's what you mean. But he will waste. And wasting takes the mind with it. The body can recharge. The magic can refresh, but if left too long, the mind..."

I held up my hand. "Don't finish that thought. Just tell me Blade can help."

"He can. Blade's blood has enough magic. He'll take care of Mica. But I wasn't just coming here to tell Blade about Mica."

He tapped his pocket as though he were searching for keys. "We have much to cover before the Days begin if we're to have a chance of success."

I nodded and sank into the hard-back chair beside the table. "Fine." I tapped my nail on the glass, letting it ring out in crystalline chimes.

I was still staring at the glass, lost in thought when he dropped a familiar looking pouch in front of me.

"The cursed items," I said.

"Yes. I'm to school you on them. My father says we no longer have the luxury of not trusting you with them."

I leaned back, using my nail to shove the glass toward him. I felt wearier than I should have been at finally getting that glimpse I'd been waiting for of those items. Part of that, I knew, came from imagining Kit somewhere in the manse under lock and key, and maybe even holed up in that damn dungeon they'd kept me in.

"Sure," I said, bitterness biting through my voice. "Do let's crack on with that." I crossed my arms over my chest. "But first, since you've been able to see to your brother's welfare, maybe you'll spare a few details about my own sibling who has been torn from her normal world into this one by force." I peered up at him, a warning in my eyes. "And don't skirt the truth."

He offered me a brief, apologetic smile. "She's fine," he said in a voice that suggested he was relieved to be giving me the information. "Blissfully gorging on chocolates and soaking in a hot bubble bath probably as we speak."

I was about to ask how he could know that when he answered like he had plucked the words from my tongue. "My father thinks the Days will be announced soon. He ordered her prepared for your presentations." He cocked his head. "You're to have the same treatment, but I thought you'd want to go over the items first."

"Business before pleasure," I said, and lifted the glass, titling it toward me and sniffing it.

"Are you thirsty?" Stone asked.

I shook my head. It felt squishy, like I'd had a two day bender on Bloodmist. Whatever dregs I'd hoped to see inside were gone, the glass as empty as if it had never contained liquid. I eyeballed the bottle.

"Is she alone?" I asked, scanning the glass with a squinted eye.

"Flint is outside her suite with several guards stationed nearby. She'll be safe."

My gaze flicked up at him. "Your idea of safe or mine?"

"Flint has orders. He'll hold to them."

"That's what I'm worried about."

He pulled out the chair and settled into it, crossing one leg over the other. "If you must know, the bath was my father's idea. The chocolates were Flint's."

I raised my eyebrow, but said nothing, just placed the bottle back in the center of the table. "So will you order me chocolates or must I ask that wiry bastard for some?"

"We are all very competitive," he said in answer, then paused a moment. "Except for Mica." A shade crossed his eyes, followed by a grim set to his mouth. "The boy has no duplicity in him."

"Is it really that bad?" I reached across the table for his hand.

He squeezed my fingers. "It is. Whatever he wanted to tell you, he braved the wasting to do it."

The words made me feel sick. "I'm sorry."

His smile was wan. "You couldn't know what he'd do or stopped it from happening." He shook his head. "He has his own mind. Stubborn, so stubborn."

I knew that word. Blade had used it on me enough. "Alathir," I said, projecting my inference of its meaning into the syllables. Stubborn. It certainly fit me so I supposed it might Mica.

A look of surprise crossed his face before he mastered it. "In a manner of speaking, yes," he said as he pulled the bottle toward him. "You pronounce the term very well for a human. And for all Mica's naiveté, he is very brave. I don't know as I'd have the conviction to refuse to waste instead of using another's blood to heal. That's a special sort of courage I don't possess."

His eyes flashed, the aquamarine swirling with emotion. "Except the technical use of that term would be reserved for someone with a more intimate connection than family." The color in his eyes settled and deepened. "I might have used it on you, for example," he murmured. "If you'd let me."

It was difficult to hold in gaze while my heart was fidgeting like a squirrel in my chest. I could swear there was an entire tsunami washing over the small bones in my ears. Everything had become a whoosh of wind in there. Alathir. It did not mean stubborn at all.

"And what might you be meaning if you did refer to me?"

"My brave beloved," he said, and repeated the word with a warmth of emotion that only made my stomach hurt because it sounded wrong coming from his lips. "Alathir."

The way he stroked the inside of my palm with his thumb as he said it made me pull it gently from his grasp. I cleared my throat. The edges of my vision blurred.

All sass and snarl fled me. I coughed again, doing my best to clear my throat of the clump that had risen to choke off my breathing. Alathir. Blade had called me his brave beloved. I thought the room had grown far too small.

"We should go over the objects," I said and a flash of strangled emotion crested his face and disappeared. To disguise the knowledge that I'd seen it, I reached for the leather bag.

My grabbing for the bag seemed to free him, as with a jerk of his hand, he tapped my fingers away.

"Haven't you heard of a mummy's curse?" he grumbled good naturedly. Maybe too much so. "Let those who have magic open the nasty magic bag lest you release a gust of germy power into the air."

The way he said it indicated he wasn't the least bit worried, but the tone had far less casual humor than I bet he'd tried to inject into the comment, and so with a flourish and a reckless yank of the leather string belied any suggested caution, he tugged the bag open.

I leaned forward, scanning the contents as they spilled onto the table noisily, showing a cache of eight separate objects. There seemed to be less than I remembered the witch stuffing inside. But the gemstone I'd taken from the witch's hand was there. My gaze snagged on it. It looked bigger than I remembered.

"A ring, three coins, a corsage, a pair of glasses, and an amulet," he said, inventorying them aloud as he pointed at each. "Oh, and this rock, I guess." He gave the stone a sharp look with his eyes crinkled at the corners.

Thinking he was going to grab it, I plucked it from the table before he could touch it. "I remember this. I took it from Lilah's dead hand."

He grimaced. "I suppose if she was holding it, then it must be something."

"You don't know what it does?" My fingers closed around it, squeezing. The stone seemed to shrink and pulse back to its normal size.

"I have no idea. It wasn't there any time we opened the bag."

His gaze remained steady on my hand as I tossed the stone, testing its weight. It had warmth, I decided. "It possesses magic," I said. "I'm sure of it."

A small thoughtful sound slipped through his lips. "I wonder why it wasn't in there before."

"Well, I certainly didn't take it," I said. "I put the damn thing in there in the first place." I dropped it back onto the table, suddenly anxious. "If you don't know what it does, I'm not going to mess with it."

He murmured his agreement before setting it aside, then without further preamble he sifted through the rest of the objects with his finger, totally oblivious to any inherent danger from the magic.

As he separated each item from the group he explained what each of them did. The ring, a garish looking thing made of green stone carrying several strange looking marks along the band, drained the wearer of health and gave it to the person who gifted it.

"Not exactly what we're looking for because you'd have to get Ferranus to accept it," he said. "Not likely a fae will take a present from a human. Too suspicious." He eyeballed the stone around my own neck with a narrowed gaze.

I touched it. "Is it just as suspicious if it's the other way around?"

"More so," he said shortly. "I hope you trust the fae who gave that to you."

I might have answered that except he continued on in a rush, moving his finger to the pile of coins. "This, I believe is a ferryman coin," he said and I had a hard time swallowing the gasp that tried to worm its way free at his casual mention. It took everything I had not to reach out and pluck the thing from the table as he went on so casually, I knew he had no idea Blade owned any. "The coin allows the bearer to create a sort of hologram of themselves while their true form hides in shadow."

A ferryman coin. Something I could use to get Kit out of Fae and into a safe place without any of them knowing. I couldn't pull my gaze from the nicked and worn surface bearing a thick serpent coiling around the edge. Its head was larger than a snake's with a head like a cobra and a mouth like a lamprey's.

As if my heart wasn't beating loudly enough for him to hear, he went on like nothing was out of the ordinary, and I struggled to follow his finger as it hovered over the other two coins. "These two are a pair," he said. "One transports gold and silver from the pocket or purse where it rests to the pocket or purse of the owner who holds its partner."

"Not useful," I said, my eye running to the only two items left on the table. One, a fragile looking corsage was made of bloom I'd never seen before. With wispy, almost transparent blue petals nestled in the midst of a cluster of baby's breath and a single rose, it appeared almost ghostly.

"The flower delivers a deadly curse to one who inhales its scent," he said, "and the amulet allows the wearer to compel another to do her bidding."

I noticed he used a feminine pronoun for the amulet wearer and my gaze snapped up to meet his. He gave me a smug look, and I knew exactly what he was thinking.

"I can use that to compel him into accepting me," I said. "In case he's not interested."

"He'll be interested," he said. "But yes."

"How long does it last?" I asked, my mind on how I might use it for my own ends. "I mean, can you suggest something as a trigger to happen later or is it an immediate thing?"

"Are you planning to lay a trap for someone, Ava?"

I lowered my chin, self-consciously protecting my throat. "My sister's life means more to me than betraying your cartel. But if you're asking if I want to know its limits, then yes. I haven't lived this long by trusting blind luck."

"Glad to hear it," he said as he pinched his fingers around the chain and gestured at me to stand.

Getting to my feet, I realized my knees were shaking. This was too easy. Nothing was this easy. Something had to be wrong. I was missing something very important but I couldn't figure out what it was.

But instead of putting the amulet around my neck, he draped it over his own.

"I imagine you'll want to know if it works," he said. "Being the sort who doesn't trust easily."

My gaze locked on the stone.

"Kiss me," he said.

CHAPTER 25

I was a 'toss 'em down and get 'er done' sort of lover, the same as Gideon. On the odd occasions I found a man in a bar and took him home, the kissing was a necessary prelude to the event I wanted most. Namely, a fast bounce in the hay that would leave me unwound for another week or two.

If kissing in the back of a cab or at the door of my apartment would get me that, I was all in, but it didn't go on for long, and I'd found that most men didn't seem to miss it.

I expected to give Stone a speedy, perfunctory peck. What I delivered sent a flush of heat to my cheeks that had my fists clenching at my sides. My entire body went stiff and still I couldn't stop.

It was Stone who released me, gently breaking the kiss. I felt his desire thick and hard against my hips. At first, when his hands slid to my waist, I thought he planned to pull me closer, but he went rigid all of a sudden and then eased me off him. I realized with horror, I'd all but climbed onto him in my eagerness to fulfill the compulsion.

So released, I lifted my chin, exposing my throat instead of lowering it in a way that would block my pulse from his view.

"Do that again," I said, "And I'll slit your throat."

He swallowed and pulled the amulet back over his head. "I would expect no less from you, Ava," he said without meeting my eye. He began gathering the coins, the ring, and the flower in one hand for deposit into the bag, but before he could do so, I laid my hand on his. Slipping my fingers into his palm, I placed my other hand over his, cupping his grip with both my hands.

I looked into his face with all earnestness. "Thank you, Stone," I said.

His features smoothed out. "For what?"

"For trusting me," I said, and plucked each item from his fist, tossing them into the pouch. "For checking on Kit. For not making me feel like a fool when you found me with Blade."

When he swallowed, it was through a tense throat. "I told you, Ava," he said. "I care about you."

I smiled. "I know. I believe you." My palm fell to the table, beside the gemstone, in a curled fist. "The stone," I said. "Can you leave that?"

He looked down at it where it sat beside my curled fingers. "Since it wasn't there to begin with, I'm guessing it wants to be with you." This in a thoughtful voice that made me feel guilty.

When he looked back up at me, I thought I saw a thin line of color swallowing up the aquamarine, but I knew he wasn't Blade in disguise. His scent was all Stone, all caramel and butterscotch. My imagination, my desires, seeing what it wanted. And oh how that hurt to admit.

"I'll leave it," he said and with a sigh, he heaved himself to his feet. "The rest of the objects will be placed in your trousseau for your presentation."

Which meant Terran didn't trust me enough to leave them in my care. Fine by me. While I didn't like the very damsel-ish, old world notion of a trousseau, I let the comment slide in favor of what he'd seemed to think I would enjoy the most.

"And my bath?"

"One of the lesser fae has already been charged with getting that ready." He grinned. "And I'll see to the chocolates."

My fingers trailed to my throat, touching the stone Blade had given me. I noted his eye followed. "Don't bother with the chocolates," I said. "That sounds too much like a gift."

A mischievous smile teased his mouth. "Smart girl," he said and swept out the door, leaving me with the echo of a warning he couldn't know he'd given me.

My eyes roamed to the bottle still on the table as well as the empty glasses. I didn't remember downing all the booze. Had the necklace come before or after?

It occurred to me that I'd not got a good look at the necklace at all. Curious now that I'd given it more thought, I crossed the room to the mirror. Blade had said it would just look like my skin when I wore it. I tried to remember if Stone had noticed it and couldn't.

My reflection showed me looking far more harried than I would like, my eyes gleaming with a sort of mania. I supposed that was to be expected, knowing Kit was now in the same Fae sideshow I was in. And after the incident with Blade and Stone's kiss, I would have been surprised if I looked unfazed. But my reflection showed no true evidence of a necklace unless I looked really hard. There was the faintest of smudges, like a blurred area of a picture where the weight seemed the heaviest, and I let my fingers trail to it and lift the stone from between my breasts.

A delicate chain rose along with my fingers. Made of gold, it didn't look sturdy enough to hold the weight of the stone at the farthest part of the loop.

With a twist of my head, I slipped the chain and stone over and let it lay in my palm.

My breath caught in my throat as it phased into view.

It was stunning. A long, crimson droplet made of amber. Filigree laced the edges of the clasp in circular whorls that looked like someone had stamped Os over and over again on the clasp. Every few links of chain, a tiny fragment of blue amber caught the light.

But what lay inside the large crimson amber was what caught my attention. A wink of blacksteel peered out at me from its capping over a jagged, revolting looking tooth.

Slavin's tooth. That bastard half-trow prick who'd taken me to the catacombs.

My face heated at the memory of digging that tooth out of his mouth, of palming it until I couldn't bear to hold it any longer. I'd thought it lost. My heart swelled with emotion enough to make my eyes sting, thinking the dark enforcer had found it and kept it and had it turned into something more unique than a trophy I'd seal into a cabinet in the back of my closet.

It was both the most horrific and thoughtful gift I'd ever received.

Wear it to remind me what I was, Blade had said.

I had only to remember my reaction to him when he'd kissed me, so much different than the long, languid smooches with Stone, to know what it meant. That he knew me as well as I knew myself.

I was a monster. And monsters did monstrous things. This gift was a talisman to draw my own sort of power from, to remind me of the courage I needed if I was to take down the most powerful fae in the realm and still walk away. If I was to get my sister out as well.

That kind of courage had fled me after I'd realized I was out of my depth here in Fae. I'd thought it gone in the catacombs and had acted out of desperation and survival instinct. I'd begun to believe I was a tool to be used here. A Patsy. A damned damsel.

This necklace reminded me what I was, exactly as he'd said. I wasn't a mere tool. I wasn't a mere mortal without skill, at the mercy of powerful creatures who possessed magic. I was me. Hunter of monsters. Survivor of addiction. A damned bad ass who danced to no one's tune.

I turned the stone over in my palm, watching how it slid in and out of focus, changed color, blended with my skin and back again as it decided whether it was supposed to camouflage or stand out. A remarkable piece of jewelry. Too remarkable, really, for a mere mortal to have been gifted it.

A fae bearing gifts, especially a powerful one like Blade, might have ulterior motives.

The hunter in me picked up her head. Just what was the dark enforcer offering me with this gift? And what was his motive in serving me that wine?

I dropped the necklace back over my head, and watched it disappear. Then I turned my attention to the thing in my other palm, the thing I'd taken from the pouch as I'd slid item after item into the sack under Stone's watchful eye.

The serpent on the coin's face stared back at me in accusation. I'd used him, I knew. Batted my eyelashes, used his feelings for me to blind him to the sleight of hand I'd used to pluck the ferryman coin out of the cache, distracted him with the gemstone, that truth be told, I could have cared less about.

Kit was out there somewhere, and I was going to be sure she did not follow me to the Iron Court. I had no idea how the magic worked, but I had to trust that if Blade had passed one to three women to share, that it would simply do what it needed to.

I tucked the thing in my pocket and headed to the door, thinking I'd have to work my way in a grid through the manse until I found Flint and his cronies, and therefore, Kit's suite. My gut clenched at the thought that I should start in the dungeons, but I couldn't imagine her bathing and eating chocolates in a place that Terran used to feed the City its pain.

I'd memorized the path to Terran's suite and the layout of the cellars and the way to the dining room, but I'd not been in any other part of the manse. So it stood to reason that I had to go where I hadn't been.

Blustering out into the hallway would be a ludicrous plan. But it wasn't too far off the correct path. I dressed in a shirt and trousers I found in the armoire, all black, as though they'd been put there specially for me. I found my boots inside as well and pulled them on. Then I waited for the servants to come.

When they did, three of them, bearing buckets of steaming water, I let them trail back and forth until the water was a froth of steam rising from the copper, all the while glancing to the hall, taking the measure of the burly males I saw lingering outside. Four of them. All watching the females with keen eyes.

Before the servants herded back out, I grabbed the blasted book that kept appearing and moving on its own from the fireplace where it lay open like a hound's tongue.

"Terran gave me this book to study," I said to the one who seemed to be in charge.

She eyeballed it. "I don't read," she said.

"That's fine," I told her. "I do. And it has some very important information in it that might help young Mica. I hear he's unwell?" I cocked my head at her thoughtfully. "I think this might help."

She reached for it with the intent to grab it from me, but I pulled it away. "I need to show him where the remedy is," I said. "Since you don't read, I'd hate for it to get lost in translation."

It took her a moment, but she finally nodded. "I'll show you where his suites are. But you'll have to convince the guards to let you go. I don't want to get in trouble."

No problem, I thought. I didn't bother with niceties. Just told them Terran's book had a remedy for the young male and that things were dire unless I could get there in time. The leader, a male who reminded me very much of Slavin, except much bigger, waved me on with a glare, telling me if I wasn't back in twenty minutes, he'd have to come looking for me.

It took at least five minutes for the woman to show me to Mica's wing because we all but ran the whole way. By the time we stood in front of double doors with a knocker that spanned them both, I was winded.

"I'm wanted in the kitchens," she said as she jerked back-wards. A motion as if someone had tugged on an invisible leash.

I couldn't have asked for a better happenstance.

"Go," I said with a smile. "I'm fine. I know my way back."

I was already making plans to backtrack and take the hall-way I'd noticed to another wing when she nodded, a harried expression on her face. I watched her bustle back the way we'd come. One more moment, I thought, to make sure she was gone, and then I'd creep toward that other hall.

Except I heard sounds coming from the suite and I turned to face the door. It was the slightest bit ajar. Voices leaked from within, one was baritone, familiar, and made my heart skip as it moved along the air currents to my ears.

My hand went to my throat automatically as I recognized Blade's voice. Something about not getting caught inside, which I found strange. He'd been sent for. I leaned closer.

The other voice was a musical lilt, the kind that came from a young girl.

"I don't want to go just yet," she said. "I want to paint his nails."

"Not now, my young one. He's sleeping."

"But maybe he'll want to see the pretty colors when he wakes."

"There's no time, love. You know you're not supposed to be here."

I thought I heard a foot stomp. Barely able to help myself, I peered through the gap.

The room looked very much like it belonged to Mica. It was filled with bouquets of flowers on every table, most of which had turned brown and dried. Three walls were comprised of shelves of books that stretched from floor to ceiling, broken only by one very large window covered by purple velvet curtains, and a broad Grey brick fireplace.

Each wall of books possessed its own sliding ladder made of the most gorgeous tiger wood. Bean bag chairs clustered around the fireplace with thick velveteen blankets tossed over them. A richly ornate desk squatted in one corner with an equally ornate oil lamp casting a mellow glow over a sheaf of papers and a pile of books. I thought I recognized the lovely illuminated pages of The Diary of an Unnamed Queen spread open beneath the lamp and scanned the desk for the other tome, the book on alchemy but didn't spy it among the ephemera.

And in the midst of that very Mica-like chamber, Blade and a very young female sat at a small table, a teapot between them and small plates of what looked like crackers and cheese. Both she and Blade held delicate pink teacups and saucers in their hands, his pinching a tiny handle with large, awkward fingers.

I almost choked on my own spit when he lifted the cup to his lips and made a loud slurp that set her to giggling.

He set the cup down on its saucer with a clinking sound before he leaned back in his half-sized chair, a gargantuan beast in a doll house. Bull in a china shop didn't quite fit.

"I don't want to wait for him to wake up," she said in a trembling voice as she set her own cup down so gently it was obvious she was taking great pains to appear a lady. She sounded like she was fighting tears. "What if he wakes to those ugly nails he had when last he visited? He might be sad. I want him to be happy."

Blade leaned forward, his eyes flashing as he reached out to fondle a lock of bright, red hair. "You've left him lots of bright color on his pillow," he said. "He'll know you were here when he sees the locks of hair you placed there. That will make him happy. And I will tell him you wish him well."

"You promise?"

He laid a hand on his heart. "May I be struck dead from my own power should I fail to give him your love. Now is that enough? Will you return to your rooms now, Phaedre?"

I couldn't see her face, but I could see her nod. Those auburn locks bounced and my heart squeezed at just how innocent she must be.

Like I had in the Velvet Boar bathroom, I felt terribly ashamed to be spying on this intimate moment. The things I was seeing, hearing, those things were as intimate as the acts he'd committed with Jasmine but for different reasons. I had the feeling if he caught me watching this time, I'd not get away with a smirk and an arrogant offer.

I had to get out of there. Just as I was backing away, she turned around and I was captured by the horror of her face.

CHAPTER 26

I sucked back in the shocked gasp that wanted out at the sight of slanted eyes far too big for her face. Set way too far apart for her to be considered pretty, they were also thyroid bulbous and gawking with lids that barely closed down over them when she blinked.

Those eyes roamed the room and focused with laser intent on me pressing my nose into the gap in the door. She'd seen me, I knew. A look of surprise took her features and with a sharp hiss, she just...popped out of existence, taking the table, chairs, and teacups with her. Blade was left to collapse to the floor in an undignified heap.

It was a moment only, but it was enough to see the fullness of her features well enough to recall it later in description. Her nose had a crook that leaned toward her left ear. Long canine teeth protruded from full red lips that were far too adult for what I knew was still a child. Her forehead went on too far before her gorgeous hair sprouted out around tiny nubs that looked very much like a doberman's perked ears.

She'd be considered grotesque in the human world. A sort of changeling from the old world in a pretty froth of lace. Probably entered into the carnival world had it been an earlier century.

I shrank back as quickly as she'd evaporated, my heart in my throat. My chest rose and fell too quickly. I thought I might be hyperventilating. And it wasn't from the shock of seeing the girl. It was the shock of seeing Blade, his tenderness, the earnest look on his face as he touched Phaedre's hair.

The dark enforcer would know someone was in the hall, surely. There'd be no other earthly reason she'd disappear like that. He'd know and he'd come to investigate and he'd see me standing there like a peeping Tom and God only knew what he'd think of me then.

But no command came. And in relief, I rolled away, pressing my back against the wall by the door.

I made a hasty scan of the hallway, noting the direction I'd be going and the mental pathway back here and down to my own suite. A countdown began in my mind, calculating the moments I'd been gone, the amount of time I might have left before the guards came looking for me. They'd come right here, I knew, since that was what I'd told them.

If I didn't make it back, I'd be discovered and so would Kit.

I had to hurry.

"What are you doing here, Ponytail?"

I swung to the sound of the voice, my heart in my feet. I'd not heard him even approach the door let alone open it, but there he stood. All magnificent six feet four of him. He wasn't leaning on the door frame as he did so often nor did he fill the frame. He looked...anxious.

All I could think to do was hold out the book. "I thought Mica might need this."

His gaze slid to the book held between us. "You think my brother might want a book about rocks?"

I pulled the tome closer, peering down at it. "Is that what it is?" I said, unable to keep the surprised note out of my voice. "Huh."

"What do you want, Ava?"

"I told you—"

"You lied," he said, advancing a step toward me in a most predatory manner. "How long have you been standing out here, spying?"

My shoulders automatically came up. "I wasn't spying."

"No?" he asked. "And I suppose you saw nothing inside."

His hands slid behind his back, like he was hiding something. I took a chance, stepping toward him this time.

"What I saw," I said, prowling the rest of the few feet between us with the same animalistic intent he so often employed. "What I saw was a grown ass, nasty as hell fae playing tea party."

He might have looked guilty for all of a second before he schooled his features once more, but I'd seen the shift. I knew whatever he was doing, it was forbidden for some reason. "Let me see your hands."

The arrogance slid over his features again. "Why? You want to see if they still have your juices all over them?" He took a step forward to meet me, a challenge in his eyes.

But I knew he was deflecting. Whatever I'd seen inside Mica's rooms, whoever Phaedra was, he wanted that knowledge kept secret. So I met his gaze with a lifted chin even though my belly was trembling, even though some part of me was quivering with remembered desire. Even if the lust in his voice was so thick my knees went to sandbags.

"You're afraid," I said.

"I'm afraid of nothing."

"Who's Phaedra?"

At that, he had me barreled all the way across the hall and against the wall. The book dropped from my grasp and fell to the tiles with a thud long before my back hit the wall. One of his hands circled my wrist, the other planted itself over my head. My shoulders splayed over the plaster, I held his gaze with courage, and yes, just the tiniest amount of desire. My throat was thick.

But I wasn't scared.

"I asked you a question, hellhound," I said through the tightness squeezing my throat.

For a moment, I thought he'd say nothing, then he drew back. He let go of my wrist but his hand remained above my hand. So...released. Sort of. My gaze slid to that hand caging my head along the wall. Each nail sported a bright pink shade of polish.

"She says I'm too dark all the time," he rasped. "That I need some color to remind me to be happy." He swallowed, watched me keenly, the crimson coils around his irises flaring.

I all but sagged from the weight of his confession and yet he didn't seem ashamed or embarrassed. Just...resigned. He didn't want anyone to know, and yet he kept one nail painted. To honor her, I supposed. It was hard to wrangle up an accusation knowing that.

So I did what I swore I'd never do. I let myself trust him.

"I was looking for Kit," I said.

He canted his head at me. "No taunts?"

I shrugged nonchalantly even though I was still so surprised I was all but speechless. His eyelids shuttered to half mast. "Kit is fine. I told you I won't let anything happen to her."

I snorted because anything besides a snide comment made me far too uncomfortable. "Is that the Mad Hatter or the hellhound speaking?"

Rather than being offended at the taunt, a smile stole his mouth and he lowered his head to mine. His breath smelled of cinnamon, making my traitorous thighs clench. "There she is," he said. "The human female who can't let herself feel what she really wants because she's too afraid."

"Only a fool denies fear," I said. "It's what we do with it that matters." I thought of Kit and all the things I'd done because I was afraid she'd never forgive me. Yes, afraid. I could admit that now. "Fear is healthy. It keeps us honest."

"And are you being honest, Alathir?"

My head snapped up at the term. "Don't call me that."

The slant to his head made him look curiously like the hellhound. "You know what it means."

My lips pressed together. I hadn't meant to reveal that.

"I need to get back to my rooms," I said.

He leaned in closer, his torso hovering an inch over mine. In a heartbeat, his hips would grind against mine and I'd surrender. I knew I would. The space got too claustrophobic. I tried to shove him off me.

"Who will complain if you're here with me, Ava?" he asked in a low voice. "Stone? Are you worried what Stone will think? He's already seen you with me, remember. He knows what we are even if you don't."

I froze. "What do you mean: what we are?"

He ran his nose along the column of my throat. "I've smelled it on you since the moment we met, my Alathir, but I didn't realize the truth until you fought the wendigos at my side. I knew it the instant I saw you broken in the catacombs. Did you not feel it when we shared the wine?"

My knees let go. I had to scrabble at the wall with my hand to keep from collapsing, and even as I sagged like a torn sack of grain, his knee slid between my legs, propping me up. Pinning me, straddled on his thigh. I had to lean against him or fall sideways.

"The wine," I said. "What did you do to it?"

"I told you it was a special vintage."

"What. Did. You. Do. To it."

"Many things, Ava," he murmured, his head dipping low, his voice turning to a rasp. "All meant to protect my mate."

Whatever hold I had on my control fled me then. My mouth dried up. The hackles raised on the back of my neck. And damn if the center of me currently propped against his muscled thigh didn't grow moist and warm.

Fuck. This had gone too far. Way too far.

"I'm no one's mate," I said. "I came here because I was forced. I came because my sister's life is on the line. A sister now imprisoned in your family's dungeons."

"Suites," he said, correcting me with an indulgent grin. "She's housed in a luxurious suite, being watched over by a doting male."

I sucked the back of my teeth at the ridiculously minimizing description.

"You're mad," I said, pulling out information from my knowledge bank that could explain this shift. "You suffered a wasting back in the bookstore. You didn't heal in time. Your mind is gone."

His hand left the wall, finally, to slide between the plaster and the small of my back. The warmth of it there made me want to melt when he splayed his fingers over my spine. I managed to resist. Barely.

"I'm too old to waste, Ponytail. Only the young suffer such illness. I have all my faculties and then some." He pulled me closer, dropping his knee so I was supported by his arms and his body, and I felt exactly what he meant by 'then some'.

"There was a drop of my blood in that wine, Ava," he murmured, dropping his mouth to my neck and trailing his lips along my skin in a whisper to my ear. "Only my mate would have reacted the way you did, matching my ferocity, my violence."

"You drugged me?" Something horrible caught in my throat, an emotion so intense it sent a ripple of nausea over my skin.

He drew back and caught my gaze and in the depths of his, I saw both agony and rapture. "I had to know, for certain, Alathir. And it wasn't a drug. I would never do that to you."

I stiffened. "You know how it was for me," I said. "It felt like a drug. Felt...more."

When I tried to pull away, he tightened his hold. "That was your blood calling to mine. It was the bond making itself known. Believe me when I say I've struggled with that knowledge, fought it like you have, but not because I don't want you. Fuck I want you. But I know humans don't feel the bond the way we do. It's possible all you feel for me is lust and the desire to control a beast that you can't kill."

"You drugged me," I said, my jaw tight and aching around the loosening of those words. "You did it without me knowing."

"Would it be so bad, Alathir?" he asked. "If that was how you could feel, a hundred times that rapture, to rise to heights of ecstasy you've never gone to before... wouldn't you want it?"

I ached all over as he said those words. My cells cried out for that sort of ecstasy. The addict in me craved it. Of course I'd want it. I wanted him more than I'd wanted anyone.

But I knew something of that sort of rapture. I knew the agony when it peeled away.

"No such rapture comes without a fall," I said, my gaze dropping to his throat and pinning to the pulse I saw hammering there.

His hand pressed tighter, drawing me closer still. "Only angels fall, Ava, and we are not that. We are something other. Something more."

"You are other," I said, closing my eyes against the burning intensity of his. "Not me. "

He dropped his mouth to the space beside my lips, brushing over my skin. My whole body buzzed like honey bees swarming, fanning me with their wings. Even so, I couldn't speak through the tightness in my throat.

"I'll hold you tight to me, Ava," he murmured. "If you go, I go. Trust me. If you fall, I'll be there with you, the updraft of a great fire to keep you safe."

I just shook my head, doing my best to hold back. I trembled with the exertion to resist, and his lips whispered lower, touching down on the flesh just below my jawline, feathering its way to the lump in my throat.

"You want me to plead, Ava?" he said against my skin. "Because I will. I've never had to beg in all my days for a woman's touch, but I'll beg for yours," he murmured, forcing my chin up with a finger to meet his gaze as he pulled his mouth away. "Give me just one night, this night, so I can dampen the fire that burns beneath my skin for the want of your touch every damn time I'm with you and know you only see me as a monster."

Each word was a razor to my skin. To imagine that was all he thought of himself. The thought of him with Phaedra, with Mica. The paint on his nails and the delicate way he slurped at a toy teacup.

"I don't think you're a monster," I said in a breath. "You are many things, but you are not that."

The serpent of crimson circled his irises. The silver limning them flared. "Praise from a hunter the likes of which I've never heard," he murmured in a teasing growl. "And yet you resist."

There were no words for the gutted feeling in my stomach, the fear that clutched at my bowels. I shook my head, confusion making me mute. He was right. I wanted to give in. I wanted that moment of rapture. He was so damned magnificent. The sheer power coming off him in waves called out to my marrow. It wasn't a matter of trust that held me back.

I knew right then why I'd fought my own emotions and refused to see how deeply he cared about me, and it wasn't because of Kit. It wasn't because I was worried he'd do me harm over the blood oath. It wasn't any of the things I'd argued to myself or told myself or wanted to believe.

It was because he would be an addiction. Far stronger than Bloodmist ever could be. I'd lose myself in him. The heights of rapture he spoke of, the fire burning within, the monster craving just one moment of surrender...no more perfect description of addiction ever existed.

And that terrified me.

Protests aplenty rose to my lips. Words of surrender too. The indecision, the paralysis of wanting so badly to both give in and refuse held me there in an icy moment of torment. If he said one more word, I was sure I'd fling myself over the precipice, be damned what came.

But he didn't say another word. Because he wasn't a monster, he didn't press me further. I almost wanted him to. I wanted to close my eyes and just give in to the trust that danced at the edge of my soul, trying to cast light on the darkness within just as it illuminated all those hulking trunks filled with every horror I'd lived through.

I sucked in a breath. One more moment and he'd release me and this would be over. I'd have made it through. I could hold my own. I could stand against the temptation.

But then he touched me. Nothing much, just a brush of the back of his finger along my cheek as he released me. A soft, accepting whisper of skin on skin.

And I dove off the edge.

I stole his hand from alongside my cheek, twisting it in mine and placing it on my breast beneath the hem of my shirt. Even as the warmth of his skin met mine, it dragged a low, rasping moan from him. My chest felt too tight as I burrowed beneath his clothes to plant my palm against his heart, felt the jerk of his muscles and the heartbeat beneath.

My heart hammered against his palm. I was sure we matched beat for beat.

He tensed all over. "What are you doing, Ponytail?"

"One moment," I said. "Take it."

There was no space between the words and his mouth claiming mine. Just that same, marrow-curdling desire that claimed us both so savagely, I was ready to let him take me right there against the wall, just so long as he took me.

I didn't care for bedding and sheets and sweet nothings. I just wanted him. All of him. Hard and punishing and absolving all at the same time. I'd deal with the aftershocks later. Just like I'd dealt with every other drug I'd ever succumbed to.

His hands roamed beneath my shirt and cupped my breasts. A moan escaped me, whether it was dread or excitement, I couldn't tell.

"Close your eyes if you have to, Ponytail," he growled beneath his breath. "I'm about to burn down every wall you've ever built and it isn't going to be pretty."

That was it. The only warning I had before he scooped me off the wall and clawed me closer. Somehow he managed to hold me against his waist and tug at the laces of his trousers at the same time. My legs coiled around his waist, holding to him tightly enough that, braced against the wall, I could work my buttons, pull my shirt up, drag my bra out of the way to give his lips full rein of my breasts.

It was savage and beautiful at the same time. I was lost to it all. So lost that when Blade froze and went suddenly rigid, I tried to drag his head back to my breasts, confused as to why his lips weren't on my skin anymore.

"Mica best be dying, Stone," he said over my head.

"You would know better than me," Stone drawled, unafraid, and even smothered behind Blade's body I could still make out the disappointment that ran in the subterranean currents of it. Disappointment. In me.

Yet, for the hurt in his voice that I would have spared him if I could, all I could think was fuck. Not again.

I went completely still for all of three seconds as the humiliation rose to flush my face. It was like being caught by Kit with a crack pipe to my lips the day after she'd saved me from the dealer's rope.

It was a struggle to peel myself away from Blade because he fought my release. But he did let me drop my feet to the floor, and I buried my face in his warm chest so I could let the heat of embarrassment subside.

His breath washed over me in waves as his chest heaved with the exertion of barely suppressed control. A dizzying moment when I was spun along with him as he put his back to Stone, hiding me from his brother's bald view.

It took several moments for me to regain my composure. My fingers trembled, but I managed to move them toward the hem of my shirt, to pull it down chastely if not somewhat guiltily.

Blade's hand came down on mine, halting my work. "Don't," he said to me and in his voice was a quiver that suggested he was working hard to control himself. "After I murder my brother, I'm going to take you naked and screaming to my rooms if I have to, and we're going to finish what we started."

"That's not going to happen," Stone said.

I peered around the massive shoulders that kept me corralled out of sight. Blade looked back over his shoulder. His every muscle was tense. The area around his jawline was white.

"I don't think it's a good idea to cock block the dark enforcer for the second time in one day, brother," he said.

Stone crossed his arms over his chest. "Keeping you out of Ava's pants was not my intention, brother, although I won't say I'm sad about doing so. Father sent me to find you."

"Why?" A curt, rude tone to the question. I had the feeling he wanted to commit violence right then. "Does he suddenly care about Mica, or is he rabid over the idea I might offer him my blood?"

"The Days have begun," Stone said with a grim line to his mouth. "Word came a few moments ago."

"The days..." Blade let the words trail off as he worked his brain around the shift in topic. I thought I understood what Stone meant long before he did, and everything in me sagged. He must have felt it because he peered down at me.

In his face, I saw exactly what I knew flitted across mine. The knowledge that I'd be herded back to my suites. Bathed and pimped and primed for the inevitable showing like a horse at an auction. The thought of an auction made the hairs rise on my neck.

The reality slammed home like a brick, and I pushed away from him. I squared my shoulders, taking the moment to adjust my clothes and find some dignity. I couldn't look him in the eye. Not now. I couldn't imagine what I was thinking. I owed Stone a debt even if he didn't know it.

"How long before we're presented?" I asked, rubbing my arms over my sleeves as they'd suddenly grown cold.

Stone's pitying look did nothing for my mood. "In the morning," he said. "The king has called for the bells to be rung at dawn."

"There's more," Blade said as he faced Stone, his gaze narrowing as he took in the way his brother kept fidgeting back and forth.

"Father wants me to present her," he said, skimming me with his gaze. "Flint is to present Kit. And you are to remain here."

"No place for the dark enforcer, I suppose," Blade said and I thought he took the news very well, considering. Only clenching his fists at his sides and unfurling them twice before letting them rest. "I suppose he also orders us to his audience," he said through clenched teeth, and Stone nodded.

"I'm sorry," he said and he really sounded as if he meant it. "Ava must return to her room until Father calls for her. And we are to meet him in the cellars."

My mouth went dry at the mention of the cellars. Being called for would mean he wanted to impress upon me all the dangers my sister would be in should I fail to achieve the goal. If I knew Terran the way I knew most monsters, he'd do his level best to impress me.

But I wasn't scared of that. Days ago, maybe. When I'd been an ailing addict who had lost track of who I really was. Back when I felt like Prometheus losing my liver to the sharp beak of a raven each day. But now, I remembered there'd been heroism to his tale at one time. Once, he'd done the impossible.

I let my fingers trail into the pockets of my pants. The coin was still there. I traced its edge with my nail and wondered if it shouldn't have sent me reeling along a portal somewhere at its mere touch, if a changeling shouldn't be standing in my place, and I worried it was a dud.

Maybe it wasn't even the real thing anyway.

But it didn't matter. I had only to touch the stone at my neck to remember what I was. Never mind the near plunge into a newer, more dangerous addiction, I would climb the mount and do the impossible even if I suffered for it later.

So as both Stone and Blade pivoted on their heels, ready to descend from their mount to the cellars below to meet with their god, I aimed my feet in the direction of the hall not yet scoured. Because I was a hunter.

And it was time my sister knew that.

—the end for now—

<u>Keep reading</u> to see what happens when Ava meets the king

Author Thanks

I always rely on the same eagle-eyed favorite readers to beta read and find the usual pesky typo. Caroline Jenkins, Denise Sherman, Evelyn Dotson, and Joann Colantino.

But there are also some who give me critical feedback to help me finesse the story. Those readers, bless their hearts, have no idea how much I appreciate them.

Debra Martin, Kerry Taylor, and Julie Pederick. You made such a difference in the story. I can't thank you enough.

Then there's readers like Crystal Crystal Amason, who was the first stranger to make me feel like my little ditties were worth reading, and whom I now keep in my mind's eye when I write.

I really appreciate you all.
-thea-

www.ingramcontent.com/pod-product-compliance
Lightning Source LLC
Chambersburg PA
CBHW020651120726
47906CB00001B/221